CONTROLLED BURN

SHANNON STACEY

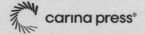

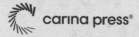

ISBN-13: 978-0-373-00290-0

Controlled Burn

Recycling programs for this product may not exist in your area.

CONTROLLED BURN

Acknowledgments

Thank you to Angela James and Carina Press for your constant support.

**Also available from Shannon Stacey
and Carina Press**

The Kowalski Series from Shannon Stacey

Suggested reading order

Also available from Shannon Stacey and Harlequin

**And stay tuned for *Fully Ignited*, the next book
in the Boston Fire Series from Shannon Stacey,
coming soon**

ONE

"FIVE BUCKS SAYS she requested Ladder 37 when she called 911."

Rick Gullotti glared at Gavin Boudreau, then shook his head. "That's bullshit."

They were back at the station after a run and, as the lieutenant of Boston Fire's Ladder 37, he had to stay in the bay with the guys and take care of the gear. Even if they were being idiots. In the bay next to him, the guys from Engine 59 were doing the same. Stowing the gear, checking tanks and supplies. The ladder truck and the pumper engine that shared the three-story brick firehouse always rolled together, and the guys of L-37 and E-59 operated well as a team.

A team whose members loved to give each other shit, Rick thought as Scotty Kincaid yelled from the other side of the bay. "That's the fourth time that woman's needed the fire department in six months, Gullotti. Must be rough when all your emergencies happen while you're still in your lace nightgown."

"Maybe it's you she's after," Gullotti called back.

"It wasn't me she hugged with so much…gratitude."

Yeah, that had been awkward. He didn't mind being offered cookies or invited to stay for lunch, but the hugging he usually managed to avoid. Thankfully he hadn't taken his bunker coat off, so the feel of a curvy woman in satin and lace hadn't gotten through, but he was going to have to be more careful in the future.

"She was definitely grateful." Chris Eriksson— who was one of the older guys in the house, but avoided promotions due to an extreme aversion to paperwork—paused in the act of wiping down L-37's bumper to smirk at him.

Rick's phone vibrated in his pocket, and he pulled it out, anticipating a summons from upstairs. It wasn't going to take long for the story to circulate, and he knew they'd have to come up with a way to gently discourage the woman's attempt to date via frivolous emergency calls. Not only was it a waste of time and money but, if it escalated, she could accidentally burn down her house.

But the text was from Karen Shea. She was a nurse he'd dated for a while before she met a guy who had the potential to be the one she wanted to spend the rest of her life with.

They just brought Joe into the ER. Stable, but he took a fall and Marie got upset.

Shit. He'd rented the third floor of Joe and Marie Broussard's house for years, and the elderly couple had become more than just landlords. They were like family, and worry settled in the pit of his stomach.

We're wrapping up after a run. I can sneak over for a few mins.

I'll tell them. Marie's having tea and Joe's griping about having to wait for scans.

They were okay, then. And he knew Karen would keep an eye on them until he got there.

"Tell me you didn't give her your number," Eriksson said, nodding at the phone in Rick's hand.

"Who?"

"The grateful lady in the lace nightgown."

"Hell, no. It's Joe and Marie. They're in the ER with Karen."

"Damn. Is it serious?"

"Joe fell and she got upset, I guess. Nothing critical, but I need to tell Cobb I'm heading out and get over there. If a call comes in, bring my gear and I'll meet you there."

"Will do." Chris snorted. "And we'll leave you some of this grunt work to do, too. Trust me."

The emergency room wasn't busy, so he asked if Karen was free instead of asking for the Broussards. He wanted more information before he saw the older couple. About five minutes later, Karen came into the waiting room and smiled at him.

He gave her a quick hug because they'd stayed friends, but a flash of light caught his eye. There was a diamond ring on her left hand, and he took hold of her fingers to give it a look.

"That was fast," he said.

She was practically beaming. "Yeah, but when it's right, it's right. And we have a little incentive to make it legal."

It took a few seconds for her words to sink in, and he realized she was pregnant. Genuine happiness for her came first, but on the heels of that was a pang of regret. He really liked Karen and he wished they'd had whatever chemistry it was she shared with the lucky guy she was going to marry.

But how many times had he heard himself referred to as *not the marrying kind*? More times than he could count, even if he wasn't totally sure what that meant.

"Congratulations," he said, making sure she could see his sincerity on his face. "He's a good guy."

"He is." It looked as if she was going to get all misty-eyed, but then she put her nurse face back on. "Okay. I probably shouldn't have texted you. Marie's calmed down and it's looking like Joe's going to be punted out as soon as the scans are done. But her blood pressure was up and she looked a little dizzy when they brought them in."

"Always text me," he said. "Where did he fall?"

"At the bottom of the stairs. He was trying to measure to see about putting in a stair lift so Marie can get upstairs to her craft room and he says his sock slid on the hardwood tread because she didn't get all the Murphy Oil Soap wiped up."

Rick sighed and rubbed the back of his neck. "The house is too much for them. And Marie won't let me hire a cleaning service for them no matter how hard I push."

"I hate to tell you this, but Joe's doctor was here making rounds, so the ER doc pulled him in. They want to talk about elder care options."

"It's probably time to start having those discussions, I guess. If he sets up a time, I can be with them and keep them honest. They're still in denial when it comes to their limitations."

Karen hesitated, then exhaled. "The other nurses and I call you because we know you, but Joe and Marie haven't updated their legal information. Dr. Bartlett already left a message at the last known contact for their son."

"They called Davey?" Rick shook his head. "That douche bag probably won't even return the call."

"I just thought you should know before you see them."

"Do they know? About the call, I mean?"

"I don't think the doctor's been in to follow up with them yet, so probably not."

He should tell them himself, before the doctor did, so Joe and Marie wouldn't be taken off guard. Their son was a painful subject and they were already having a shitty day. "We should probably make sure Joe isn't making a break for it."

Recognizing the change of subject for what it was, Karen led him through the security doors and down the hall to a curtained-off room.

Marie stood when she saw him and held out her arms. Rick hugged her, some of his worry eased by the steadiness in her slim, tall figure. Even at seventy-eight, Marie was strong. Neither of them was as strong as they used to be, though, and it was becoming a problem.

"They shouldn't have called you," Joe grumbled

from the bed. Rick let go of Marie to put his hand on the man's shoulder. Taller and four years older than his wife, but not quite as thin, Joe had once been rugged as hell. Age and a stroke had taken a toll, though, and Joe was having trouble reconciling with the fact he wasn't fifty anymore.

"If a call comes in, I'll have to go, but we'd just finished a run. Pretty lady in a lace negligee thought she smelled smoke."

"Same one as last time?" Joe asked, leaning back against the stack of pillows.

"Yup."

"You said she was pretty," Marie said. "Maybe you should ask her on a date. She obviously likes you."

"Jesus, Marie." Joe scowled at his wife. "You can't encourage that or half the women in the city will be setting their tablecloths on fire."

Rick laughed and sat on the exam stool, leaving the visitor's chair for Marie. Hoping it would be a few more minutes before the doctor came back, he listened to the familiar banter between the two people who'd come into his life as landlords and become like family. And he tried to figure out how to tell them the hospital had reached out to their son because Joe and Marie knew as well as Rick did that Davey probably wouldn't reach back.

JESSICA BROUSSARD PARKED her rental car at the curb and flexed her fingers because they practically ached from her death grip on the steering wheel. Driving in Boston was certainly no joke.

Having learned through previous experience that navigation systems weren't infallible, she squinted to make out the brass numbers tacked to the front of the tall blue house. Then she looked at the address she'd punched into the GPS and took a deep breath.

This was it. Her grandparents' home.

The flight from San Diego to Boston had given her plenty of time to obsess about all the ways this trip made no sense. Whenever her father was unavailable, Jessica checked his voice mail in order to keep Broussard Financial Services running, but she hadn't known what to do about the call from the Boston doctor. Reaching out to her father had resulted in a brusque demand for her to deal with the problem before she even got a chance to tell him it was personal.

But she couldn't deal with it. The doctor wouldn't speak to her about Joe and Marie Broussard, the grandparents she'd never met, because she wasn't on the form. And, when she was tossing and turning at two in the morning, she wondered if it was because they didn't know she even existed. The plan formed—seemingly brilliant as many insomnia-born plans were—to deal with her father's problem and to meet the people David Broussard had barely spoken of, and never kindly.

A curtain in the house twitched, and Jessica realized she'd been staring. It was time to get out of the car, or drive back to the airport and force her father to call the doctor.

She climbed out of the car, bracing herself for the blast of cold air, and walked toward the front door as a pickup drove past and then turned into the drive-way. Jessica paused with one foot on the bottom step, but the man who got out of the truck definitely wasn't one of her grandparents.

"Can I help you?" he asked, walking toward her.

"I'm looking for Joe and Marie Broussard."

He nodded. "I'm Rick Gullotti. I rent the apart-ment upstairs. They expecting you?"

No, they most definitely were not. That two-in-the-morning plan had also included not giving the Brous-sards the opportunity to tell her not to come. "No, they're not. But I'm…their granddaughter. Jessica."

The man froze in the act of extending his hand to shake hers, and his eyebrows rose. He had great eye-brows, which was ridiculous because when had she ever noticed a man's eyebrows before?

"I wasn't aware they have a granddaughter," he finally said, and she could tell he was trying to be careful with his words.

"To be honest, I don't know if they're aware of it, either."

"Okay." He dropped his hand. "Do you mind if I ask why you're here? Is your visit related to the doc-tor calling Davey?"

Davey? Not once in her entire life had Jessica heard her father referred to as anything but David.

She took her time answering, assessing her op-tions. On the one hand, it would be easy to dismiss him as a tenant who should feel free to mind his own business. But on the other, he knew her grandparents well enough to call their son Davey and she didn't know them at all. When it came to moving them into a better living situation and getting the house on the market, he could be her strongest ally.

"The doctor refused to talk to me and my father is unavailable. If Joe and… If my grandparents add me to their paperwork, I can help them navigate their options."

After a long moment spent staring at her as if trying to read her mind, he nodded. "I'll introduce you."

When Jessica stepped down to let him go in front of her, she realized how tall he was. She wasn't sure she had an actual type, other than a preference for men taller than she was, but circumstances had led to her last few relationships being with younger men. Judging by the hint of gray peppering his short, dark hair and scruff of a beard, Rick Gullotti definitely wasn't younger. His blue eyes were framed by laugh lines, and she got the feeling he laughed a lot.

Worn jeans hugged his bottom half, and a T-shirt did the same for the top. He'd thrown a hoodie on over it, but it wasn't zipped—which meant he *had* to be crazy—so his body was well displayed. *Very* well.

"How can it be this cold already?" she asked, trying to divert her attention away from the view before she said something stupid, like asking him just how many hours per day he worked out to look that amazing.

Rick shrugged. "It's that time of year. It's going to be warmer the next few days—maybe back up to fifty—and then there's snow in the forecast. Welcome to Boston in December."

"Snow." She'd gone on a ski trip once, during her college days. There had been a fireplace and alcohol and as little snow as possible.

"I hope you brought boots."

"I won't be here that long."

He gave her a hard look she couldn't quite decipher and then opened the front door without knocking. She followed him in, trying to block out her father's voice in her head.

Crass. Alcoholic. Bad tempers. When she was eleven, she'd had to do a genealogy project in school. *They're just not our kind of people, Jessica, and you're upsetting me. I don't want to hear about this nonsense again.* That was the last time she asked about her grandparents. Her project was entirely fictional and earned her an A.

"Rick, is that you?" she heard a woman call from the back of the house, and Jessica's stomach twisted into a knot. "Did you get the… Oh. You have company."

Jessica looked at her grandmother, emotions tangling together in her mind. Marie was tall and slim, with short white hair and blue eyes. And Jessica knew, many years from now, she would look like this woman.

"Where's Joe?" Rick asked, and Jessica was thankful he seemed to want them together because it bought her a few more seconds to gather herself.

"He's in the kitchen. Come on back."

When Marie turned and walked away, Jessica looked up at Rick. He nodded his head in that direction, so she followed. Other than a general sense of tidiness and a light citrus scent, she barely noticed her surroundings. Her focus was on her grandmother in front of her and an awareness that Rick Gullotti was behind her.

Her grandfather was sitting at the kitchen table, working on some kind of puzzle book with reading glasses perched low on his nose. When he looked up, he frowned and then took the glasses off to stare at her.

"I found Jessica outside," Rick said. "She says she's your granddaughter."

Marie gasped, and Jessica felt a pang of concern when she put her hand to her chest. "What? She can't be."

"If her hair was short, she'd look just like you did years ago, Marie," Joe said, and she wished she knew him well enough to know if the rasp in his voice came from emotion or not.

"I can't believe Davey wouldn't tell us he had a baby."

"Davey hasn't told us anything in almost forty years."

"I'm thirty-four," Jessica said, as if that explained everything, and then she immediately felt like an idiot. "I'm sorry. I should have called first."

"Did Davey send you because that damn doctor called him?"

"I came because of the call, yes." She couldn't bring herself to admit yet that her father had no idea she was here or why.

Silence filled the kitchen, and she became aware that the Broussards had a real clock hanging in their kitchen—the kind with a second hand that marked the awkward seconds with a *tick tick tick*.

Jessica was torn. The logical analyst voice in her head—the part of her that had earned her a cushy corner office in her father's investment business—wanted her to set up a time to speak with them about the doctor's call and then check into the hotel room she'd reserved. But her inner eleven-year-old wanted to hug her nonfictional grandmother.

"It's a long flight," Rick said, stepping out from behind her so she could see him. "You hungry?"

His quiet words breaking the silence also seemed to break the tension, and Marie gave her a shaky smile. "Have a seat and tell us all about yourself. Rick, are you going to stay for a while?"

"I'll stay for a little bit," Rick said, and though his voice was even enough, the look he gave Jessica made it clear he wasn't just a tenant in this house and he wasn't sure what he thought of her yet. "I want to hear *all* about Jessica."

TWO

RICK WASN'T SURE exactly what to make of Jessica Broussard. The only thing he knew for sure about Joe and Marie's surprise granddaughter was that she smelled pretty damn good for a woman who'd just flown across the entire width of the country.

She didn't look too bad, either. Her long, blond hair was in a long and straight ponytail, and if she was wearing makeup, it was subtle. A soft sweater that looked more fashionable than warm reached her thighs, which were encased in black leggings that disappeared into similarly nonfunctional boots. The soft leather might make her legs look amazing, but they weren't keeping her feet warm. And she was tall enough so it wouldn't be awkward to kiss her.

Not that it mattered, since he had no intention of kissing Jessica. But, being tall himself, it was something he tended to notice about women.

But what he didn't know about her was why she'd flown all the way from San Diego to Boston at the drop of a hat to show up on the doorstep of people she didn't even know.

"I'm really not hungry," Jessica said, pulling out a chair to sit. "But I'd love a glass of water if it wouldn't be too much trouble."

"It's no trouble at all." Marie pulled out the chair next to Jessica's. "Rick, would you get Jessica a glass of water, please?"

Smiling, he opened the cabinet and took down one of Marie's "company" glasses, rather than grabbing one of the plastic tumblers they usually used. After rinsing it out, he filled it with ice and water from the fridge.

"Thank you," Jessica said when he set it down in front of her. But she didn't take a sip immediately. She wrapped her hands around it as if she just needed something to do with them.

Instead of taking the fourth seat at the table, Rick leaned against the counter and folded his arms across his chest, watching her.

"What do you do for work, Jessica?" Marie asked, and he felt a pang of sadness at the anxiety in her voice. She would try not to show it, but the woman was a wreck on the inside.

"I work for my father, actually, at Broussard Financial Services. We do financial planning and manage investments and things of that nature. As his vice president, I handle everything when he's unavailable, so of course I returned Dr. Bartlett's call yesterday. It sounded urgent."

"Are there other people in the office?" Marie asked. "If you're here, who's running things now?"

"We do have staff. And I have my laptop. Other than rescheduling a few face-to-face meetings, most of my work can be done remotely."

"Let me ask you something," Joe said, fiddling

with his reading glasses. "Does your father know you're here?"

"No, he doesn't," she answered after a long silence, and Rick got the feeling she didn't want to answer the question. The granddaughter they didn't know showing up in Boston unannounced when their son couldn't even be bothered to return a call was interesting, but he really hoped she wasn't up to no good in some way. "The doctor couldn't discuss your situation with me because I'm not on the form, but my father is unavailable, so I decided to come in person."

Unavailable. She'd used that word outside, too, and he wondered what it meant. Most people would say he was on vacation or at a remote fishing cabin or chained in a basement somewhere. The use of *unavailable* seemed deliberate, meaning she didn't care for them to know what Davey Broussard was up to.

"I feel bad that you came all the way out here," Marie said. "Dr. Bartlett overreacted and shouldn't have called."

"Needs to mind his own damn business," Joe muttered.

Rick cleared his throat. "Maybe he did overreact this time, but it's not a bad idea to go over your legal papers and discuss your options once in a while."

"We can talk about all that tomorrow," Marie told them. "Right now I want to hear about my granddaughter."

Rick did, too, actually. He watched her slowly relax as she told them about growing up in San Diego. She'd graduated second in her class and gone to the Uni-

versity of Denver for her degree. Then she'd joined
her father's company and worked her way up to second in command, poised to take the reins when he
retired. She'd never been married, but she owned a
lovely condo and drove a convertible Audi.

He wondered if Joe or Marie would press for the
details she'd left out. There was no mention of her
mother or siblings. Had she wanted to join her father's company or was it simply expected of her? For
almost an hour he stood there while they talked, but
she never said anything that wouldn't be out of place
in a professional bio.

"I'm so glad you're here," Marie said after a while,
resting her hand on Jessica's arm. Rick watched the
younger woman's gaze settle on the touch, her smile
a little on the shaky side. "I should start supper. Is
there anything you don't like? Or do you have any
food allergies?"

"I… No. I like most foods and I'm not allergic to
anything that I know of."

"Oh, good. I have a lasagna in the freezer. I can
pop it in the oven so we can get you settled in while
it cooks."

"Oh, I appreciate the invitation, but I really should
go and get settled into my hotel. Is there a time we
can get together tomorrow to talk?"

Rick and Joe exchanged amused looks when Marie
held up her hands and shook her head. "Oh, you don't
need a hotel, honey. We have a guest room upstairs. It
has its very own bathroom and everything."

"That's really generous, but I already have a res-
ervation."

"No sense in wasting money like that," Joe argued.

"I'll be working a lot, too. Just me and my laptop,
you know?"

"You can work here," Marie said. "We have really
good internet so Rick can talk to all of his girlfriends
on Facebook."

"Hey!" He laughed, shaking his head. "I don't have
girlfriends on Facebook. And that's not why we have
internet."

"Imagine what people would think if my granddaughter stays in a hotel," Marie pushed.

"None of your friends know you *have* a granddaughter," Jessica pointed out.

Joe snorted. "Trust me, they will."

Rick pushed away from the counter and walked
toward the table. "You may as well just give me the
key to your car so I can bring your bags in."

"Go ahead and pull the car into the driveway, too,"
Joe said. "Get it off the street."

"I…" Jessica gave Rick a look that was clearly a
plea for help, but there was nothing he could do for
her. Marie had made up her mind and she was possibly the most stubborn woman he'd ever met.

"I would really like for you to stay with us," Marie
said quietly, touching Jessica's arm again.

Her granddaughter just nodded, her smile less anxious this time, and pulled the rental's key out of her
sweater pocket to hand to Rick.

After parking the very compact car in the shadow

of his truck, Rick popped the trunk and pulled out her suitcase. Then he wheeled it around to the other side of the car.

He wasn't sure what to do about the stuff on the front passenger seat. While he'd noticed she had a small pocketbook on a thin chain across her body, she'd left a tote bag and some other stuff in the car.

After a moment's hesitation, he zipped the expensive-looking sunglasses into the case he found and dropped it into the top of the bag. A pen and a tin of mints went in after it, and then he looped a scarf through the tote's handles.

He lifted the tote out of the car and noticed a small legal pad had been under it. The house's address was scrawled across the top, so she'd probably pulled the pad out to enter it into the navigational system. But the list of addresses under Joe and Marie's house, written in much smaller letters down the page, caught his eye as he was in the process of putting it in the bag.

The street names were all familiar and when he read the abbreviations and dollar amounts listed with each one, he realized they were meant to be comps— lists of houses for sale in the area that might have a comparable value to Joe and Marie's.

So it looked as if their granddaughter had amused herself on the plane by researching their home's worth. What she might not be aware of was that, with an actual backward, two-car garage—with accompanying driveway—and spacious third-floor apartment, he'd take a wild guess at high six-figures.

Or maybe she *was* aware of it and the amount factored into her urgent need to meet her grandparents after thirty-four years. For all he knew, her *unavailable* father had something to do with it.

He didn't want to believe it, though. He'd seen her face when Marie had walked into the room and Jessica wasn't going to be winning any poker tournaments anytime soon. She'd been trembling. It was subtle, but he'd noticed. And there had been a lot of emotion in her big-eyed expression. He didn't know her well enough to read them, but it was obvious meeting her grandmother meant something to her beyond dollar signs.

Jessica Broussard was definitely a mystery, and the only thing Rick was certain of was that, for Joe and Marie's sake, he was going to have to keep a close eye on her.

A WAVE OF relief had washed over Jessica when Rick walked out of the kitchen. The entire time she'd been talking to Joe and Marie, trying to make a connection with her grandparents, a part of her had been distracted by the man leaning against the counter.

He hadn't been looming, exactly, but he was a big guy and made for a definite presence in the room. His arms being folded had stretched his lightweight sweatshirt across his shoulders, and when he crossed one ankle over the other, it had the same effect on his jeans and thighs. He was very, very distracting.

And then he'd laughed, turning her somewhat wary awareness into a much more potent, very different kind of awareness. His laugh was not only warm and rich, but loud, and she realized she didn't have men in her life who laughed like that. Her father rarely laughed at all, and the men around them tended toward polite laughter.

"It breaks my heart to have to ask this because I feel like I should already know," Marie said, breaking into Jessica's thoughts, "but is your mother that girl he met at college? I don't remember her name now and he never brought her home to meet us, so I can't even tell you what she looked like."

"My mother's name is Emily and I know they met at college, but I don't know if she's the same one." She took a long drink of water, wishing there was a way to avoid telling the rest. "She left us when I was three, so I don't really remember her."

"Oh." Marie fell silent, giving her the sympathetic look Jessica had come to expect years ago on the rare occasion her mother was brought up. "Did he remarry?"

That made her laugh, though it sounded harsh and humorless. "Several times. He's currently in the process of divorce number four."

And, even though he invariably brought those failed marriages down on himself, divorces were hard on her father and one of the reasons the reins of BFS were currently in her hands.

She didn't even want to imagine how he was going to react when he learned she'd handed those reins over to the staff. Not totally, of course, but she'd delegated like she'd never delegated before in order to manage this trip, and her father wasn't going to like anything about it.

"I'm sorry to hear that." Marie sighed. "I've always tried to imagine him happy, even if he didn't keep in touch."

Why? The word was on the tip of Jessica's tongue, but for some reason she didn't ask the question. If her grandparents felt anything like she did on the inside right now, they all had enough on their emotional plates without digging into the reasons behind their estrangement from their son.

"Davey hasn't been happy a day in his life," Joe said, his voice gruff with some emotion that went deeper than anger.

Every time she heard the name Davey, Jessica's mind tripped over it. These strangers knew her father, but they seemed to know a different version of him and that fascinated her. She wanted to know more about him.

She heard the front door and then the thump of footsteps on the stairs. Rick must be bringing her bags upstairs, and she fought down a rush of panic. Was she really staying here? With her grandparents?

"We should get you settled in," Marie said, standing up. "Being on a plane all day like that must be exhausting."

Jessica couldn't disagree, especially considering the amount of anxiety that had accompanied her, and the shift in time zones wasn't going to help. She followed Marie to the stairs, but paused halfway up when a framed photo caught her eye. She'd barely noticed all the family pictures on display, but this one had been blown up.

Even though he was just a child—young enough to show off two missing front teeth in a huge smile—Jessica had no trouble recognizing her father. And Joe and Marie hadn't changed very much, either, even though Joe had been a little beefier. They all looked so happy, smiling for the camera, and the ache in Jessica's stomach intensified.

She had a few pictures of her mother. There was even a photo of them together, taken just before her third birthday. They'd both been looking at the camera with solemn eyes. Jessica's mouth had been turned down in what looked like sadness and her mother's lips had been pressed tightly together.

There were no happy family portraits on David Broussard's walls.

When she heard Marie pause at the top of the stairs, she forced herself to look away and climb the rest of the steps. Maybe later she'd look at all the framed photos and try to get a handle on her emotions before having any conversations with her grandparents.

Halfway down the hall, they passed Rick, who was heading back for the stairs. He smiled at Marie, but some of the sparkle went out of his eyes when he turned it on her. "I put your bags in your room."

"Thank you." She already knew she'd lose some sleep trying to solve the mystery of Rick Gullotti. Was he afraid she was there for nefarious reasons? Or did he have nefarious plans of his own that her presence could derail?

Marie led her to the last door on the right, which was standing open, and Jessica saw it was a slightly barren but very clean guest room. Her suitcase and her tote were set just inside the door, and she saw that he'd thrown the stuff she'd had on the seat into the bag.

"I don't think it's too dusty in here." Marie pulled off the sheet draped over the bare mattress before walking to a closet. She pulled out a pile of fresh bedding and together they made the bed.

"Can I ask you a question?" Jessica asked when they were almost done.

Marie smiled at her from across the bed, but her eyes were wary. "Of course."

"How did you get my father's business number to put on your forms? I know he's had the number a long time, but…not *that* long." Somehow she doubted making sure they had his current contact info was high on her father's priority list.

"Sometimes I type his name into the Google on the computer at the library," Marie said, a hint of sadness creeping into her voice. "I'm not very good with computers, but I clicked on the first thing in the list it gave me and it was a website for his business—and yours, I guess. It has a phone number so I put it on the form, and there's a picture of him, too. I look at it a lot."

Jessica had no idea what to say to that, so she kept her mouth shut, but it made her sad to think this woman had been pining for her son. A son who seemed to harbor no good feelings toward her at all. She tried to remind herself that people changed and almost forty years was a long time.

Although, her father never seemed to change.

"There." Marie ran her hand over the quilt to smooth out a wrinkle, and smiled at Jessica. "It's no five-star hotel, but I think you'll be comfortable."

"I know I will. I'm glad I'm staying." And she was. It was going to be awkward, of course, but distance wouldn't help make it any less so.

They started toward the door, but at the last second, Marie turned to face her again. "I know this is probably weird for you, but would you mind if I gave you a hug?"

"I...I'd like that."

When Marie wrapped her arms around her, Jessica sighed and rested her head on her shoulder. Tears blurred her vision, so she closed her eyes and let herself soak in the emotion.

She knew the coming days would be a mess. Her father would be angry. There would be doctors, real estate people and perhaps lawyers to talk to with her grandparents, and there would probably be some emotional conversations about the family's past.

But for now, she was content to hug her grandmother.

RICK WALKED THROUGH the door of Kincaid's Pub and just the sight of Tommy Kincaid and "Fitz" Fitzgerald sitting at the bar relaxed him. Both retired firefighters, they'd been a fixture in the place even before

Tommy bought it, enabling Fitz to claim the back stool by right of best friendship.

Kincaid's wasn't pretty, but firefighters had made it their own decades before—even before Tommy bought it—and it was like a second home for the guys of Ladder 37 and Engine 59. Memorabilia and photos from the local stations decorated the place, along with a signed photo of Bruins legend Bobby Orr screwed right to the wall to keep anybody from walking off with him.

Lydia Kincaid was behind the bar tonight and she waved to him when he walked in. She'd left the family business—and Boston—for a while, but came back to help out on a temporary basis a few months before. Temporary until she hooked up with Aidan Hunt, who was assigned to Engine 59 with her brother and his best friend, Scott. The firehouse had been a little tense when that relationship news broke but now, almost four months later, the drama was forgotten. Scott and Aidan were as tight as they'd ever been and Lydia had a diamond on her left hand.

And she had a beer in her right hand, which she set down on the bar next to the one she'd poured for her brother. Scotty was alone, so Rick walked up and draped his arm over his shoulders. "You hanging out with all your friends?"

"Screw you. I thought Aidan might show up, but Lydia's making him do responsible adult shit, I guess."

His sister rolled her eyes. "He's grocery shopping because we like to eat. He said he might stop by to shoot some pool later, or he might not."

"I figured he'd spend more time here, not less," Rick said. "Since you're here."

"I don't go hang around the firehouse just because Aidan's there."

He shrugged. "True. But he was hanging out here long before you became the reason why."

"He'll probably be in, unless there's an animal documentary on. Then he'll sit down and end up asleep."

Rick watched her mouth curve upward in an affectionate smile and took a few swallows of beer as she walked away. He was happy for her. He'd known her for years, since she was Scott's sister and she'd been tending the bar since he was old enough to drink. And he was happy for Aidan, too. He was a good guy.

"You're antsy tonight," Scott said, and Rick realized he was tapping his fingers against his mug. "What's up?"

"My landlords' granddaughter showed up from San Diego today."

"Joe and Marie have a granddaughter?"

"That's what I said when she showed up."

"And?" Scotty prompted when he didn't offer up any more details.

"And what?"

"Where has she been? Why is she here now?"

Rick filled him in on what little he knew, pausing now and then to sip his beer. It didn't take him very long to tell the story, of course, since he had a lot more questions than answers when it came to Jessica.

"So she's basically vice president of a financial management company, but she gets on a plane to Boston with no advance notice because her father got a call about her grandparents, who she's never even met?" Scotty frowned. "That's a little weird, don't you think?"

"I'm not sure what to think. I don't like the fact she's already researching the value of the house, though."

"What I can't believe is that they haven't updated their legal situation in how many decades? From what you've told me, their son wants nothing to do with them."

Rick nodded. "Yeah, but what else are they gonna do? With Davey out of the picture, it's just the two of them."

"And you."

"No." Even the suggestion Joe and Marie would disinherit Davey in his favor made him uncomfortable. "When push comes to shove, I'm their tenant. It's bad enough they cut me such a break on the rent. They don't need to be giving me more than that."

"They're not just giving you a break on the rent for no reason, though. They want to keep you because they trust you and because you take care of the house. And the yard. And pretty much everything else a son would do for them."

"I don't want the house. Or their money. I just want them to be comfortable and safe. If that means selling the house to find them something more manageable or to pay for one of those assisted-living places, so be it. I'm a big boy. I can find a new place to live."

"So you're just going to stay out of it?"

Rick took a long drink, considering the question. "No. Maybe Jessica's here because her father's unavailable, whatever the hell that means, and she wants to help out her grandparents and maybe even get to know them. Or maybe they got a phone call and saw dollar signs. I'm not going to sit back and watch father and daughter shuffle Joe and Marie off to some shit hole and take control of their finances."

"I don't know your landlords as well as you do, but they don't seem like the type to fall for something like that."

"I hope you're right," Rick said. "But their son left a big hole in their lives and... If you could have seen Marie's face when it hit home that Jessica was really her granddaughter. They're vulnerable, even if they don't see it."

"We don't have another shift until Tuesday morning, so you'll be able to keep an eye on her."

"And what woman are you keeping an eye on now?" Lydia asked. She'd been passing by, carrying a couple of empty mugs from some guys at the end of the bar, and she stopped in front of them.

"Not that kind of keeping an eye on," Rick said. "I don't have my eye on anybody in that sense right now."

Her eyebrow arched. "It's not like you to be single for long."

She walked away before he could respond, but he wasn't sure what he'd say, anyway. It made him a little uncomfortable to hear her say that, he realized. He dated a lot. So what? He was single and his relationships almost always ended mutually. Most of his ex-girlfriends were still women he considered friends.

Like Karen. He turned his head to face his friend. "Did you know Karen's engaged?"

Scotty nodded. "Did she tell you or did you hear it somewhere? I don't think too many people know yet, actually."

"I saw her ring when I was in the ER for Joe and Marie yesterday."

"She tell you the rest of it?"

"About them having a baby? Yeah." Rick took a long swallow of his beer. "I'm happy for her."

"Really? Because you look kind of like a man who's one more beer away from writing a bad country song on the back of a bar napkin."

"Sure, I liked her. But it wasn't a forever kind of thing." He shrugged. "The first time I saw her with the new boyfriend, I knew there was something between them we didn't have."

"You will someday. Probably."

Scott Kincaid was probably the last guy he should be talking about relationships with, but there was nobody else around. "What do you think *not the marrying kind* really means?"

Scotty snorted. "Hell if I know, but I've been told more than once if you look it up in the dictionary, you'll find a picture of me."

"Maybe next time a woman says it, I should ask her to be more specific."

"I'm not sure I want to know."

Rick wasn't sure he did, either. But seeing how

happy Karen had been lately made him see how big a difference there was between having a woman in your life and having a woman you wanted to spend the rest of your life with.

Once the issue with Jessica Broussard had been resolved, he was going to have to give some serious thought to making himself into the marrying kind. Whatever the hell that meant.

THREE

JESSICA OPENED HER eyes and blinked at the sun shining through the frilly white curtains. She'd struggled with sleep issues her entire life, so she had room-darkening drapes in her bedroom at home and only ever knew what time of day it was by looking at the clock.

There was certainly no doubt it was morning right now. And it was her first full day in Boston, in her grandparents' house.

She rolled onto her back and stared at the ceiling, surprised she'd slept at all. The last thing she remembered was the clock ticking over to one o'clock as she tried to reconcile the Joe and Marie she'd met yesterday with the crass, alcoholic, bad-tempered people her father had refused to talk about.

Even given the fact people changed and her grandparents were different now than when they'd raised their son, Jessica's gut told her something wasn't right about the way he'd cut his parents out of his life. Maybe she'd always suspected that, but it had taken something of a perfect storm for her to face it. She'd become painfully aware most of her friends had married and started families, while she was still acting as her father's business partner and hostess, and she wasn't sure how she felt about that. At thirty-four, she needed to figure out if she even wanted those things, or if she liked her life just how it was.

There had been a lot of introspection, though. And a realization that, when her father eventually passed away, she'd be alone. Then the call had come from Boston. And her father had been unavailable to stop her from getting on the plane.

Maybe she'd find out that, once the element of surprise wore off, Joe and Marie weren't very nice people, after all. If that was the case, she could just get on a plane back to San Diego. She'd be sad, but at least she'd know her father had been right all along.

Now she desperately wanted a cup of coffee, but she wasn't sure what would happen when she went downstairs. Marie might not mind if she went through her usual morning routine of catching up on stock movement and financial news on her phone while waiting for the caffeine to kick in. Or she might want to chat and make breakfast together. As lovely as that sounded, business came before family. She'd learned that at her father's knee.

Ten minutes into scanning reports, though, and the craving for coffee burned through her good intentions. Coffee was too ingrained in her morning routine to attempt productivity without it. After getting dressed, she grabbed her phone and her laptop and went down the stairs.

Her grandparents were sitting in the living room when she reached the bottom, and they both looked over at her. Joe was sitting in a leather recliner, a mug of coffee on an end table next to it. And Marie was seated on the couch with her feet up on the coffee table, flipping through a magazine.

"Good morning," she said, feeling awkward all over again. She really shouldn't have let Marie talk her out of staying at a hotel.

"Good morning," Joe said, and then he turned back to the television. It was turned up pretty loud, so she guessed they didn't really do morning small talk.

Marie smiled. "Good morning, honey. There's coffee in the carafe. And I left some muffins and a few slices of bacon on a plate for you. There's a paper towel over it. If you want eggs, I can fry you up some."

"No, thank you. A muffin will be plenty."

"You can go ahead and do your computer stuff at the kitchen table if it's comfortable. We're watching our morning shows for another hour, at least."

"Thank you."

Once she'd fixed her coffee and inhaled a cranberry muffin and two strips of bacon, Jessica sat down at the kitchen table and got to work. It wasn't ergonomically ideal, but she wouldn't be spending enough time on the computer to worry about it today. Not only did she use her phone a lot, but she felt as if it would be rude to ignore her grandparents on her first day there.

By the halfway point of her second coffee, she'd cleared her inbox and exchanged a few emails with Sharon, her father's secretary and the woman who'd be doing the heavy lifting as far as keeping the office up and running. There were several messages from clients to respond to, but overall things were quiet.

Most people were wrapped up in ski trips and the up-coming holidays once December hit.

She jumped, almost bumping her coffee cup, when the back door opened and Rick walked in. He'd skipped the sweatshirt today and she admired the way his navy T-shirt clung to his upper body before forcing herself to look at his face. He looked tired.

"Good morning," she said, watching him walk to the coffeemaker.

"Morning. Where are Joe and Marie?"

"In the living room watching television. Marie said they have morning shows they usually watch, so I could go ahead and work at the table." And speaking of work, why wasn't he at work? She hadn't expected him to be around until later in the day, if at all. "Do you have a job?"

He stopped in the process of pulling the carafe off the brew plate to look at her. "Excuse me?"

She felt the heat in her cheeks. Polite conversation was usually a lot easier for her, but there was something about Rick that made her feel awkward. "I'm sorry. I was surprised to see you because I guess I just assumed you'd be at work today, but I didn't mean to be so abrupt about it."

"I'll be at work tomorrow if there's some reason it matters."

Jessica wasn't sure what he meant by that, but there was some bite to his tone. "Are you upset that I'm here?"

After pouring himself a mug of coffee, he set the carafe back in place and then turned to face her. He leaned against the counter, just as he had the day before, and looked at her over the rim of his mug. She waited, saying nothing, while he drank a few sips of coffee.

"No." He cradled the mug in his hands and shook his head. "I'm not upset. But I find it a little funny you think two people who didn't know you existed twenty-four hours ago will just put their legal and financial affairs in your hands."

Her eyes widened as what he *wasn't* saying sank in. "You think I'm here to take advantage of Joe and Marie?"

"I really hope you're not, for their sake, but I don't know you so I'll probably be around a little more than you thought, just to keep an eye on things."

She tried not to take offense, but the implication she was running some kind of con on her own family stung. "Or maybe you're unhappy I'm here because *you* want to be in charge of their legal and financial affairs."

He snorted. "Sorry, Jess, but you're barking up the wrong tree there."

Jess? When was the last time anybody had called her that? High school, maybe. She couldn't remember, but she knew she'd gone only by Jessica in college because her father had explained it was a stronger name, and she'd probably be taken more seriously.

She didn't correct Rick as she usually did other people, though, and she wasn't sure why. "It's a valuable piece of property and it's obvious you've been helping them maintain it for quite some time. It's not unreasonable to think you might feel entitled to something."

"Maybe it's not unreasonable, but it's wrong."

There was no way to force trust. "So I guess we're at an impasse and we'll have to take each other's word for it."

"For now." He pulled out the chair directly across the table from her and sat down. "I'm a firefighter. That's my job."

"Really?" Now that he was sitting in front of her, she realized the small logo on his T-shirt's pocket said Boston Fire.

"Yeah. I work two twenty-four shifts each week and I don't have a second job like some of the guys, so I'm around quite a bit."

"Is that a warning?" She smiled to let him know she was joking with him, and was relieved when he smiled back.

He had a great smile. It softened the hard angles of his face and deepened the laugh lines around his eyes. He was even scruffier today than he'd been yesterday, and for the first time in her life, she got the appeal. It was too easy to imagine how that gray-flecked scruff would feel against tender skin.

"You okay?"

She wished he'd stop arching his eyebrow like that. It was distracting. "I'm fine. Just a little warm, I guess."

"Maybe because you're wearing a coat."

Jessica looked down at the thick, fleece zip-up

she'd bought on a whim at the airport. "It's not really a coat, exactly. And it's cold here, remember?"

"That was yesterday, and you were outside. We heat the inside with these newfangled things called furnaces."

She laughed and unzipped the fleece so she could pull her arms free of it. "Are you from here? Do you have family nearby?"

"My parents still live in Fall River, where I was born. It's about an hour and a half south of here. And I have an older brother, who lives and teaches high school science in the next town over from them."

"So he's not a danger junkie, like you?"

There went that damn eyebrow again. "Danger junkie?"

"Don't you have to be a little bit of a danger junkie to be a firefighter?"

"Or maybe I became a firefighter because I'm a safety junkie." He took a sip of coffee, his gaze locking with hers.

She wasn't sure she bought that. "Maybe a little of both."

"Oh, Rick, it's you." The eye contact was broken when Marie spoke, and they both looked toward her. "I thought I heard talking, but I wasn't sure if Jessica was doing one of those video meeting things."

"We do have a setup for video conferencing in the office, but I mostly talk to the team by text. It's easier. Except for my father, who hates texting. He either calls or summons me to his office."

Marie's mouth pinched a little at the mention of

her son and that bothered Jessica. Her father—and the company—was a huge part of her life, so she tended to talk about him a lot. If hearing about him made her grandparents unhappy or uncomfortable, that was going to be a problem.

"Joe made a couple of phone calls and we can see the doctor next week, because he wants to follow up after the fall he took anyway, and we're waiting for a return call from our lawyer. It's been a long time since we talked to him. I hope he didn't retire. Anyway, can you stay that long?"

Jessica hesitated. Things were going smoothly in the office and her accounts were all in order. Even though it was only her second day away from the office, she felt confident everything could be handled in her absence. Truthfully, with technology the way it was, it almost made no difference whether she was in her office or in a kitchen in Boston. But eventually her father was going to surface and when he did, he was going to be livid.

She looked at the hopeful expression on her grandmother's face and smiled. "I can stay."

THE NEXT DAY, Rick stepped over a hole in the charred roof and walked to the edge to look down at the scene on the street. They were six stories up, so he had quite a view of the neighborhood. There were probably a dozen engines jammed around the corner lot, along with support vehicles and the police cruisers. The bystanders were wandering away now that the fire was out and there was just the boring stuff left.

Roof fires were never fun, but there had been no injuries and it hadn't spread. As long as none of them tripped over a line and fell through a hole or a weak spot, all would be well.

Jeff Porter was sitting on the brick fascia, and Rick hoped like hell it wouldn't crumble out from under him. Porter was a big guy. "All clear?"

"Yeah, we can start picking this shit up anytime we're ready," Rick said. "I'm just taking a few minutes to relax. It's pretty quiet up here."

"I hear that."

It was warm, though the weather wasn't going to last long. The temperature was already dropping and there was snow in the forecast, but for now they were seriously overdressed. Rick slid off the big bunker coat and tossed it next to Porter's before turning to watch the guys from E-59 head down L-37's ladder with hose in tow. He stood with hands tucked in his suspenders, soaking in the sun.

"Took the wife to Kincaid's for lunch yesterday," Porter said. "I hear your landlords have a surprise granddaughter."

Of course he'd heard. By now, everybody probably had. He'd told Scotty. Both of Scotty's sisters—Lydia and Ashley—worked the bar at Kincaid's. And they were both with guys assigned to Engine 59. Lydia was engaged to Aidan, and Ashley was married to Danny Walsh, the engine company's LT. And each of the guys had helped him with some project or other at the Broussards' over the years, the most recent being

the handicapped ramp in the back of the house, so
they knew Joe and Marie in varying degrees.

"Yeah, her name's Jessica. She showed up day before yesterday."

"Must be awkward."

"It is. Joe and Marie are over the moon to have her
there, of course, but they're all still dancing around
the issue of Davey."

"That's their son, right? Her dad?" Rick nodded.
"How long is she staying?"

"Not sure yet. They've got some meetings next
week, I guess, but she's kind of a big deal at her old
man's company from the sounds of it, so she'll have
to go back to San Diego eventually."

"San Diego." Porter snorted. "Went there once.
Hated it."

"Next time don't take your mother-in-law. Or the
kids."

They were laughing when Rick got a heads-up
from Danny Walsh that relaxation time was over and
they needed to hustle. Their trucks were blocking another company from leaving and they wanted to un-
clog the streets before the elementary school up the
street dismissed.

Once they'd repacked and made the drive back
to the house, they backed the ladder truck and the
pumper engine into the side-by-side bays and went
through the post-run routine of checking and re-
stocking equipment, and cleaning the trucks. Rick
and Danny went up to the second floor to take care
of some paperwork, while the rest of the guys went

up to the living space on the third floor of the old brick building.

He did step into the bathroom and wash away the soot he'd managed to get on his neck and up one side of his face. But he knew if he went up and made himself a coffee or pulled up some couch for a few minutes, he wasn't going to drag himself back to the hated desk.

By the time he made his way upstairs, he could smell the big pot of chili that had been simmering for most of the day. There were some drawbacks to feeding a building full of guys chili, of course, but Chris Eriksson's recipe was too good to resist. And anything that simmered, slow-cooked or could be shut off and reheated made for a good meal because the dispatchers couldn't say, "Hey sorry, but they're eating so it'll be an hour or so."

The somewhat outdated space on the third floor never felt as small as it did at mealtimes, when the guys all came together. Cobb had come up, getting a break from the office in which the chief oversaw both companies. His own guys from Ladder 37. Jeff Porter. Gavin Boudreau. Chris Eriksson. And the guys from Engine 59. Danny Walsh. Aidan Hunt. Scott Kincaid. And the kid, Grant Cutter. All together, they made a good team, and they were like brothers.

Then Rick watched Grant jostling for space in front of the shredded cheese and crackers with Gavin—who was only a few years older—and felt old. In some cases he was starting to feel more like an uncle or other mentor to the younger guys, and he wasn't sure he was ready to be *that* guy yet.

Once he'd scored a bowl of the chili and topped it with some shredded cheese and garlic salt, Rick went into the living room to watch the news while he ate. Most of the guys would hang in the kitchen and shoot the shit, even if it meant standing while they ate, so he was able to grab a seat on the battered love seat with Aidan. Jeff and Scott were on the big couch, and Cobb was sitting in one of the wooden rockers.

Because they were all busy eating, he was able to watch the news in peace. There was footage of the roof fire and they watched the district chief give a statement for the cameras. Rick knew him, of course, but it wasn't Cobb in front of the cameras because they'd been called out when additional alarms were struck, so the scene wasn't theirs. But he knew Joe and Marie would ask him about it later anyway since they were sitting in front of their television watching the same news broadcast.

He wondered if Jessica was watching it with them. Probably curled up at the opposite end of the couch from her grandmother, maybe wrapped in the fleece blanket Marie kept draped over the back of the couch once the weather turned cooler. Even though they'd had a decent couple of days, the chill had to be a bit of a shock coming from San Diego.

"What's so funny, Gullotti?"

Rick jerked his gaze to Cobb, who was scowling at him, his dark and caterpillar-like eyebrows almost meeting over his nose. "What?"

"They're talking snow in the forecast and you're the only guy in the room grinning like somebody just told you there are naked twins waiting for you in the bunk room."

"Oh, I didn't even hear the forecast. I was thinking about something else."

"What's her name?" Scott asked with a smirk.

Jessica. "Maybe I was thinking about the time you got stuck going through a window and I had to push you through like that cartoon bear."

Before Scotty could come back with a smart-ass response, the alarm sounded and they all groaned. Rick shoved his way into the kitchen to dump his bowl in the sink and then joined the stampede down to the bays.

As he stepped into his boots and pulled the suspenders on the pants up over his shoulders, he hoped this wouldn't be a long call because chili was a bitch to clean up after the fact. And as he grabbed his bunker coat and helmet off their hooks, he wondered what Jessica would think if she saw him on the late news in all his gear. A lot of women tended to find firefighters sexy, but he had no idea if she was one of them or not.

Rick swung up into the seat, scowling. He also had no idea why he cared.

AFTER DINNER WAS EATEN—far earlier in the day than she was accustomed to—and the dishes were washed, Jessica excused herself to her room. She'd heard her phone ringing in the distance while they ate, and that particular ringtone was only assigned to her father.

She hadn't answered it, of course, but she hadn't heard the voice-mail tone. That meant, if she didn't call him back very soon, he'd try again.

"Are you going to come watch the news with us?" Joe asked before she left the kitchen. "We watch the six o'clock news together every night."

"The news?" She almost said no, because checking in on financial news online would be a more productive use of her time than watching highlights of budget fights and Boston sports games on the television. But there was something about the way he said it that made it sound less like a polite question and more like an invitation to join them in a family activity. "Sure. I'll make sure I'm finished in time."

The smile on his face made her smile in return, thankful she'd made the right call. "Great. We'll make extra decaf tonight."

At least their third-floor tenant wasn't around tonight, she thought as she went up the stairs to her room. Not that she didn't like him. That wasn't the problem at all.

The problem was that whenever he was in the room, she had to resist the urge to look at him. She kept telling herself it was because he was tall and broad at the shoulder. Of course he'd draw the eye. But she'd also found herself wondering if his hands were as strong as they looked and what the scruffy beard on his face would feel like against skin, and she was pretty sure neither of those things had anything to do with how much space he took up in the kitchen.

Jessica had just closed her bedroom door behind her when her cell phone rang again, vibrating in her pocket while playing the distinctive ringtone that signaled a call from her father. Sighing, she pulled it out. She'd been hoping to do a quick sweep of her email and make sure nothing was happening at the office before calling him back.

Talking to him had been inevitable. While she hadn't expected him to step foot in the office for several more weeks, at least, he usually checked in with her or Sharon every so often. As tempting as it was to mute the ringer and let his call go to voice mail, Jessica knew he'd only keep calling back until he got through to her. And he would get angrier with each attempt.

"Hi, Dad."

"What the hell do you think you're doing?"

So he knew where she was, which meant he'd called Sharon before calling her. "I called to tell you about the message from the doctor, but you chose not to listen."

"What is it you think you're going to accomplish?"

"You told me to handle it. I'm handling it." More or less.

"Jessica, why didn't you tell me my parents are involved?"

Because he hadn't given her a chance to talk before barking out his demands and hanging up on her, like usual. But she recognized by his tone that he wasn't in the mood to admit any fault on this one. All she could do was try to keep anything emotional off the table. "I wanted to solve their problem for you as quickly as possible, and coming to Boston seemed like the most efficient way to accomplish that."

"I expect your assistance when it comes to the company, but this is personal. My family is none of your business."

Jessica was glad they were having this conversation by cell phone so he couldn't see her actually look at the phone and cock her head sideways in an are-you-serious-right-now kind of way. "I'm your daughter."

"I know who you are. And you're also vice president of Broussard Financial Services."

"I am your *daughter*," she repeated. "I *am* your family. That makes your parents—who are my grandparents, by the way—very much my business."

He was quiet for a few seconds, and she waited, knowing he was pondering the best route to take. "I told you a long time ago that they're not our kind of people, honey. And you know how much I depend on you in the office. I can't do it without you. I can hire somebody to help out my parents, but nobody can run this business for me like you do."

In the past, she would have given in. Not because she was flattered. Regardless of the truth in what he said, she knew he was saying it to manipulate her. For years she'd been telling herself that she let him get away with it because it made *her* life easier, not because it was actually effective.

But she wasn't finished in Boston. The initial awkwardness of staying in the house with her grandparents was wearing off, and she was enjoying getting to know Joe and Marie. Their conversations were still of the getting-to-know-you variety, though. They were almost comfortable enough with each other to maybe start having some heart-to-heart discussions and if she left for California now, it might not happen. Who knew when her father would free her up to return to the East Coast again?

They seemed hale and hearty enough to Jessica, but she reminded herself she was here to discuss their elder care options because Joe had ended up in the emergency room. And they were both on a variety of medications. If she returned to San Diego and something happened to one of them before she could get back…

"I prefer to stay and continue working remotely while helping Joe and Marie consider their options," she said firmly. "I have my laptop and my phone. That's all I ever use in the office, and they have good Wi-Fi and don't mind if I work at the kitchen table. The staff texts me when they need to and, as you know, that's how they usually communicate with me, anyway."

"They don't mind if you work at the kitchen table," he repeated in a flat voice, and she realized she'd given away the fact she wasn't talking to him from a hotel room. "Where are you staying?"

"I'm staying at their house. With Joe and Marie." The silence went on so long, Jessica glanced at her phone's screen to make sure the call timer was still running and he hadn't hung up on her. "The office is fine, Dad. Everything's running as smoothly as usual. Sharon and I are in contact several times per day. And, as I said, I'm perfectly set up for remote work."

"What about me? This isn't an easy time for me, Jessica."

A lifetime of conditioning kicked in and she nodded her head, but when she opened her mouth, the words wouldn't come out.

She didn't want to go home, but she knew she wouldn't get anywhere with him by playing the sentiment card. Instead she tried speaking his language. "They've already set up meetings for next week. Imagine how it would look if word got out you weren't willing to help your own parents with their affairs. It could be a PR disaster if word hit the right circles."

"My parents do *not* travel in the right circles."

Jessica closed her eyes and said a silent apology to Rick. "Their tenant could be a problem. They're very close and he's protective of them, so I wouldn't put it past him to cause a fuss. And he works for the city, so he probably knows a lot of people."

It was the truth, even if she knew her father wasn't envisioning a firefighter, but rather a guy in a suit at the city hall. She was in a tough spot because she wanted to stay with Joe and Marie a while longer. But she also couldn't lose her father and possibly derail her career for people she'd just met, no matter how much she wanted to get to know them, so it would be a balancing act.

"You have clients," he said, but she could hear the weakening in his voice. He was probably nearing the point where he'd give her what she wanted just so he could get off the phone and have a drink.

"My clients are being taken care of. And Sharon's the only person who knows why I'm here. Everybody else believes I'm wooing a potential client."

"The meetings are next week?"

"Yes. I haven't set up a meeting with a real estate agent yet, though, but hopefully I'll find one who can come out on short notice."

"Don't get too close to them," he warned. "Keep our personal business to yourself. But I'll let you stay until this matter's resolved so I don't have to hear about it again."

She let the statement of granted "permission" slide. "Thanks, Dad. I'll talk to you soon."

Once he'd hung up, she sat on the edge of the bed for a few minutes to calm herself. Her father was always draining to a point, but never so much as when he was drinking.

After a few minutes, she opened her laptop and lost herself in her inbox and stock reports. She kept an eye on the clock in the corner of the screen, though, so when it was almost six o'clock, she saved everything and went down the stairs.

Joe was in his chair and Marie at her usual end of the couch. And there was a mug of what she assumed was decaffeinated coffee sitting on the coffee table in front of the other end. She smiled a greeting and then curled up in the corner before reaching for the mug.

"Thank you," she said, and then took a sip.

"Are you okay?" Marie asked. "You look tired all of a sudden."

"My father called. He didn't know I was here and he's concerned about my not being in the office while he's unavailable." There. That was mostly the truth. She didn't see any reason to tell them he was more upset that she was with *them*.

"Do you want to talk about it?"

"Maybe another time," she said. "It's time for the news, anyway."

Because she seemed to live in a constant state of not-quite-warm-enough, even in the house, Jessica pulled the blanket off the back of the couch and tucked it around herself as the news began.

"Oh, I wonder if Rick will be on TV," Marie said as they started into a story about a roof fire.

Jessica didn't lean toward the screen, but she tried not to blink as they ran footage of the fire somebody had taken with a cell phone. She wasn't sure how she would tell which one was Rick with all the gear on, but she tried not to blink anyway.

And when she didn't see him, she tried not to be disappointed. And she *really* tried not to wonder if she'd see him tomorrow. According to Joe, Rick worked a twenty-four-hour shift and then had forty-eight hours off. Then he worked another twenty-four hours and had seventy-two off. This was his second of the week, so he'd be home for several days.

And he'd already made it clear he intended to keep his eye on her. She just needed to remember it was because he didn't trust her and not let herself develop a crush on the man. She was too old for crushes. And, in this case, it couldn't end well.

FOUR

THE NEXT MORNING, Jessica was dressed and ready to head downstairs by seven-thirty, since that seemed to be when Joe and Marie ate breakfast. She wasn't much of a morning eater, herself, but she recognized that Marie wanted to feed her and there was no sense in disrupting their routine.

As soon as she walked into the kitchen, she felt as if the vibe had changed somehow, as if they'd been talking about her and stopped when she came downstairs. Joe wasn't a cheery morning person to begin with, but this morning he spent a lot of time staring into his coffee cup. And Marie's lips kept pressing together as if she was trying not to say something that would be upsetting.

She'd set down three plates of scrambled eggs and toast before it appeared to Jessica she couldn't hold it in anymore. "Can I ask you something about Davey?"

Jessica nodded, pushing some eggs around on her plate. "Of course."

"Did he tell you we were dead?" Marie's voice was almost a whisper.

Jessica froze, her heart breaking at the question. How painful it would be to have a child who'd rather pretend you were dead than admit you were alive and just didn't want to see you? "No. He never said that."

The breath seemed to rush out of her grandmother's lungs. "Oh, good. We thought maybe that was why... Well, it doesn't matter. You're here now."

Jessica took a big, bracing gulp of coffee because it was time to put it all out there. She'd rather do it now than have her grandparents thinking she hadn't *wanted* to know them. "I asked about you sometimes when I was little. But it made Dad angry, so eventually I stopped asking. He said...he said you weren't our kind of people. That you were crass and drank a lot. I was a little girl, so I never questioned what he said. But when the doctor called...I wanted to meet you."

The hypocrisy of her father damning anybody for drinking burned in Jessica's stomach, but she took a bite of her toast to calm it. Marie dabbed at her eyes with her napkin, but she was smiling. It was Joe who spoke, though, after a gruff clearing of his throat.

"I guess during Davey's teen years, things were a little hard. Work was tight and we hit a rough spot in our marriage. I made some mistakes. We fought a lot and I drank too much. I admit it."

"Davey was always different," Marie said quietly. "He always wanted better and I always felt like he was embarrassed of us."

That sounded like her father and Jessica had certainly felt as though her father was judging her and finding her wanting a few times in her life. "I guess he hasn't changed very much."

"We've mellowed with age," Joe said. "I won't deny that. But the last time he was home, your grandmother was hurt that Davey wouldn't bring his girlfriend home to meet us."

Marie shook her head. "Joe, don't."

"She has a right to know," he said, looking across the table at Jessica. "He said he'd never bring a girl to this shit hole and called Marie trash. I'm not proud of it, but I put my hands on him. I put him up against the wall and told him if he couldn't respect his mother, he could leave. He never came back."

"He was young and stupid," Jessica said, and then she covered her mouth with her hand. "I'm sorry. I shouldn't be trying to defend him. It's a habit, I guess."

"We reached out to him a few times," Marie said, "but there was nothing. It was like there had never been a relationship with us. Eventually it hurt too much to keep trying, but I always hoped when he was older and had his own kids, he'd come around."

"He's very…self-centered," Jessica said quietly. "And I'm so sorry his relationship with you has been so painful."

"Has he been a good father to you?" Joe asked.

"Yes," she said without hesitation. "Not perfect, of course. Who is? But we're close and he's done the best he could. I have a great life."

"That's what matters, then." Her grandfather gave her a warm smile, which she returned.

Even though he tended to wreak havoc on her senses, Jessica was relieved when the back door opened and Rick walked in. She could take the hard conversations in small bits, but she wasn't used to emotional talks.

"Hey, everybody," he said, and Jessica noticed he did a bit of a double take when he looked at Marie. She was smiling, but her eyes were still a little wet and her cheeks flushed. "How's everybody doing this morning?"

"We're good," Marie said. "Do you want some breakfast? I can whip up some more eggs with no trouble at all."

"I already ate. Today seems like a good day to get some errands done and I was thinking I'd drag Joe along. We need to make new plywood tents for your bushes in the backyard because we trashed the old ones last year, remember?"

"I meant to ask you about that, but I forgot," Marie said. "I have a list somewhere."

"Didn't you just work twenty-four hours?" Jessica was surprised to see him looking maybe a little tired around the eyes, but mostly ready for a day of yard work.

"We sleep between runs," he said. "Last night was quiet. Trust me, there are days when the only thing I do when I get home is strip off my clothes and crawl into bed."

"I can imagine," she said. Good lord, she could imagine him stripping without any effort at all. "I mean, I can imagine working twenty-four hours if it was busy would be hard."

"Oh, today's Saturday," Marie said. "Joe and I

are supposed to go to a barbecue lunch for Valerie's grandson's birthday today."

"A barbecue?" Jessica almost dropped her fork. "It's winter. You guys do know it's winter, right?"

They all laughed, and then Joe shook his head. "It's not even cold yet. If the hamburger doesn't freeze between the time you walk out the door to the time you put it on the grill, it's warm enough to barbecue."

"I'll take care of the bushes," Rick said, walking toward the coffeepot. "You already told Valerie you'd be there and you know how she is. Every time you see her for the entire year, she'll find a way to take a dig at you for missing the party."

"Yes, that's true." Marie looked at Jessica. "Do you want to go?"

Besides the fact she didn't feel nearly hardy enough to stand around outside eating burgers with strangers, whether the burgers froze or not, she didn't feel up to facing the questions that would inevitably come her way. "I'm a little behind on work, actually. If you don't mind, I'll take the time to catch up."

"Good call," Joe muttered. "Valerie's husband has two degrees of grilled burgers. Raw on the inside or hockey puck."

"Rick going in and out won't distract you or keep you from working, will it?" Marie asked.

Jessica looked at Rick, who was watching her with those blue eyes. Oh, Rick going in and out would definitely distract her. "He won't keep me from working."

He raised that damn eyebrow of his and grinned, as if she'd just issued a challenge.

If a woman did all of her work on her cell phone and laptop, why she needed to have a pen was beyond Rick. But Jessica had one and it seemed like every time he walked through the door, she was sitting at the table playing with her damn pen.

He'd seen her tapping it against her bottom lip, which naturally made him notice her bottom lip and how utterly kissable it looked. She tapped it on her teeth. And on this trip inside he saw she appeared to be concentrating on the screen particularly hard while she sucked on the cap.

And, dammit, he forgot what he'd gone inside for. That was assuming he'd even had a reason and wasn't subconsciously coming up with excuses to see Jessica. Grabbing a drink had made sense. Another trip inside to rummage through Marie's junk drawer for a permanent marker had made sense. But since he lived upstairs, there were only so many reasons he needed to be in there.

"Hi," she said, dropping the pen onto the table, and he realized he'd been staring at her. "Do you need something?"

That was a good question. He'd obviously needed something since he'd gone inside, but seeing her lips puckered around the pen had wiped his mind clear of everything except her mouth. He had to say something, though. "I wanted to see if you could give me a hand for a second, but you're obviously busy."

"No, I'm not." She closed the laptop so fast he got the impression she'd been looking for an excuse to be done. "It's time for a break, anyway."

"Great. Appreciate it." And now he had to come up with something for her to do. "You don't have any paper."

"Excuse me?" She got up and pushed her chair in. "Do we need paper? I have a legal pad upstairs if we do."

"No. We don't need paper for what we're doing." Of course she had a legal pad. She'd been using it to figure out what her grandparents' property might be worth. "I just thought it was funny you have a pen, but nothing to write on."

Her mouth twisted in a wry smile. "I quit smoking six years ago. I'm a fidgeter by nature and quitting seemed to make it worse, so I was constantly fidgeting with the pen. After a while I realized having that keeps me from wanting to get up out of my chair constantly, so I always have a pen in my hand when I'm working."

And in her mouth. "Congratulations on quitting. It's not easy, from what I've heard."

"Thanks. It wasn't easy to quit, but most of the time I'm proud of myself." She laughed. "Sometimes I wonder what the hell I was thinking because the cigarettes sure made life easier, but I know better."

"Joe used to smoke cigars, until Marie made him quit. Does your dad smoke?"

She shook her head. "Never has, that I know of. I started in high school, when it seemed like a good diet plan. Don't comfort eat. Just comfort smoke instead."

He wasn't sure what to say to that. He wanted to ask her why she'd needed comfort. Or tell her she certainly didn't have to worry about a diet plan because her body was pretty damn perfect just as it was. But neither were any of his business, so he just smiled and led the way to the backyard.

She trailed her hand down the railing of the handicapped ramp Joe and Marie used. "This looks fairly new."

"Yeah, some of the guys from my station helped me build it a few months back. The front steps can be a bitch in the winter and the back ones needed replacing. Seemed like a good time to do it." He picked up the two pieces of plywood he'd built a frame around and formed them into an A shape. "I'll show you how to hold them while I screw the hinges in."

"Okay." Either she didn't realize this wasn't something he really needed help with, or she didn't care. "What are these for?"

"They make tents over the bushes so the weight of the snow won't crush them or break the branches off."

She stopped in the act of bending over to look at the plywood panels. "You get that much snow?"

"Sometimes."

When she had the two pieces of wood lined up, Rick bent to drive in the screws. It put their heads very close together and, when he inhaled, he could smell her shampoo or soap or something. It wasn't strong enough to be perfume, but it was enough to be distracting.

Together, they made quick work of the first two, but he didn't like the way the third lined up. Rather than risk his drill slipping and catching her fingers, he set it down and put his hands over hers to adjust her hold on the wood.

The touch must have startled her because her head jerked up. Her face was so close to his, he would barely have to lean forward to kiss her. And with her hands so small and soft under his, and her gaze locked with his, he really wanted to. As if she could read his thoughts, her face flushed and her lips parted slightly. Unless he was totally misreading the signal, she wouldn't slap his face for trying.

But it would be a huge mistake, so he very reluctantly dragged his attention back to the task at hand. "Here, hold it like this so I don't accidentally nick you with the drill."

Jessica nodded and dropped her gaze back to their hands. He wasn't sure if the sudden scowl was one of concentration or if she was thinking about what had just passed between them. Or hadn't, as the case may be.

As soon as her fingers were in the right place, he removed his hands from hers and picked up the drill again. The sooner they were finished with this, the sooner he could stop calling himself every kind of an idiot for making up a stupid reason for having her out there in the first place.

She helped him do the fourth frame and then stepped back as he put them in place over Marie's more delicate bushes. Rick was keenly aware Jessica was watching him as he screwed a small cross member on each one so they couldn't collapse if the snow was heavy enough to shift the hinges.

"It's snowing!"

He turned to see her with her face turned up to the sky, watching scattered flakes fall. "Yeah, they said we might get some flurries off and on before the actual snow starts."

"Is it true that if you stick your tongue to a metal pole, it'll stick?"

"If it's cold enough, hell yes, it'll stick. We responded to three calls for that last winter."

Her eyes widened, making him chuckle. "You're kidding."

"Nope. And now that all the kids want funny videos or selfies for the internet, they do dumb shit like that all the time and we get to lecture them while saving them from themselves. Licking metal poles seems to be popular for some reason."

"So how cold is too cold?"

"It's definitely not cold enough yet." He put his hands on his hips and looked at her. "Is licking a pole on your list of things to do while in Boston or what?"

As soon as he said the words, his inner twelve-year-old boy snickered, but he hoped she wouldn't catch the accidental innuendo.

"I have no intention of licking any poles while in Boston, thank you." Yeah, she'd caught it. He could tell by the way her lips tightened in an effort not to smile. The tiny quirk at the corners gave her away, though.

He *had* to stop paying so much attention to her mouth. After putting the battery drill back in its box, Rick wrapped the cord around the circular saw and put them both, along with the square and a few other miscellaneous tools, back in Joe's toolshed. After he'd snapped the padlock closed, he turned, expecting Jessica to have gone back into the house.

But she was still in the yard, frowning at the snow flurries that were barely worth noticing. "Joe and Marie will get home before the roads get slippery, right?"

He smiled. "Yeah, they will. This is just a flurry, I promise, and the roads won't be affected. The snow's supposed to pick up some later in the day. And speaking of driving, do you need to do something about that rental?"

"No. I already talked to them because I anticipated having it for a few days, but since it was already open-ended, they don't really care. I'm not sure about driving it in the snow, though."

"You don't need to. Joe or I can drive you if you absolutely need something before the roads are clear. It's still early in the winter, so you shouldn't have any problems."

"You don't worry about Joe driving?"

It took him a second to realize she probably meant because of his age and not because of the snow. "Not really. There have been a couple of times Marie or I have had to taxi him around, but unless his doctor tells him he's done driving, there's no reason he can't."

"And the doctor isn't concerned?"

"Not that I've heard. It seems to be living arrangements he's concerned about."

She sighed and tilted her head way back to take in the three-story building. "It's a lovely house, but it's so big."

"They like it. And I can tell you right now, they'll fight to stay here."

"Be honest, though. If you move out, can Joe and Marie still take care of the property without you?"

That was a tough question to answer. He definitely didn't want them doing some of the stuff he took care of. The idea of Joe up on a ladder cleaning the gutters, for instance, made him ill. And he didn't know if they could afford to hire people to do all those tasks because he'd never asked about their finances. They were none of his business.

"I don't know," he said, going for honesty. "But I don't plan on going anywhere anytime soon."

"What if you fall in love and get married and want to start a family?"

Maybe that had been on his mind a little lately, but it didn't appear it was going to happen anytime soon. "Don't worry, I'm not the marrying kind."

She rolled her eyes. "That's what all guys say and then, bam, wedding rings and minivans."

"No minivans. An SUV, maybe." He didn't really want to think about what vehicle he'd cart his hypothetical family around in and preferred to talk about her. After fending off that urge to kiss her, he needed to put a little more distance between them again. "Joe and I spend a lot of time talking, just so you know."

"What's that supposed to mean?"

"Just that if you try to push them in the direction

you want them to go instead of the direction *they* want to go, I'll hear about it."

Jessica looked at him a long time, her mouth in a grim line, before she shook her head. "I know I can't make you trust me, but they're my grandparents. I'm not going to try to screw them out of anything."

"You've been with Davey for thirty-four years. You've been with Joe and Marie for three days. Can you blame me for wondering where your loyalty lies?"

"Says the man who's sunk a lot of time and hard work and maybe even money into a property that he has no claim to other than through the affection of its owners."

It should have pissed him off, but he found himself smiling. He admired the way she stood her ground without letting temper get the better of her. "As long as we both have Joe and Marie's best interests at heart, we shouldn't have a problem."

"I guess we'll just have to wait and see how it turns out, but you *can* trust me," she said, and then she walked up the ramp and back into the house, letting the screen door slam behind her before she closed the big door with a solid thud.

Rick bent to pick up the scraps of wood with a sigh. With the Broussards' future on the line, he definitely hoped their granddaughter was right. He wanted to trust her. But he needed to trust her for the right reasons, and neither her mouth nor the dreamy expression on her face as she watched the snowflakes fall were the right reasons.

One thing he was certain of was the fact he didn't

want Joe and Marie to come home and find out he'd pissed off their granddaughter. Once he'd picked up the yard, he'd go inside and make sure he hadn't offended her too badly.

JESSICA TRIED OPENING her laptop, but she gave up after ten minutes or so and closed it again.

For a few crazy seconds outside, she'd thought Rick was going to kiss her. There was something about the way he looked at her—especially her mouth—that made her sure he wanted to.

What a disaster that would be, she thought. Since a few minutes later, it sounded a lot as if he was accusing her of wanting to take advantage of Joe and Marie financially, kissing Rick could only add to the weird emotional place she'd found herself in.

To distract herself from the sexy firefighter she absolutely couldn't kiss, she reached across and picked up the puzzle book sitting open on her grandfather's end of the kitchen table, along with the pencil. She'd already figured out that Joe loved his puzzle books, but only the language puzzles. The math ones were rarely even started, never mind finished.

Even though she submersed herself fairly quickly in numbers, she heard Rick's footsteps outside before the door opened. She was thankful because it gave her a few seconds to focus on not looking as if she'd been thinking about kissing him.

"Hey," he said, closing the door behind him. "Sorry if I'm bothering you again, but I just wanted to make sure you're not too mad at me."

It took her a few seconds to realize what he was talking about, and then she smiled. "I'm not mad. I mean, I didn't like the implication, but I understand where you're coming from. Plus I'm doing Joe's math puzzles and I'm one of those weird people who find numbers soothing."

He looked at the puzzle book and then arched an eyebrow when he realized she'd already finished the puzzle. "I guess if you're in charge of taking people's money and making it into more money, you must be pretty good at math."

"I am. My father made sure of that."

"How do you make sure somebody's good at math? Isn't that a you-are-or-you-aren't kind of thing?"

"He told me when I was a little girl that I have a natural aptitude for it."

Rick grinned. "Of course you do. Your grand-mother taught advanced high school math for almost forty years."

"Really? I guess numbers must run in my family. I don't know why, but I just assumed she was a homemaker. Maybe because she's so good at it and Joe seems so…old-fashioned, I guess."

"It's only been a few days, Jess. You and your grandparents aren't going to learn everybody's life stories overnight."

"I don't know why I didn't ask, though. Or why she wouldn't have mentioned it, since math's a big part of my job."

He took up his usual position, leaning against the kitchen counter. "I think she just wants to know about you so much she doesn't think to tell you much about herself. They're still wrapping their minds around the fact you even exist, you know."

She nodded, feeling as if there was a lump of emotion clogging her throat. "He made them sound pretty horrible, you know. And it made him so angry when I asked about them that I stopped. Maybe I should have kept asking."

"You were a kid. And why wouldn't you believe him? You were only getting one side of the story and you had no reason to doubt what he told you." He shifted his weight, crossing one ankle over the other. "I'm a little surprised you never reached out to them when you were an adult, though."

"It would have made my father unhappy."

"A lot of things make parents unhappy. They get over it."

"Do they?" She fiddled with the pencil, rolling it between her fingers before tapping it on the book. "I guess my mother didn't get over it, since she never came back."

His expression turned serious, and he inhaled deeply through his nose. "I'm sorry about that. It's a pretty shitty thing for a mother to do, but I highly doubt you were the one who made her unhappy enough to abandon being a mother."

Jessica shrugged, trying to hide how much she wanted that to be true. "Maybe not. But what I do know is that my mother took off, and was an only child whose parents had both passed. My paternal grandparents were supposedly awful people, and stepmothers come and go. When you only have one person in your life who's family, you try not to piss him off too much."

He nodded his head, as if he could see her point. "Since we're kind of on the subject, what does unavailable mean?"

It was tempting to pretend she didn't know what he was talking about, but it was a core word in her vocabulary. *I'm sorry, but my father is unavailable at the moment...* "He drinks. Which is really ironic considering it's one of the things he holds against his parents. Or Joe, at least."

"So Davey's an alcoholic?"

"It sounds so weird to me, the way everybody here calls him Davey. He's always David now. Not even Dave." She paused and shoved her hands into her coat pockets. "And I honestly don't know if he's an alcoholic. He'll go a long time without drinking at all. Or he'll have a few cocktails here and there at social events. But if things get rough he...binge drinks, I guess you'd call it. He just disappears and spends days drunk. Sometimes weeks. He's *unavailable* right now because my most recent stepmother is about to join my previous three stepmothers in the ex-wives club."

"Ouch."

"He's not an easy man to live with." That was a bit of an understatement.

"Yet you've built your entire life around him."

There was no censure in his voice. No inflection implying she was an idiot. It was just a statement of fact, but it still made her wince inside. "I've built my life to suit *me*, but he is the only family I've ever had before now. We're a team."

It was a habit to defend him, she supposed. She'd done it often enough with the staff and trying to play peacemaker with his wives. But it was also the truth. Other people, including her mother, had come and gone, but she and her father had always been a team.

"Family should be a team," Rick agreed. "And I'm glad you're taking the time to get to know Joe and Marie because they're your family, too. And they're good people."

"I think so, too."

"Good. While I'm thinking of it, I'm going to check the filters on the furnace because I think it's time to change them out. It's in the cellar, though, so I shouldn't be in your way."

Jessica stood and pushed the puzzle book and pencil back to Joe's end of the table. "I'm probably going to do some laundry or something, anyway. I'm not in the mood to sit in this chair today."

"Sitting at the desk doing paperwork is the only part of the job I don't like," Rick said, shaking his head. "I don't know how people who work in offices stand it."

"Well, I don't have to climb giant ladders and risk my life in smoke and fire. So there's that."

He laughed as he walked toward the door to the cellar. "Good point."

Because the rich sound of his laughter did funny things to her nerves, Jessica gave a little wave and walked out of the kitchen. Everything in her life seemed to have changed so much and so fast with that one voice mail from Joe's doctor, so she knew she had to be careful about being vulnerable emotionally.

She needed to squash this attraction she seemed to have for Rick, and the best place to start was probably getting out of the kitchen and not staring at the cellar door, waiting for him to reappear.

FIVE

JESSICA LOVED EXPLORING the house. Every time she looked around, she seemed to notice something new. And since she was too antsy after her conversation with Rick to sit in front of her laptop, she went into the big living room.

She'd already looked at the framed family photos scattered around. There weren't many, and she got the sense Marie hadn't been much for taking pictures. The staircase wall had pictures of her dad, and she'd spent some time yesterday looking at them. There was very little of the boy growing up in the variety of frames in the man she knew. He'd been cute with no front teeth, but it was obvious he didn't like having his picture taken. And there were no photos of him at all after his senior portrait, in which he glared sullenly at the photographer in front of what looked like a department-store studio backdrop.

It was the treasures that she really enjoyed. Her father wasn't a knickknack kind of guy, and certainly wasn't sentimental about things, so she'd grown up in a very uncluttered household. But on display in Marie's curio cabinet was all manner of things. The bride and groom figurine from her grandparents' wedding cake. A clay cup her dad had made them in clementary school. A gilt-edged teacup so old the fine age cracks made the flowers look almost mosaic. According to Marie, it had belonged to Joe's grandmother and was the only piece of china left from the set that had come from Nova Scotia with her.

Today she wandered to the bookshelf and, tilting her head, scanned the spines. There were a lot of old Westerns and Agatha Christie titles, which made her smile. And on the top shelf was a framed newspaper article. She realized it was a picture of a firefighter and leaned closer.

All of the gear obscured the identity of the man helping an extremely pregnant woman onto the ladder while the black smoke billowing from the window framed them. But the caption told her it was Rick, and that the woman's water had broken halfway down the ladder and her daughter had been born in the ambulance on the way to the hospital.

"That was a helluva day."

Jessica turned at the sound of Rick's voice, caught off guard because she hadn't heard him come back up the cellar stairs. "They were both okay?"

"Yeah." He tucked his fingers into the front pockets of his jeans and shrugged. "Three stories up on a ladder with the most pregnant woman I'd ever seen was already hairy. Then her water broke and she started panicking. There was no way to throw her over my shoulder, so she just leaned back against me while I tried to get us both to the ground in one piece."

His gaze was fixed over her shoulder, probably on the framed clipping, but he had a faraway look. Jessica couldn't wrap her mind around the fact doing stuff like that was his job. "Is it always like that?"

He snorted, shaking his head. "No, thank God. We get our share of fires, but there are accidents and medical calls. Cats stuck in trees."

"Why did you become a firefighter? And don't tell me it's because you're a safety junkie. If you wanted safety, you'd probably be a teacher, like your brother."

"*My* teachers would be horrified at the thought." He gave her a grin that made her whole body tingle. "Guy I played hockey with sometimes was at the fire academy and there was some trash talking and, to make a long story short, I became a firefighter to prove I could. Almost like a dare. I guess I still do it because it pays good, the benefits don't suck and I really can't imagine myself doing anything else."

She wanted to ask more, but they heard the faint squeak of the back door's hinges, followed by Marie's voice. Despite being disappointed her conversation with Rick was at an end, since he'd turned and walked away, Jessica was relieved her grandparents were home. She knew it was silly to be worried about a few snowflakes, but she also knew that the older people got, the worse their reflexes were.

Following Rick into the kitchen, she listened to them all talk about the barbecue. The conversation mostly consisted of news about a lot of people Jessica didn't know, so it was tempting to grab her laptop and go upstairs. It had been several hours since she checked her email and that might have been a record for her.

But she liked the easy rhythm of their interactions. They even seemed to have their own individual spots for talking. Joe sat at the table, with his word search book open in front of him. Marie puttered around the kitchen, getting ready to make dinner. And Rick, as usual, leaned against the counter.

Because it seemed the logical thing to do, Jessica had sat in the chair she'd been using since she arrived on Wednesday. While Joe, Marie and Rick were almost a family unit, it made her feel almost as if she belonged to have a usual spot, too.

But she jumped in her chair when her phone, still sitting on the table next to her laptop, rang. It was her father's ringtone, and his name flashed on the screen. The others looked at it, since it was hard to ignore the sound, and she realized Marie could see the name when her body stiffened.

"Sorry," Jessica said softly, tapping the option to send his call to voice mail, and then flipping the switch to silence her phone in case he called again. He almost certainly would.

"You can answer that, you know," Joe said. "It could be important business."

"It's nothing that can't wait." It would be too awkward to talk to him while they were in the room. "It's not like Rick's job, which is literally life-and-death."

"And cats in trees," he added, making Joe and Marie laugh.

The bubble of tension popped, and Jessica smiled. "Can't forget the cats."

"I should head upstairs," Rick said a few minutes

later. "I left laundry in the washer and I hate when I forget it's in there and have to wash it again."

"You'll come down and eat supper with us, won't you?" Marie asked.

Jessica saw him hesitate as his gaze met hers. Then he looked away with a sigh. "You don't need me underfoot. And besides the laundry, I've got a list of other stuff waiting to get done."

"You took care of my bushes today. And I'm making stuffed manicotti."

He groaned. "You know I'm a sucker for any of your pasta dishes."

"Come back down in about two hours, then."

Jessica watched him go, and then snatched her phone off the table when it vibrated loudly against the wood. She should have anticipated that. After rejecting her father's second call, she cradled the phone in her hands under the table where it wouldn't be as noticeable if it went off again.

"I'm going to go watch some television, I think," Joe said, pushing himself up off his chair. He winced a little as his knees straightened, but he gave Jessica a wink. "I get nervous when I'm the only man in the kitchen."

Marie snorted. "You should be. And Jessica probably needs to go upstairs and deal with work stuff, anyway."

Yes, she needed to. But after a few seconds, she shook her head. Then she powered off her phone completely and tossed it on top of her laptop. "Actually,

I've never made stuffed manicotti. If you don't mind teaching as you go along, I'd love to help."

The smile that lit up her grandmother's face made Jessica's heart ache, and she knew she'd made the right choice. She'd probably still regret it when she finally had to return to her father's phone call, but for right now, she was going to hang out in the kitchen and cook a meal with her grandmother.

After the men vacated the kitchen, they got to work. Jessica wasn't surprised Marie didn't have to pull out a recipe card or cookbook, though she did promise to write it down for Jessica after dinner if she liked it.

"This was one of your dad's favorite meals growing up," her grandmother said.

"It still is, actually. I probably would have made it before now, except when we dine together, it usually doubles as a business meeting. It's a lot easier to do that in a restaurant."

"Do you cook at home for yourself, though?"

"Sometimes, but definitely nothing like stuffed manicotti. I have an indoor grill I love and I'll toss a quick salad to go with whatever meat I grilled for dinner. I'm not very creative, I'm afraid."

"And none of your stepmothers taught you how to cook?"

Jess sighed. "Most of them haven't been very fond of me, I guess. I'm a big part of my father's life and he would defer to me a lot even for household decisions."

"Why haven't you ever married?" Marie said, popping the lid off of a tub of ricotta cheese. "If you don't mind my asking. I'm being very nosy, I guess."

"Confession time. I don't really care how to make stuffed manicotti. I just wanted to spend time getting to know you and the kitchen seems like a good place, so nosy is kind of the point. I found out from Rick that you taught math in high school and I can't believe I hadn't already asked you that."

Marie laughed. "I think I've been hogging all the questions. But I'd really rather hear about your love life than my teaching career, that's for sure."

Jess snorted and shook her head. "I wouldn't call it a love life. I date, of course. But for some reason, most of the men I've gone out with have been younger than I am, maybe because they're not beating the *time to start a family* drum."

"And you're not ready for that yet?"

"I think I'm getting there, but not quite yet. And besides the age issue, there's my father. The men I've dated have either wanted a chance to work with my father or they've been scared spitless of him. It's really annoying, so I haven't dated much at all lately."

"You'd be surprised how many friends I have with grandsons that would be perfect for you."

Jess side-eyed Marie, who laughed at her. "I have enough on my plate right now."

"Oh, but let me tell you about this one young man. Well, young meaning forty-five or so."

Two hours of blind date dodging and a lot of laughter later, Jessica found out why Rick had been willing to forego doing his own chores to come back downstairs for dinner. Even though the ones Jessica had stuffed looked a little messy, the manicotti tasted amazing and she ate until she couldn't bear to put another bite in her mouth.

Then she leaned back in her chair with a groan. "I can't keep eating like this. I swear my jeans are already getting too tight and I have a closet full of pencil skirts. Those are *not* forgiving."

"What's a pencil skirt?" Rick asked from across the table.

"They're long, like midcalf length, and they hug your...let's just say they're somewhat form-fitting." When he raised an eyebrow, she tried not to blush. "They're flattering, but they won't be for long if I keep having seconds of everything Marie cooks."

"You have a beautiful figure," her grandmother said, and Jessica didn't miss the slight nod of Rick's head before he quickly turned his attention back to his plate.

"Not for much longer. Our office building has a fitness center in it, so I usually work out at the end of the day. Only for half an hour or so, but I can gather my thoughts and sweat out any frustrations before heading home. And it keeps my jeans from getting too tight, I guess."

"Rick, you belong to a gym, don't you?" Marie asked. "Even though she doesn't need it as far as I can tell, you should take her to work out with you if it makes her feel better."

Jessica's imagination coughed up an image of a

shirtless, sweaty Rick and the instant hot flash made her feel anything but better.

RICK HAD JUST put a big chunk of stuffed manicotti into his mouth and he took his time chewing it. He didn't need a flashing neon arrow to see what direction Marie was going with that question, but he had a suspicion the place he had a membership to and the San Diego office building "fitness center" Jessica used were on totally opposite ends of the gym spectrum.

"Sometimes," he said once he couldn't put off swallowing his food any longer. "We have some workout equipment at the station, so I don't really get to the gym very often. I probably talk about it a lot more often then I actually see the inside of it."

Marie set her fork down and took a sip of her drink before turning her laser focus on him. "There aren't any of those gyms just for women nearby, I don't think, and I don't want Jessica running around the city trying to find one. But I don't want her going to your gym with a bunch of strange men all by herself, either."

"It's honestly okay, Marie," Jessica said, but Rick knew it was a lost cause. "I don't think I'll actually outgrow my jeans before I get back to San Diego."

"But you use it to clear your mind, too, and it's probably stressful being out here while you have a business to run all the way across the country."

The obvious answer would be for Jessica to go back across the country and just run her business, but Rick wisely kept that suggestion to himself. "I can take you to the gym. You want to go tomorrow?"

"I…" She gave him a look across the table that clearly said she wasn't sure she wanted to at all, but she *was* getting the hint that Marie wasn't going to give up on the idea. "Okay."

"How's ten o'clock? It's not far. Down the street and around the corner, so we can walk. And there's no place to change, so wear what you want to work out in."

"Sounds good."

"That's settled, then." Looking very satisfied with herself, Marie picked up her fork again. "Since you're going to the gym tomorrow, do you want another manicotti?"

Once they were done eating and the kitchen had been cleaned up, Rick made his second escape of the day. They'd invited him to watch television with them, but he'd reminded them he had stuff he needed to get done.

It wasn't entirely true. He didn't have much of a to-do list other than the laundry and some light house-keeping, but he'd pretty much had his fill of Brous-sards for the day. They were exhausting, really. He'd been worried about Joe and Marie for so long, he should have been relieved to have Jess there to take up some of the slack. But he couldn't help but won-der if it had been a coincidence that they were meet-ing with the doctor on a Tuesday, when they knew he'd be at the station.

And then there was Jessica. He found it difficult to

concentrate around her and, when he wasn't around, he found himself looking forward to seeing her again. That was a disaster in the making. If she was anybody but Joe and Marie's granddaughter, he'd probably have asked her out to dinner already. He'd get to know her and maybe, if the attraction was mutual, do something about the growing ache that intensified every time he was around her. But the last thing this situation needed was the two of them getting entangled in any kind of a relationship. He wasn't sure how Joe and Marie would feel about it but, good or bad, it would change everything.

After finishing his laundry and doing some other chores, Rick stretched out on his couch and did some channel surfing. Nothing caught his interest, so he stopped flipping on an action movie he'd seen at least a dozen times and tossed the remote onto the coffee table.

He woke up just before six the next morning with a stiff neck and groaned. A nice king-sized bed in the next room, and he slept on the damn couch. Being able to sleep anywhere, in almost any position, made his job easier, but it sure sucked when he did it at home.

Before jumping in the shower, Rick made himself a coffee and walked to the window. The snow hadn't amounted to much and it would probably melt off on its own by noon. He'd sweep off the ramp and throw some sand down before Joe and Marie left for their traditional Sunday brunch at the senior center, but he could ignore the rest.

He scrambled a few eggs and dropped a couple of slices of American cheese on top to melt while he toasted an English muffin. Then he showered and threw on a pair of sweatpants and a T-shirt that was so old the Boston Red Sox logo was almost worn away. If he was taking Jessica to the gym, he may as well get a workout in, too. It wasn't as if he could stand around and watch her, whether he wanted to or not.

At nine-thirty, he pulled on a hoodie and went down the back stairs to take care of the ramp. That didn't kill enough time, so he swept off the vehicles while he was at it. And, when the back door finally opened and Jessica stepped out, he laughed.

She stopped halfway down the ramp and scowled at him before looking down at the parka that covered her from neck to knee. "There's snow. Snow means cold, so Marie lent me one of her coats."

That was a February kind of coat, but she was a California girl, so he just grinned. "As long as you're comfortable. You ready?"

They walked in silence for a few minutes while Jessica looked around the old neighborhood. It was a nice neighborhood, if a little shabby in places, and geared toward families. There were no plazas or big box stores in sight, but there was a market on almost every corner and a lot of small shops along the main street.

"Since you have to work on Tuesday, is there anything in particular you'd like for me to ask the doctor?" she asked as they rounded the corner onto a side street.

"At this point, not really. Mostly I'd just like to know if he has any specific concerns, you know what I mean?" As far as he knew, the appointment was mostly a formality. A follow-up for Joe's fall and to replace Davey with Jessica on their paperwork. "If there's something serious going on they're not telling me about, I'd like to know."

She was quiet for a moment, and then he caught the sharp nod of her head from the corner of his eye, as if she'd made a decision. "If there's something going on, I'll make them tell you."

Rick didn't miss the phrasing. She wasn't going to tell him herself, maybe not wanting to break their confidence. It annoyed him a little that she'd be in the loop but he wouldn't be, but he also had to respect the fact she was taking this—and her newfound loyalty to her grandparents—seriously.

He stopped in front of a metal door with chipped blue paint and the gym's logo. It was dimly lit and smelled like sweaty socks, and there were a few guys already working out. Jessica didn't hesitate. She simply looked around as he led her to a long bench that had hooks hung over it. They only had one locker room and it looked like a science project gone bad, so Rick never used it. He stripped off the hoodie and hung it on a hook before looking at her.

"You ready to sweat?" he asked.

She nodded, but didn't meet his gaze, which he found amusing. Then she unzipped the parka and shrugged it off.

Jess in gym clothes wasn't something he'd really given a lot of thought to. Now he was afraid he wouldn't be able to think of anything else for a long damn time.

No baggy sweats and shapeless T-shirt for her. She had on tight black leggings that hugged every single curve. Her calves. Her thighs. Her hips. And, when she turned slightly, her ass. Most definitely her ass. And she was wearing a similarly body-hugging tank top with a scooped neck that showed a hint of cleavage. Her arms were bare and toned, and still tanned whereas most of New England's citizens were already losing their summer color for the winter.

Whatever she did in her fancy executive fitness center, it was definitely working for her.

"I ran to the store after supper last night and picked up a few things." She scowled, looking down at the new clothes. "When I go home, I'll either have to buy and check a second suitcase or mail a box back to San Diego."

Rick could tell by the silence that he wasn't the only man in the room appreciating Jessica's choice of workout gear, but he forced himself not to turn around and glare at anybody. "As you can see, we don't have a lot of fancy stuff. Weights. There are a few speed bags and a couple of heavy bags if you want to hit things. There are two bikes over in the corner. And more weights."

"I think I'll just spin for a while."

He frowned. "Spin?"

"The bikes. I'll just ride the bike for some cardio."

"Ah, okay. I'll probably lift some weights for a while."

"Hey, Gullotti, you got any tickets for the game on you?" a guy called from across the gym.

"Not on me, but if you stop by the station, any of the guys can hook you up."

"What game?" Jess asked after the other guy had nodded his thanks.

"Charity hockey game," he explained. "Fire versus police."

"Oh, I've heard of those. They're a big deal."

Rick smiled. "Yeah. This isn't the big battle of the badges game. Just a smaller neighborhood game to raise money for Toys 4 Tots. And most of the people not only buy the tickets, but they bring toys, too. It's a tradition and the turnout's always good."

"Is it soon?"

"Next Saturday."

"Oh." She looked thoughtful for a few seconds. "Do Joe and Marie go?"

"Every year. I can get you a ticket if you think you'll still be around," he offered, even though he was pretty sure she'd head west once the doctor appointment was out of the way. She didn't need to be there for the lawyer, and Joe and Marie weren't anywhere near ready to consider a real estate agent yet. If at all.

"I haven't taken a vacation in years," she said. "I'd like to see a hockey game, I think. Especially with Joe and Marie. I'll stay that long."

Even though she sounded sure of the decision, he could see the worry in her eyes and the set of her mouth. Her old man was *not* going to be happy with her. "I'll save you a ticket, then. Joe and Marie will love having you there."

He wasn't so sure how he felt about it, though. Watching her walk to the exercise bikes, her ass perfectly displayed by the yoga pants or tights or whatever the hell they were called, was excruciating. And the longer she was around, the harder it would be to keep telling himself he didn't want her.

Deliberately choosing a weight station that didn't have him facing the exercise bikes, Rick wondered how long he'd have to work out in order to wear his body out to the point it didn't react to Jessica. But he knew, no matter how much he made himself sweat, he didn't have that kind of time.

SIX

"TODAY WOULD BE a good day to drive over to Brookline and pick out a Christmas tree."

Jessica glanced over at her grandmother from the stove, where she was scraping and folding eggs in Marie's big cast iron skillet. She'd never made eggs this way—scrambled in a little of the leftover bacon grease—and eating them was going to cancel out what little good she'd accomplished at the gym yesterday, but they were going to be worth it. She hoped. When Marie made them, they were delicious, but this was Jessica's first attempt without help.

"You mean a real tree?" she asked. "Wouldn't it be easier to have an artificial one?"

"Easier, maybe, but we both like the look and smell of a real tree, so as long as we have Rick to help Joe carry one in and set it up, we'll stick with tradition." Marie pushed another four slices of bread into the toaster and smeared butter across the slices that had just popped. "I know you have to go home for the holidays, but if we get a tree now we can at least share a little Christmas spirit while you're here."

"What are you scheming now, woman?" Joe asked as he walked into the kitchen, no doubt lured in by the smell of bacon and coffee.

"Did Rick mention having any plans today?" Marie asked instead of answering the question.

Jessica turned off the burner and divvied up the scrambled eggs between the three plates on the counter as her grandparents discussed whether or not they should bother Rick and argued about how long the tree had lasted last year and if they should wait another week. She had a feeling Joe would lose on that point, since Marie's primary motivation seemed to be sharing the experience with her.

She wasn't sure she could take another day with Rick, though. It was one thing to be attracted to him and indulge in a very secret fantasy crush. But when they'd built the plywood frames for Marie's bushes, he'd looked as if he was going to kiss her. And then, at the gym, they'd both spent the entire time trying— and failing—to pretend they weren't sneaking looks at each other. If he felt the attraction as strongly as she did, separation might be the only way to resist temptation.

And it was Monday, though the only way she'd been sure when she woke up that morning was by looking at her phone. Since her grandparents were retired and Rick's work schedule was so different from the norm, she was having trouble keeping track of what day it was. While she'd done a round of email responses and market research reading before they started breakfast, she'd need to video chat with Sharon later. And she needed to check on the many end-of-year processes, especially the tax forms.

"What kind of Christmas tree do you like, Jessica?"

She realized Joe was talking to her. "I don't know. Aren't Christmas trees pretty standard things?"

He laughed. "Besides the fact there are a lot of different kinds of real trees to choose from, there are also artificial ones. Some even come in weird colors. Those don't seem like Christmas decorations to me, but young people don't always embrace traditions."

Jessica dealt out the toast and bacon Marie had made to each of the plates with the scrambled eggs and carried them to the table. "I have a small artificial tree, and it's the kind with the lights already strung on it, but it still looks traditional. My father likes the fiber optic trees and the one we use for the office party has colors that change in time to a music playlist. It's fun, I guess, but not one I'd want in my home."

"You need to experience a real tree," Marie said. "Joe, after you finish your breakfast, call Rick and see if he's busy today."

Three hours later, Jessica was bundled into her grandmother's parka and warm boots and sitting in the backseat of Rick's pickup with Marie. She was sitting on the passenger's side, behind Joe, so she had a perfect view of Rick's profile as he drove. He looked relaxed as he drove through what looked to Jessica like an insane network of narrow streets, talking about sports with Joe.

Marie chattered away about the neighborhoods they passed through and Jessica was able to pay attention well enough to say the right things at the right times, but she couldn't stop herself from looking at

Rick. He hadn't shaved that morning, and she was free to admire the scruffy line of his jaw. When he smiled at something Joe said, his eye crinkled at the corner.

"Oh, there's a wonderful secondhand store near here," Marie said. "It's all high-end and designer stuff, so of course it's all barely worn before they get rid of it to make room for the newest trends. A friend was telling me about all the bargains she got on school clothes for her grandchildren."

"It's always nice to save money," Jessica said, watching Rick as he took a big gulp of coffee from the travel mug he'd brought. His throat worked as he swallowed, and she had a crazy urge to run the tip of her finger down over his Adam's apple.

As the truck rolled to a stop at a red light, Rick turned and looked back at her. The questioning arc of his eyebrows and the amused tilt to his mouth told her he was definitely aware of her watching him. Blushing, she turned her head and looked out her window.

"I bet we could find you some nice winter things there," Marie continued, seemingly unaware of the silent look Jessica and Rick had just exchanged. "Some sweaters, maybe."

Jessica laughed. "I'm definitely going to have to ship boxes back to San Diego. There's a limit to how many suitcases the airline will lug across the country for me."

"Why wouldn't you just leave the winter clothes here? You have the closet and the dresser, and we can always get some of those vacuum bags to store the

sweaters and things in if it's going to be a while between visits. Oh, and you can pick out new bedding,
of course. It's been so long since we redid that room
it's not even funny."

"It's fine," Jessica assured her, but her chest ached
a little at the thought of the room not being a guest
room, but being *her* room. And it did make sense to
leave the winter clothes there because, as she smiled
at her grandmother, she knew that she'd be making
frequent trips between San Diego and Boston for what
she hoped would be many years to come. "And you're
right about leaving the winter clothes here. That way
I won't be carrying them to California and back for
no reason, since I definitely won't wear them there."

Left unsaid was the possibility she wouldn't have
a room for long. While leaving behind the few cold-
weather belongings she'd accumulated wouldn't be
an issue, she wouldn't make herself too much at home
while their future in the house was still uncertain. But
if they moved into a smaller place, it wouldn't stop
her from visiting. She'd either stay at a hotel nearby
and pack her suitcase for the weather, or she'd rent a
small apartment or look into a time-share or whatever she had to do.

When they arrived at what looked like a real
farm—something Jessica hadn't expected to see
within a short driving distance of her grandparents'
neighborhood—she was touched by the care Rick
showed in helping Marie climb out of his truck. Then
he walked around the front end while Joe was getting
out and offered his hand to her.

After a moment's hesitation, she put her palm over his and their fingers curled together as she stepped out onto the running board and then hopped down. When her feet hit the ground, though, he didn't let go right away. She met his gaze as the touch lingered, and the awareness hung between them. He didn't want to let go of her hand and she didn't want him to.

"Ten bucks says we look at every tree on the lot and end up buying one of the first three she looks at," Joe said.

After holding her gaze for a few more heartbeats, Rick released her hand and turned away. "No way in hell I'm taking that bet. This isn't my first Christmas-tree-lot rodeo with you two."

But it was Jessica's first time, so she tried to shake off the lingering effect Rick's touch had on her nerves and lose herself in the experience. Joe wasn't kidding when he told her there were all different kinds of Christmas trees. Some had tinier needles than others, and some had almost a bluish tint. There were tall, elegant trees, and round ones so full it would probably take yards and yards of garland to make it from top to bottom.

"Jesus, Marie, that tree would take up half the living room," she heard Joe say, and she laughed at the massive tree her grandmother was checking out.

Rick leaned close enough to speak quietly in her ear, putting his hand to the small of her back. "He says that at least twice every single year."

She could barely concentrate on the words he said with his mouth so close to her ear. And even through her thick coat, she could feel the weight of his hand. "They're a funny couple. I can't imagine being married to somebody as long as they've been married."

"At the rate I'm going, I'd have to live to be a hundred and thirty or so."

She laughed, then started walking as her grandparents moved on to another stand of trees. Rick moved with her, his hand still on her back. "I think you must have some fundamental flaw I haven't seen yet in order to still be single. Don't most women think firefighters are sexy?"

"I think they find the idea of firefighters sexy, but the reality can be tough. Long shifts. Sometimes the hours are erratic. There's a lot of worrying and waiting when you're married to a firefighter. And all of that's before you start factoring in the emotional toll the job can take on the guys. Sleep problems. PTSD. Alcoholism. Anger management issues. The long-term toll on our health."

"You're right. That's not sexy." She tilted her head back so he could see her smile. "You should tell people you're a financial advisor. No excitement there. We don't have sexy T-shirts, though."

"I have a newfound appreciation for the sexiness of financial advisors, actually."

She turned her attention back to her grandparents when a hot blush spread across her cheeks. There was nothing subtle about his flirting now, or the hand on her back, and she was suddenly anxious. With five more days until the charity hockey game, there would definitely be enough time for them to get into trouble before she went back to San Diego. And she wanted it—wanted *him*—but there was no denying it would be a short-lived fling that could have long-term repercussions.

Watching Joe and Marie squabble over a tree she seemed to think was too scrawny, Jessica reminded herself she was here to help them conduct business. And their interests might not align with Rick's. Being Joe and Marie's granddaughter was already a huge conflict of interest. This thing that may or may not be happening with Rick would be even worse.

"What kind of Christmas trees do you like?" she asked, feeling a need to change the subject.

"I like them all, from scraggly little Charlie Brown trees to big old city square trees. My very favorite real trees are ones that are well-watered and have yearly inspected light strings on them. And no extension cords."

She laughed. "You're right. You're totally a safety junkie."

"I can't help it. And as for my own personal tree, I rarely get one. I usually work Christmas Day, and I spend Christmas Eve with my family in Fall River or with Joe and Marie. I have a ceramic one from possibly the 1970s that plugs in and has little light-up bulbs that Marie gave me, and that's enough."

"Rick, what do you think of this one?" Marie called, and he let his hand fall away from her back. "Joe says it's too fat."

He shrugged. "It's a little…round, to be honest. I think it'll either block part of the television or it'll block any light coming through the window, depending on where you put it."

Marie sighed. "Jessica, what do you think? You should pick one you like."

Jessica was new to family politics, since she'd only really had to worry about keeping one person happy for most of her life, but she figured the best way out of this was to suggest a tree neither Joe nor Marie had already presented a case for. "There's one we just passed that seems like a perfect height and it's not too round. And it has that bluish look that's really pretty."

Fifteen minutes later, the tree had been run through a machine that wrapped it in netting. After Rick put it in the bed of his truck, Jessica closed his tailgate while Joe helped Marie into the passenger seat.

"Nicely done, by the way," Rick said in a quiet voice. "That's the quickest I've ever seen them agree on a tree."

"If I ever join a dating site, I'm going to make that a test question. Do you like tall and skinny Christmas trees or round, fat ones?"

"A smart man will respond with whichever tree my wife falls in love with."

She wasn't sure about smart, but she was pretty sure that was the answer a guy like Rick would give. She hadn't known him long, but she'd known him long enough to know that he'd choose whatever put a smile on his family's faces.

An ache spread through her body, and she gave him a quick, tight smile before going around him to get in the truck.

Whoever finally won Rick's heart was going to be one very lucky woman. It kind of sucked that, thanks to their circumstances, she didn't have a shot at it.

RICK WASN'T SURPRISED when Marie tried to veto the traditional practice of letting the tree sit for a while to let it settle. She was all in on Christmas while she had Jessica there.

"You have to give it twenty-four hours to let the branches fall," Joe told her. "You know that."

"The sooner we get it all decorated, the longer Jessica has to enjoy it."

"I'll be here at least through the weekend," Jess said. "And I'll probably take a lot of pictures and make them my screensaver at work so I'll feel festive and think of you every time I'm at my computer."

"I suppose you're right." Marie sighed and looked at the tree, still in the netting and leaned against the wall.

Rick smiled from his spot on the couch. It was fun watching Jess figure out how to make both of her grandparents happy without actually taking one's side over the other. It was a skill she was developing pretty quickly considering she'd only known them for a week.

He had to believe it was because she felt genuine affection for them. Maybe she'd come to Boston with the intention of pushing them into selling the house and getting her hands on a slice of that valuable real estate pie, but he couldn't be sure. What he could be sure of was the fact she was seriously bonding with her grandparents and their genuine well-being would be her primary consideration going forward.

"We can at least get the decorations out," Marie said.

"I'll go drag the boxes out of the garage," Rick said, thankful to have something to do. "We can put it in the stand and give it some water, plus we can inspect the lights. Jess, you want to give me a hand?"

She looked startled for a second, but recovered quickly. "Sure."

"The storage loft in the garage doesn't have a light because I need to replace the bulb socket and keep forgetting. I just need you to hold a flashlight for me."

He wasn't sure why he'd made the request. There were windows at either end of the loft and enough light filtered in so he'd managed to drag the Halloween decorations out and put them away without a flashlight. It was just like the plywood frames for the bushes all over again. He didn't need her help. He was just using it as an excuse to spend time alone with her.

It would be awkward to back out now, so he waited while she shoved her feet into sneakers and put a sweatshirt on for the short walk to the garage. After unlocking the side door, he flipped on the main lights and led her to a narrow wooden staircase at the back of the garage. The loft was basically just plywood over ceiling joists, but it was dry and a lot easier to access than the attic space in the house.

"Wow, there's a lot of stuff in here," Jessica said as the flashlight beam danced around the boxes, plastic totes and miscellaneous junk stacked high.

"Yeah, but it's more organized than it looks. Stuff that probably should have been thrown out fifteen years ago is in the back, under the eaves. The closer you get to the center, the more recently the stuff's been used. The front's mostly decorations for the various holidays."

Suddenly Jess squealed in a choked, horrified way that made it sound as if she was being strangled, and Rick turned, hoping she hadn't cut herself on anything. Non-adventurous, indoor sort of people tended to go a long time between tetanus shots.

But when he saw her face, he couldn't hold back the laughter. She must have strayed too far into the corner because she had a mess of cobwebs in her hair and across her face and chest.

"Where's the spider?" she asked in a small voice.

"What spider?"

She narrowed her eyes at him. "What do you think made the cobwebs? A stray cat?"

"They're probably old. Like a spider starter home, and it's already moved on to something bigger and better." He set down the box and moved toward her. "Are you afraid of spiders?"

"Not usually, but I'd rather not have one on my face. And I hate cobwebs."

"Stay still. I'll get them off." He wiped the sticky strands off her face first, his fingertips skimming over her soft skin. Her lips parted slightly when he touched her, and he found himself staring at her mouth.

She shivered slightly, but he couldn't be sure if

it was from his touch or if she was still freaked out about the spiderwebs, so he quickly picked the few off her sweatshirt and wiped them on the corner of a box.

There were more in her hair, and those weren't as easy to get out. Most of them he was able to lift off with his fingers, but a few he had to kind of scrape out by running strands of her hair between his thumbnail and the knuckle of his index finger.

After brushing the last of the cobwebs off on the box, he ran his fingers through her hair to make sure he'd gotten it all. Her hair was as silky as it looked, and he loved watching it slide through his fingers in the dim light of the loft. And what the hell. She hated cobwebs, so he did it again, just to make extra sure.

"I think you're just playing with my hair now," she teased as the last strands slipped free.

"Maybe." He grinned. "You never know, though. Spiders can be sneaky bastards."

"I wasn't complaining."

Her voice was soft and he heard the invitation in it. This time when he buried his fingers in her hair, he didn't slide them free again. He pulled her closer and watched her lips part.

And when she lifted onto her toes, her head tilted back in obvious invitation, he lowered his mouth to hers. Her hands ran up his arms and over his shoulders, pulling him close, while he gripped her hip with one hand and kept the other entwined in her hair.

He dipped his tongue between her lips and she opened to him with a sigh that made his entire body tighten in response. Kissing her was everything he'd imagined it to be, and he'd spent a *lot* of time thinking about it. Deepening the kiss, he felt a rush of satisfaction when she moaned against his mouth.

Then her fingernails grazed the nape of his neck and for a few seconds all he could think about was getting her naked and kissing every inch of her body. But on the heels of that thought came the awareness that they were in a filthy storage loft and he was *not* supposed to be putting his hands on her. Or his mouth.

Reluctantly, he broke off the kiss and took a step back. She opened her eyes, her gaze soft with desire. Hooking her bottom lip with her teeth, she looked at him as though she'd also forgotten they were surrounded by boxes, dust and cobwebs.

"Shit." He ran his hand over his hair and blew out a breath. "I shouldn't have done that. We should forget it happened."

"I don't think I'll be forgetting that anytime soon."

She said the words in a light tone, but he could see the confusion in her eyes. "I'll take that as a compliment, but we both know this is a bad idea."

Jessica tilted her chin up, looking him in the eye. "Is it?"

"Don't you think so?" His mind coughed up the whole list of reasons why he should keep his hands off of this particular woman…but maybe he was wrong.

"I guess you're right. It's not like you and I could go anywhere and I wouldn't want Joe and Marie to feel like they're caught in the middle."

Well, damn. That had definitely been on his list of

reasons not to kiss her and the fact she agreed meant he probably wasn't wrong. "Yeah. So we'll forget this happened and try not to do it again."

"Like I said, I'm pretty sure I won't forget it, but I agree we should try not to do it again."

At least she looked as disappointed as he felt. "Let's get these Christmas boxes inside so Marie can start the festivities. And try to stay out of the cobwebs, okay?"

"Ha-ha. You're a funny guy, Rick Gullotti." She gestured at the rows of boxes. "Hurry up before the spiders figure out we're wrecking the joint."

SEVEN

THEY MET WITH Joe and Marie's doctor on Tuesday, in a very cramped office that made Jessica feel slightly claustrophobic. She was just glad Rick had to work because she wasn't sure the room would have held them all. She was also afraid she wouldn't be able to concentrate with him there after that kiss, but mostly it was the small room.

Or maybe it wasn't actual claustrophobia, but the magnitude of being there and trying to help these two people she barely knew but had almost instantly fallen for to figure out what they were going to do with their lives.

Managing investments for her clients was a high-pressure job. Not even for a second did she ever forget there were families depending on that hard-earned money and she took that responsibility very seriously. But she'd never had an emotional connection to a client before, and it was making her stomach feel queasy.

Once introductions had been made, the doctor didn't waste any time getting down to the business at hand. "It's time to consider downsizing. From what I've heard, that house is going to be too much for you pretty soon."

Jessica listened to the doctor, but she was watching Joe and Marie through the corner of her eye. They were sitting in chairs directly across from the doctor, but she'd been given a chair wedged in slightly ahead and to the side of them, so she could see them both.

And they didn't look very happy. Joe looked as if he might get stubborn about it, but her grandmother's mouth trembled until she pressed her lips together.

"Maybe if somebody lived with you, it would be different," the doctor continued. "But you've had a stroke, Joe, and you fell the other day. And Marie, with your blood pressure and that arthritis flaring up more and more often, do you want to be trying to keep up with that house? Going up and down those stairs?"

"Rick lives with them," Jessica pointed out.

"Rick being the third-floor tenant?" When she nodded, he started tapping his pen lightly on his legal pad. "Does Rick clean the house? Is he on hand to run up and down the stairs for them at any hour? Can he hear if one of them calls for help?"

"Maybe we could get those necklaces with the buttons you push in an emergency."

"I'm not wearing any damn necklace," Joe muttered.

"And Rick's a firefighter," Jessica continued, figuring that was a fight for another time. "He knows CPR and, well, whatever else firefighters have to learn when it comes to first aid, which is probably a lot."

"A firefighter." The doctor nodded. "So he works long shifts, then. They moved to a 24-hour shift recently, didn't they?"

"Well yes, but…" She let the sentence trail away, not sure what she should say. Or if she should say anything. Her intention had been to determine what was in Joe and Marie's best interests, not to help them further entrench themselves in a house they possibly shouldn't be in anymore. She thought she'd be able to stay impartial, but maybe she couldn't.

"What about you, Miss Broussard?"

"Call me Jessica, please. And what about me?"

"She lives in San Diego," Marie said. "She's just visiting so we can get the paperwork straightened out. We want you to meet her and know you can contact her personally in the future, instead of our son."

Jessica belatedly realized the doctor had been asking her if she would be able to take care of her grandparents, and she was thankful Marie had jumped in. She wouldn't want to say no directly, but it really wasn't feasible. Her life was in California. She had a home and friends and a business there.

And her father, she thought, wincing at the fact he'd almost been an afterthought.

"Look, this isn't a decision you have to make today." The doctor finally stopped tapping his pen and leaned back in his chair. "It's a dialogue I like to have with my patients *before* it becomes an urgent issue. It gives you a little time to work through it in your minds. Maybe imagine yourself in a cute little assisted-living condo in a social community. No worrying about mowing the lawn or shoveling snow or doing repairs on anything. No stairs."

They didn't have to worry about most of that, Jessica thought, since Rick took care of everything for them. But no matter how much they liked him or he liked them, her grandparents shouldn't be dependent on their tenant when it came to whether or not they were capable of staying in their house. As she'd told him, he might fall in love and go off to have a family of his own. And he was a firefighter. Something could happen to him on any given day. If he got hurt on the job and was laid up, she had no doubt Joe was the kind of guy who'd try to make do on his own rather than ask for anybody else's help.

"I think it would make more financial sense, too," she heard herself saying, and everybody turned to look at her. "The upkeep and utilities for that house must be astronomical, especially the heating costs. Between the value of your property and the savings you'd see, you'd probably be very comfortable."

"I'm comfortable right where I am." Joe crossed his arms, glaring at the framed medical certificates over the doctor's head.

Marie sighed. "He said we don't have to make the decision right now, but it's something we'll have to think about."

"You're both in pretty good health, all things considered," the doctor said. "But wearing yourself out taking care of a house that's substantially larger than the two of you need could change that."

Once that conversation hit a dead end, Marie and Jessica were sent out to the reception area so the doctor could take a look at Joe and make sure there were no lingering concerns from the fall he'd taken. Then they did the paperwork to remove David Broussard from their forms and make Rick and Jessica their emergency contacts, with her listed as the next of kin.

As they walked out of the office together, the mood seemed a little grim, and Jessica wasn't sure what to say. She wasn't sure there was anything she *could* say. She'd come here with the intention of treating Joe and Marie like clients. After explaining their most beneficial option was to sell the house and move into something more sensible in both a management and financial sense, she would help them implement the plan and then keep her thumb on the process long-distance from San Diego.

But they weren't clients. They were her grandparents and they didn't want her there to make spreadsheets and bar graphs. All Joe and Marie wanted was to get to know her. They wanted a granddaughter and if she pushed too hard, she'd disappoint them.

With a heavy sigh, Jessica climbed into the backseat of Marie's car. Judging by the increasingly volatile voice mails from her father, she was already letting him down. The last thing she wanted to do was disappoint her grandparents, too.

Looking out the window, she watched the neighborhood go by as they drove back to the house in silence. Maybe what she needed was another sweaty, stress-busting workout with Rick. But thinking about Rick made her think about kissing him.

Shit.

Not exactly the first word a woman wanted to hear after a kiss that had raised the bar so high she wasn't sure she'd ever be kissed like that again. But he said he shouldn't have done it and they should forget it.

She was trying like hell, but that just wasn't going to happen.

"GOD*DAMN* THIS FUCKING JOB." Chris Eriksson whipped his helmet so hard it bounced off the brick wall of a delicatessen and rolled back to him.

Rick sat against the front bumper of L-37 with his elbows propped on his knees and his head hung low. What an incredibly shitty way to kick off the tour. "We saved a kid, Chris."

"Maybe. *Maybe* we saved the kid. And *if* he wakes up, they get to tell him his mom and his baby sister are dead because the douche bag driving was shooting up heroin at ten-thirty in the morning."

Rick tried to think of something to say. It was part of his job to keep the guys' heads right, but he had nothing. The toddler wearing a pink nightgown under an obviously handed-down blue coat hadn't been strapped into her car seat correctly and she'd been DOA. The mother probably wouldn't be declared until the emergency room, but she wasn't going to make it.

They'd focused on the boy, extricating him from the mangled wreck sitting in the middle of a major intersection while the EMTs administered Narcan to the driver. That bastard was going to make it, while

the boy was touch and go, and emotion swelled in
Rick's throat. Their job was to save everybody they
could, and they did, and let the justice system deal
with the aftermath. But sometimes it was a hard pill
to swallow.

When Chris sat against the truck's tire and dropped
his head into his hands, Rick didn't miss the way
Aidan and Scott closed ranks in front of him. They
looked like they were shooting the breeze, big bunker
coats dangling from their hands, but the news cameras across the street wouldn't be able to capture the
firefighter sitting on the ground.

Danny Walsh joined Rick on the bumper. "Victims have cleared the scene. They're bringing in the
ramp trucks now."

Rick nodded. The guy who'd been driving the
sanitation truck was an acquaintance of his, and he
knew an ambulance had taken him, too. He hadn't
been hurt when he T-boned the car and drove it into
a pole before he could stop, but he'd been so shaken
up there was nothing else they could do with him.
And they'd have to run blood tests in the hospital for
the paperwork.

They watched Jeff Porter walk over to Chris and
hold a bottled water out to him. After pulling his
T-shirt up to scrub at his face, the other man took it
and unscrewed the cap. Jeff put his hand on his shoulder for a moment and then picked up the tossed helmet to set on the truck.

Chris and Jeff both had kids, and scenes like this
one tended to hit them particularly hard. He knew

they'd eventually turn their minds to the boy who would hopefully survive, but right now all they saw was the little girl who hadn't.

Danny pulled out his phone and looked at the screen for a few seconds before cursing and shoving it back in its holster. "You're not going to believe this."

"You won the lottery and we're all retiring on your dime."

"Jesus, that sounds nice. Cobb just got another phone call about the damn decorations. We're the only house that doesn't have our decorations up yet and there's been some question about our community spirit."

Rick snorted. The freaking Christmas decorations were turning into a major pain in the ass. Usually hanging them was no big deal, or even an enjoyable way to break the monotony. But when they'd changed up the way tours were scheduled, everything got messed up, including it being a lot easier to leave odd jobs for one of the other crews to take care of. Throw in a busy early winter and the decorations were still sitting in boxes in the storage room.

"The guys are pretty emotional right now. I don't know if hanging Christmas decorations would help cheer them up or make them focus even more on losing a kid today," Rick said.

Chris was on his feet now, talking to Jeff, Aidan and Scott. He'd seen Gavin and Grant talking to a couple of the cops earlier, though he couldn't see them now. Those two were younger and tended to bounce back emotionally a little faster so maybe he could pawn the job off on them.

"Cobb wants it done today," Danny said. "Said he doesn't give a shit if the entire city burns down. He hates talking on the phone and doesn't want another complaint call."

"We'll see how they are once we're back at the house. Routine helps. And food doesn't hurt. I think they'll be okay by afternoon."

"Even if it's Christmas related, busywork's better than sitting around dwelling on it, too."

"I agree," Rick said, standing and stretching his back. "We'll be here a while yet, but let's get them moving."

Routine did help and as the guys moved around the accident scene, cleaning up and repacking the trucks, Rick felt his anger at the situation seeping away. Maybe hanging Christmas decorations wouldn't be a bad way to spend the afternoon. It was fairly mindless work, but it was also hard not to feel festive when light strings were involved. And people in the community would come to watch and share stories, which served as a nice distraction.

As he worked, Rick found himself thinking about the upcoming holiday. He'd work Christmas Day, since it was his usual shift. But even when shifts rotated, he often worked the holidays, covering for guys with kids whenever he could. If possible, he went to his parents' house for Christmas Eve to celebrate with them and his brother's family. If not, he visited with Joe and Marie.

He'd bet money Jess's plans for Christmas Day were already weighing heavily on Marie's mind. They'd been alone in their house for decades, making do with celebrating with friends. In the past they'd traveled to his sister's house or one of her brothers to visit with their nieces and nephews until spending hours in the car at their age sucked the festivity out of the occasion. But now they had a granddaughter and it didn't sound as if Davey was a really festive kind of guy. Would Jessica stay that long? Or come back to the East Coast to spend Christmas with them?

According to Joe, Marie had wanted to get the Christmas tree just to share the experience with Jessica, but they weren't going to put any pressure on her to spend the holidays with them. Because Davey was such an ass, they didn't want to make her feel in any way as if she was in some kind of family tug-of-war game.

Maybe he should get her a present just in case she was around. A nice wool scarf, maybe. It was a good gift for a friend of the family and God knew she needed cold-weather stuff. But kissing her complicated things. Would she see the gift as a token because of their mutual relationship with Joe and Marie, or would she take it as a sign of something more from the man who'd kissed her?

That was a question for another day. Rick climbed up in the cab of L-37 to back it up a few feet, out of the way of a ramp truck, and tried to put Jessica out of his mind. Things were definitely changing around him, but he had a job to do.

ONCE THEY REACHED the house, Marie decided she wanted to go to the craft store, which Joe wanted no part of. "Bad enough I had to listen to a damn lecture from that old quack. I'm not watching you stand around and yap with your friends in the craft store."

"I'll go with you," Jessica volunteered, the words leaving her mouth before she really gave any thought to them. She *should* work, even though she was kind of on vacation.

Just thinking about the phone call from her father that morning made her shudder. Sharon must have finally told him Jessica was using vacation time to extend her stay long enough to go to the charity hockey game, and he'd not only been very angry, but also still intoxicated.

"You know one of us needs to be on top of things," he'd said when a simple demand she return hadn't gotten the result he wanted. "The clients depend on it."

She'd taken a deep breath and then closed her eyes. "Then maybe you should have a pot of coffee and take a shower and go in to the office."

He'd hung up on her, which he rarely did, and hadn't called her back right away as he had in the past. She'd sat with her phone for almost fifteen minutes, battling an urge to call him back and tell him she'd fly out as soon as the medical meeting was over. Then she'd turned it off and turned her focus to getting ready to meet Joe's doctor.

It was the first time she'd ever called her father on being *unavailable* or not done what he needed her to do, but she was tired of it. She wanted to go to a stupid hockey game with her grandparents.

Marie drove, which was hard on Jessica's nerves. She had to admit, though, she wasn't sure her doing the driving would have been any easier. At least Marie knew where they were going and found a parking space without too much trouble.

"We should see if the boys are around."

Jessica was confused. "Boys? What boys?"

When Marie stopped walking and waved her hand toward the other side of the street, Jessica realized she meant men. And one man in particular.

They were across from a tall brick building that looked pretty old, and had two big openings on the first floor. The huge garage doors were up and Jessica could see the fire trucks, each parked inside with a plaque screwed to the arched brickwork. Engine 59. Ladder 37.

Great. She needed more Rick Gullotti in her life, since tossing and turning and trying not to think about kissing him wasn't torture enough. Watching his muscles flex and hearing the soft grunting sounds he made in the gym had been torture, and she hadn't been able to ride the bike hard enough to sweat the desire out. And that was *before* he'd kissed her. The feelings that seeing him triggered in her body were escalating from want to need at an alarming rate.

"I thought you wanted to go to the craft store," Jessica said.

But then a man in a Boston Fire T-shirt walked

around the front of Engine 59 and happened to glance across the street in their direction. After a few seconds, he smiled and lifted a hand in greeting. "Hey, Mrs. Broussard! How you doing?"

Jessica surrendered to the inevitable and followed Marie across the street, waiting patiently while her grandmother accepted a kiss on the cheek from the firefighter. He looked younger than Rick, and had short dark hair and brown eyes.

"Jessica, this Scott Kincaid. And this is my granddaughter, Jessica."

She shook his hand. "It's nice to meet you."

"You, too. I've heard a little about you." Rick had talked about her? Jessica clamped her mouth shut, not wanting to embarrass herself by asking what he'd said. "Let me grab Rick for you."

She expected him to walk away, but he took out his cell phone and dashed off a text. A few seconds later, his phone chimed and he read the reply. "He'll be down in a few minutes. How do you like Boston so far, Jessica?"

"It's definitely different from San Diego. And colder."

He laughed and waved them inside the big bay. "It's not even cold yet, so we've got the doors open. We love fresh air and we'll keep the door at the top of the stairs closed if we've got heat on upstairs, but we keep these open as much as possible."

Jessica looked at the fire truck practically gleaming wherever the sun or the overhead lights touched it. They obviously took good care of them. "They're so huge. How do you drive them around this city without hitting anything?"

"We pretty much always have the right of way, and let's just say we *usually* drive them around the city without hitting anything."

He was walking as he talked, and she followed him around the truck, enjoying the close-up view. "Are those pictures on the internet of fire hoses run through broken windows on cars real?"

"They're real." He shrugged. "We try not to damage things because the paperwork sucks, but we're also not going to let somebody get hurt or lose half a city block because some jerk parked in front of a hydrant."

"Guess they don't do it again."

"You'd be surprised. And you should ask Gullotti about the time a call came in that there were kids trapped on the top floor of a burning three-decker. When he got there, some rookie cop trying to help secure the area had parked his cruiser in the way and wasn't right there to move it."

Jessica gave him a look of disbelief. "Don't tell me he pushed a police car out of the way."

"He pretty much wrecked the hell out of that cruiser. But that's the LT. Until he gets the ladder up, we can't save anybody, so he doesn't mess around."

"LT?"

"Lieutenant. For Ladder 37, anyway. I'm with Engine 59, so Danny Walsh gets to boss me around, but we always roll together. One pumper engine and one ladder truck."

"What about the lieutenant?"

Jessica whirled at the sound of Rick's voice, hoping the rush of heat she felt didn't show on her face. He was wearing the same navy Boston Fire T-shirt as Scott, tucked into blue uniform pants. The shirt was snug and her gaze traveled over delicious biceps before jerking back to his face.

"I was telling her what a pain in the ass you are," Scott said. "And how bossy you are."

"Yeah. Speaking of being bossy, everybody's eating. Go grab something because then we're dragging the boxes out and, unless we get called out, nobody's leaving until the decorating's done."

Scott rolled his eyes. "Good to see you, Mrs. Broussard. And it was nice to meet you, Jessica. A bunch of us are going to play pool tomorrow night at my old man's bar. You should have Gullotti bring you."

"I don't know, but thanks for the invite." Jessica watched him disappear into a back corner, where she assumed there was a set of stairs, and then turned back to Rick. "I asked him how you guys drive these massive trucks around and he told me to ask you about the police car."

"That wasn't my fault," Rick said sternly, but the corners of his mouth quirked up. "They buried me in paperwork, let me tell you."

"I'm going to go to the craft store while you two chat," Marie said. "Give her a bit of a tour and I'll be back in a few minutes."

She was gone before Jessica could protest, moving

fast for a woman who was supposed to be in declining health. Not sure what to do, she turned back to Rick. "You don't have to give me a tour. You should go eat and I'll catch up with Marie."

"Already ate. And, trust me, you don't want to be at the craft store with her. The owner's one of her best friends and they can literally talk for hours. I took her one time, when she was on a medication that banned her from driving, and I actually fell asleep in a wooden chair with my head on a pile of quilt squares on the table."

"I don't have a lot of patience for crafts, so that sounds like a nightmare. What are you decorating?"

"For Christmas. We put up lights, including some cool big ones around the bay doors. There's a big wreath we always hang above the plaques. Electric candles in the windows that face the street. That sort of thing. And each of the trucks has a wreath for the front grill."

He showed her around the trucks and all the gear, which was more interesting than she would have thought. Or maybe it was just liking the sound of his voice. Then he brought her to the second floor, where there were offices and a room where the officers slept. They skipped over most of it, though he described the rooms as they passed them.

He sent and received a text, and then led her up another flight of stairs to what she assumed was the top floor. "They know you're coming."

She heard the noise right away. Men's voices—

a lot of them—and laughter rang through the third floor, making her smile. "It looks like an apartment."

"It essentially is. In the back we have a shower room and some workout equipment, along with a couple of bathrooms. This, as you can see, is the living room, and the bunk room's through that door."

There were a couple of long couches, as well as comfortable and battered-looking chairs set wherever they fit. All of them faced a large television screen, which was currently off. She was surprised by how neat everything was and said so.

He laughed. "There are a lot of guys sharing this space. Not only the ones you can hear in the kitchen, but the other shifts that are here when we aren't. Just one person not cleaning up after himself can be a problem."

When she followed him into a huge kitchen and dining space, her eyes widened. He wasn't kidding about a lot of guys sharing the space. In chairs, leaning against counters, rummaging in the fridge. The room was full of men and Rick went quickly through their names, probably not expecting her to remember any of them.

Scott Kincaid, she'd met. And Danny Walsh, Aidan Hunt and Grant Cutter were assigned to Engine 59 with him. And with Rick were Jeff Porter—who was even bigger than Rick—Gavin Boudreau, and Chris Eriksson, who she thought was older than Rick if she judged by the gray in his beard. There was also an older man he only called Chief, who'd just bitten into a thick sandwich and waved to her from the head of the table.

Jessica smiled and gave a general wave in everybody's direction, and then followed Rick back downstairs with a sigh of relief. She didn't like being the center of attention and they'd definitely turned all eyes on her when she walked into the kitchen. Whether it was idle curiosity or whether they were trying to figure out what—if anything—she was to Rick, she didn't know, but she'd felt awkward.

"Do you think you'll get all the decorations up before you get called out?" she asked when they were back on the ground floor.

He shrugged and leaned against the side of his ladder truck. "I hope so, just so we can check it off the list. They're supposed to be up by now, but when the alarm's struck, we've gotta go. Tuesdays don't usually get too wild and crazy, but you never know."

"Thanks for the tour," she said, suddenly feeling shy. It was stupid because it wasn't as if this had been a date or anything, but she still wasn't sure how to say goodbye. "I guess I'll go find Marie and let her introduce me to her friend. I'm probably quite the gossip fodder this week."

"But the good kind," he said, not bothering to deny it. "I grabbed you a ticket to the hockey game, by the way. We can all ride over together."

"I'm looking forward to it."

"Do you want to go to Kincaid's tomorrow right? I heard Scotty ask you."

"I don't know." Did he mean as a date? Or was he

only following up on an invitation Scott had technically extended to her. "I've never played pool."

"We can teach you." She was going to respond to
that when an alarm sounded and Rick's entire body
language changed in the blink of an eye. "Gotta go."

"I'll get out of the way."

"When you go out, stay on this side of the street."
He talked to her as he stepped into tall boots with
some kind of pants scrunched into them. Once his
feet were in, he pulled up the pants and looped suspenders over his shoulders. "We swing wide coming
out and we've been known to hop the opposite curb
a time or two."

He winked at her, and then turned to grab a heavy-
looking coat with reflective stripes on it and a helmet.
She yelled a goodbye as guys flooded into the bay and
then stepped out onto the sidewalk, under a flashing
red light over the bay doors. She noticed the other
pedestrians stopped, none of them passing in front
of the fire station, and a car down the street stopped.

Faster than she would have thought possible, a
siren wailed and Engine 59's nose appeared. It pulled
out into a right turn, not quite going up on the curb,
but she saw the entire stretch was marked for no parking. The men waved to her as they went by, and so
did the guys from Ladder 37 when it pulled out. Rick
was in the shotgun seat and he gave her a grin along
with the wave.

She wasn't sure if it was the excitement of the
lights and sirens or Rick's grin that made her heart

pound in her chest, but Jessica watched the two trucks until they turned out of sight and then went to find her grandmother.

EIGHT

JESSICA WAS PROPPED against her pillow with her tablet, reading an article about a possible product recall and considering what impact it could have on stock prices, when her cell phone vibrated. It was sitting on the bed next to her, and she frowned when she saw her father's name on the screen.

Apparently he was going to be the first to flinch in their game of telephone chicken. She was surprised he'd made it all the way to Wednesday afternoon without calling with another attempt to bend her to his will. Or to tell her he'd emptied her office and all of her stuff was in cardboard boxes on the sidewalk. She took a deep breath to calm her nerves, swiped to answer and said hello.

"Jessica, it's your father."

Which she knew since her phone—the same model as his—had told her so. And she realized at that moment he never referred to himself as Dad. *Hey, honey, it's Dad.* Maybe that was why she rarely thought of him that way. He was always her father in her mind. But she called him Dad when she spoke to him directly because calling him Father would sound cold and awkward, especially in front of others. Never, even as a little girl, had she ever called him Daddy, though. "Hi, Dad."

"I'm in the office today and I don't know if I should be pleased or insulted by how well things have been handled while you're away."

She wasn't sure if it was a compliment or a prelude to letting her know he didn't need her anymore, but at least he sounded sober. He must be, since he never drank at the office. "You already know Sharon's amazing and, like I told you before, my laptop and phone don't care where I am when I use them."

"How are things in Boston?"

Did he mean her? His parents? The weather? "Fine. We met with Joe and Marie's doctor yesterday and they're in generally good health, though he thinks they should strongly consider downsizing now, rather than later when one of them has a crisis."

"Are you putting the house on the market?"

She laughed. "I can't, since it's not my house. And they're not sold on the idea yet. They're understandably reluctant to leave their home, and they have Rick upstairs."

"So there's nothing you can do there right now, then."

"I'm going to a hockey game Saturday," she said, knowing that was not at all what he'd meant.

"A hockey game." He was quiet for a few seconds, and she pictured him staring out the window as he considered what to say next. "Our holiday party is a week from Saturday."

"I know. I've been working on it with Alicia, who

has been assisting me with it for the last five years, so it's all under control. And I'll be home for that. I'm not sure what day yet, but you know I wouldn't miss it."

"I wasn't sure at all. I don't know if they've turned you against me."

Jessica sighed and wiggled down the mattress until she could lie on her pillow and stare at the ceiling. "They're not like that, Dad. They're really nice and they haven't said a bad word about you. They know you're my father and they wouldn't put me in the middle like that. They just want to get to know me."

"You shouldn't get emotionally involved with them. It muddies the business."

"They're my grandparents." Not that family seemed to mean much to him. "You know, I've seen their wedding photos and some pictures when Marie was about my age. I'm like a clone of her."

"Trust me, I know. Let me know as soon as you know which day you're flying home, okay?"

"Okay." She wanted to dig at him over the phone. To push him into revealing some emotional response to her looking so much like his mother. But he was at work, he was sober, and he was giving her some space, no matter how reluctantly. She didn't want to rock that boat. "And I'm going to forward you a few articles to read, too. We might need to strategize about a few accounts when I get back to San Diego."

"I'm looking forward to it," he said, sounding a little more chipper. "That's what we do best. We're a good team."

She smiled when she hung up, glad he was choosing to be reasonable in the face of not getting his way. He seemed content to wait until she came home for the holiday party, but she knew he'd play hardball if she tried to leave again. And that was a problem.

Every Christmas Eve, she and her father—along with his wife if he had one that year—had dinner together and exchanged gifts. He spent Christmas Day at his country club, where a charity golf game had become a tradition with the less than jolly set. She spent the day being lazy in her pajamas and watching any movies she could find that didn't revolve around Christmas and families with moms and dads.

This year she found herself wondering what it would be like to come down the stairs and have breakfast with her family and then open presents under the tree. Or maybe they were the kind of people who opened presents first and then ate breakfast.

She couldn't be here for Christmas this year. She knew that, even though it was tempting to imagine getting on a flight back to Boston once the party was over so she could spend the holidays with her grandparents. But her father sounded as if he was making an effort to accept that she was going to have a relationship with his parents, and he was also going to be alone for the first time in four or five years, since he was divorcing. Maybe next Christmas she could get away without too much guilt.

A knock startled her and she looked over to see Rick standing in her open doorway. He leaned against the jamb and crossed his arms, giving her a crooked grin. "Working hard?"

The fact he was filling her bedroom doorway while she was flat on her back on her bed threatened to put all kinds of ideas in her head, but she just smiled. "It's a strategic brainstorming session."

That made him chuckle. "Sure it is. Marie sent me up here to change the lightbulb in your bathroom, as long as it won't disturb you."

"Oh, I changed it earlier. I found some bulbs in the pantry and grabbed one." She sat up and swung her legs over the edge of the bed. "While you're here, can I ask you a question?"

He raised his eyebrow. "You can ask."

"There was an accident on the news. The guy who overdosed while driving with his girlfriend and her kids. Joe said you responded to that." He nodded, his expression shifting slightly. "How do you even do that job? I mean, how do you just forget that and move on?"

"We never forget. Ever." He shifted his weight against the doorjamb. "But we save a lot more than we lose and somebody has to do it. If we start dwelling on the times we fail, we might hesitate and we can't do that."

"Sorry. I guess that was a personal question. It's just that it was only a few hours later Marie and I were at the station and you introduced me to everybody and…I don't know. There was food and Christmas decorations."

"It was a rough morning, but we had to get through

the shift, you know? Every guy handles the hard days differently, but that's for later, at home."

"How do you handle the hard days?" Way to follow up a personal question with an even more personal question, she thought, wishing she could take the question back.

But Rick gave her a slow, sexy smile that made her sock-covered toes curl into the carpet. "There are a lot of ways to cope with stress."

"I… Oh." It was so tempting to say something provocative and get him to cross the few feet between the door and the bed, but her grandparents were downstairs.

Then he chuckled again, and she hoped it wasn't because he could read her thoughts on her face. "I went to the gym, actually, and beat the shit out of the heavy bag for a while."

"That sounds very satisfying." Not as satisfying as where her mind had taken her, but hitting the heavy bag sounded like a good way to vent. "What are Joe and Marie up to?"

"Marie's putting together her grocery shopping list for tomorrow and going through her coupons, so that means Joe's probably hiding in the garage. I told him I'd give him a hand changing the belt on the snowblower."

Jessica grabbed her phone and stood up. "I'll go hang out with Marie, then. Keep her company, at least."

"You still planning to go to the pub with me tonight? Maybe learn how to play some pool? And they have pretty good burgers, too."

"That sounds fun. It'd be nice to get out for a little while."

"Good. I'm pretty sure Marie has beef stew in the slow cooker, so if you're not there for supper it just means more leftovers for Joe tomorrow."

"I'll let her know I'm going out." Assuming the conversation was over, she started toward the door.

Rick didn't move right away, though, and Jessica had to stop short to keep from plowing into him. He looked at her for what felt like a long time, his expression frustratingly unreadable, before standing aside and waving for her to go first.

She walked down the hallway, hoping he wasn't watching her ass. Or maybe hoping he was. She wasn't sure.

RICK HAD BROUGHT quite a few women into Tommy's bar with him over the years, so he couldn't explain the low-level anxiety he felt as he opened the door to Kincaid's Pub and gestured for Jess to go in.

She was definitely a white-collar woman and Kincaid's was a blue-collar kind of bar, but he wanted her to like it. And he wanted her to like the guys, too, though he wasn't really sure why that mattered so much. He already knew that, no matter what, the guys would be nice to her and make her feel welcome.

Lydia was behind the bar, so he made that their first stop. "Hey, Lydia, this is Joe and Marie's granddaughter, Jessica."

"Hey, I heard you were in town." Lydia reached across the bar to shake her hand. "It's good to meet you. It's too bad my dad's not here. He and Fitzy had a wake to go to."

"I'm sorry to hear that," Jessica said.

"Thanks. Though, to be honest, I'm not even sure how well they knew the guy. I think they just go to see if any old flames are back on the market."

"Jesus, Lydia." Rick groaned. "I don't even want to go there."

"At the rate you're going, you'll be widow-hunting with them before you know it." Lydia threw him a saucy wink and then looked back at Jessica. "Maybe scaring him with horrific glimpses into his future will get him to settle down."

Rick gave Lydia a quelling look. The problem with all of them being like a family was that, like with real family, they didn't always know when to shut their mouths. "Funny. We're going out back. Jess, you want a beer? Or…what else is there besides beer? Soda. Coffee. Water. Juice?"

"Hey, let me do my job," Lydia said. "I'm better at it than you."

Jess said she'd have whatever Rick was drinking so once they each had a chilled mug of beer, he led the way through the mostly empty tables to the alcove where the pool table sat.

Only three guys had shown up—Aidan, Scott and Gavin—and she remembered their names, but he introduced her again just to be polite. "You all remember Jessica, the Broussards' granddaughter? She stopped by the station yesterday with Marie."

"Glad you came," Scott said, shaking her hand.

"You want to play? You can take over for me if you want."

Rick watched Jess smile at Scott and give a little shake of her head. "I think I'll watch for a while. Maybe I'll figure it out."

"Okay, but don't watch Gavin over there. He sucks."

"Noted."

Rick pulled out a chair at one of the small round tables against the wall and gestured for her to sit. Then he sat across from her and set his beer down as he rocked the chair back onto two legs out of habit. For some reason most of them did it and Tommy had learned years ago not to buy flimsy chairs.

"You don't have to sit here with me, you know," Jess said. "You can play pool with your friends and I'll watch."

"I can see them from here and I'd rather sit with you. You're prettier than they are."

"I don't know. Gavin's kind of pretty," Aidan said from his spot by the rack of cues. "But you're right. Jessica is prettier."

"Screw you, Hunt." Gavin blushed and looked over Jessica. "Excuse the language, ma'am."

"Ouch," Jessica muttered. "Ma'am? Really?"

"He can't help it," Scott said. "He calls every woman ma'am. He even called the cashier at the gas station ma'am earlier and I'd be surprised if she was seventeen years old."

"There's nothing wrong with manners," Jessica said, smiling at Gavin.

Rick watched the conversation as it went on, enjoying the way she interacted with the guys. They genuinely seemed to like her, and she looked as though she was having a good time.

When she was about halfway through her beer, she excused herself to go to the restroom and Rick couldn't stop himself from watching her walk away. The jeans, which he was pretty sure were new since she'd arrived in Boston, made her ass look amazing. Or maybe her ass made the jeans look amazing. Either way, they were a combination he couldn't look away from.

"I like her," Scotty said once she was out of earshot.

"Me, too," Aidan added.

"I swear you two are like twins. And you don't even know her."

Scotty shrugged. "It's a vibe. My gut says I like her."

"As long as that's the only part of you that likes her."

All three men looked at him, and Aidan gave a low whistle. "I guess we don't have to ask if *you* like her."

"I wouldn't have brought her here to hang out if I didn't like her, dumb-ass."

"I don't know. You keep talking about out how she's Joe and Marie's granddaughter. Like really making a point of it, so it sounds like you're stressing that you're hanging out with your landlords' granddaughter. Maybe you should just introduce her as Jessica, who's with you."

"You all know Joe and Marie, so it makes sense to let you know she's their granddaughter."

Scotty chalked the end of his pool stick. "Yeah, and you did that yesterday. And now you did again. You reminding us or yourself?"

"What the hell is wrong with you guys? No more afternoon talk shows for you three."

They went back to their game, and Rick sipped his beer, waiting for Jess to come back. Then he replayed his introductions over in his head—yesterday's and tonight's—and had to admit they might have a point. And if they did, then Scott's question was also valid.

Why did he feel such a strong, subliminal need to keep that distance between them? And was he protecting her, them or himself?

ON HER WAY back from the restroom, Jessica had to pass by the bar, so when Lydia waved, it seemed only polite to stop and chat for a minute.

"How's the pool playing going?" the other woman asked.

"Good, I guess. I think Scott's winning, though I'm not sure."

"I'm not sure how, but my brother usually wins. I think he talks so much nobody else can concentrate."

Jessica laughed. "Possibly. Who is that a picture of on the wall? It looks signed and…is it really screwed right to the wall?"

"I was going to give you hell, but I guess you get a pass since you're from California. That's Bobby Orr, one of the greatest Bruins to ever play hockey. One of the greatest of *anybody* to play hockey."

"I'll remember that. I'm going to the charity hockey game with them tomorrow, and it'll be the first time I've ever seen a game."

"With them? Oh, you mean Joe and Marie?"

"Yeah, and Rick, too. I guess we'll all go together."

"It'll be fun. I'll probably see you there, since everybody from the station sits together and the Broussards sit with Rick, so you will, too."

Of course, since she was their granddaughter and nobody could possibly miss that fact.

It was hard not to notice how carefully he introduced her as Joe and Marie's granddaughter every single time. Not as his friend. Not as a friend of the family. Certainly not as his date. He was keeping her at a distance, as if he was just doing his landlords a favor by showing her the town.

"We should go out sometime," Lydia said. "Like a girls' night out. I like to do that every once in a while since it feels like every night is a boy's night out at the bar."

"That would be fun. I don't have much free time before I go back to California, but maybe the next time I come back."

"Sounds good."

"I should get back there and see how it's going," Jessica said.

"Make them show you how to play," Lydia said. "Oh, and do me a favor and let them know I'm not walking all the way back there to take their orders. If anybody's hungry, they can come order at the bar."

When Jessica walked into the back room, she saw that Rick had abandoned the table and was leaning against the wall talking to Gavin. He smiled when he saw her and nodded his head for her to join them.

"You ready for a lesson?"

"I guess so. And Lydia said if anybody's hungry, go to the bar because she's not coming back here."

"I'll take everybody's orders up," Aidan said, and then he shrugged when they all looked at him. "Hey, I never pass up an excuse to talk to my future wife."

Jessica enjoyed the good-natured ribbing the guys gave him, though she wondered how it was that Scott and Aidan appeared to be the best of friends and she knew they worked together, but Aidan was marrying Scott's sister. She thought there was some kind of man code about dating your best friend's sister.

Showed how much she knew about men.

After they'd given Aidan a list of how they wanted their burgers, he disappeared and Rick handed Jess a pool stick. "I'm guessing you've figured out the basic rules by now."

"Use the stick to knock the white ball into the other balls to make them go in the nets around the table."

"Close enough."

Usually Jessica didn't like learning new skills with an audience. She felt awkward and she didn't like the pressure. But these guys were fun and she'd spent enough time with them tonight to know they'd definitely laugh, but they'd be laughing with her and not at her.

She tried to put her hand like she'd seen Scott do and set the stick across her knuckles. Then she jabbed it and it caught on the green table, not even hitting the white ball.

"Jesus," Rick said, "if you rip the felt, Tommy will put my balls on display in a pickle jar on the bar."

Jessica snorted. "God forbid. I'll do my best not to wreck the table, then, although I blame you since you're supposed to be teaching me how to do this."

"Tommy wouldn't waste a pickle jar on your balls, old man," Scott said. "Probably just use a shot glass."

Jessica laughed—she couldn't help it—but then squealed when Rick wrapped his arm around her waist and hauled her close.

"Think that's funny, do you?"

She playfully jabbed at his stomach with her elbow. "A little bit, yeah."

"Since I prefer my balls where they are, let me show you how to hold the cue before you get us both in trouble."

Jessica was pretty sure the way he leaned over the table with her, molding his body against hers was what would get them both in trouble. He was tall enough so her ass wasn't actually nestled against his crotch, but she knew there wasn't much space between them. And his chest *was* pressed against her back as he took her left hand in his and stretched their arms out on the table. After showing her how to hold her fingers, he closed his right hand over hers and they went over how to hold and move the cue.

She wasn't going to remember a single word he said. All of her focus was on the way his body covered hers and the feel of his hands on hers and his breath on her cheek.

"I need to hit the head," she heard Gavin say.

"We need refills," Scott said. "I'll go now so you can help carry them back."

Jessica gave a laugh that sounded breathy and full of anxiety. "Was that their subtle way of leaving us alone?"

"Incredibly subtle," Rick said before he pressed a kiss to her neck that made her entire body shiver. "This was not one of my better plans for not kissing a woman."

"And yet neither of us have moved."

When he stood up straight, she regretted saying the words. Even if it was a dumb idea, she liked the feel of his body so close to hers. But when she laid the pool cue across the felt and straightened up, he put his hand on her elbow and turned her to face him.

"It's still a bad idea," he said, his voice low.

"I agree." She stepped into the curve of his arm. "So after you kiss me, we should make another agreement about how we won't do it again."

That seemed to be all the urging he needed. His mouth closed over hers so swiftly she gasped against his lips. It was hot and urgent and she stood on her toes, arching her back to get more of him.

His hands were at her hips, holding her against his

body, and she wrapped her arms around his neck so he couldn't pull away. He nipped at her bottom lip and she moaned, wishing they were alone—really alone—and that maybe this time they wouldn't stop.

"The burgers will be—oh. Sorry."

They broke apart to see Aidan standing on the other side of the pool table, his body language making it clear he wasn't sure if he should stay or go back out to the bar.

Jessica stepped back, feeling a hot flush over her face. "Rick's showing me how to play pool."

She had to respect Aidan for holding the straight face as long as he did, for about fifteen seconds before he laughed. "I was going to tell Gavin he should ask Rick for some pointers on how to beat Scotty, but he might want to watch some YouTube videos instead."

Before either of them could respond, Scott and Gavin came around the corner, each carrying a tray of beer mugs.

"You better tip me," Scott said when he'd managed to set the tray on one of the tables without spilling the beer.

"Rick can handle that," Aidan said. "He gives good tips."

Jessica blushed again, but Rick only laughed. "Here's a tip. Don't eat the yellow snow."

As the other guys each claimed a fresh beer, Rick stepped close to Jessica and leaned close so only she could hear him. "Is this where we agree not to do this again?"

Sadly, she nodded. "That's what we said."

"Remind me next time not to agree to that in advance." He winked at her and then joined the others. "Come get your beer before one of these guys chugs it, Jess. You'll want it when the burgers come out."

She claimed her mug, and then took a seat at the table again since she didn't think she'd survive any more pool lessons tonight. But as she watched Rick joke around with his friends, she ran his words through her head again.

Remind me next time not to agree to that in advance.

Next time.

NINE

By the time the hockey game rolled around on Saturday, Rick was almost numb with exhaustion. The normal twenty-four-hour shifts didn't bother him. He could usually get enough sleep to function just fine and he liked having five days to play with. Sometimes he'd cover a tour for somebody else, but he'd been starting to play with the idea of a second job. He just needed to figure out what he wanted to do.

But sometimes the stars were out of alignment or the moon was full or maybe there was something in the water, but they ran their asses off for twenty-four hours and made do with battle naps when and where they could grab them. That had been Friday.

He'd managed to sleep for a few hours in his own bed, but what he really wanted to do was close the room-darkening blinds and hibernate for the entire weekend.

Instead, it was time to go downstairs and see if the Broussards were ready to head to the rink. There were guys from a few different stations playing, since they couldn't all play, but any firefighters from the representing stations who didn't show up with a toy better have a good excuse.

As soon as he stepped out onto his deck, he winced.

The weather was turning and there was a cold snap in the forecast. Trying not to imagine all the space heater, woodstove and chimney disasters in the city's future, he made his way down the stairs and walked through their back door.

The second he stepped into the kitchen, he realized he wasn't as exhausted as he thought. Jessica was in jeans, with her hair in a ponytail and only the lightest touch of makeup on her face. And she was wearing a navy blue sweatshirt that was too big for her, but said Boston Fire across the chest.

He wanted to back her up against the counter and kiss those strawberry-tinted lips until their legs wouldn't support them anymore and they slid to the tile floor in a tangle of arms and legs.

"Hey, Rick," Joe said, and Rick jerked his attention to the older man standing in the doorway. "I already put the toys in the trunk. I swear Marie thinks she's Santa Claus."

Rick swallowed hard and managed a smile. "It's all for a good cause. And I see you also got Jess a sweatshirt."

"Yup. Marie only has the one she wears, but I have two, so I lent her one. People need to know which side she's on."

His side, Rick thought. As beat as he'd felt this afternoon, he almost wished he was playing just so he could spot Jess in the crowd, cheering for him and calling his name.

Marie walked into the kitchen wearing a sweatshirt that matched the other two. Rick was wearing his T-shirt with a hoodie over it because he tended to run hot and crew neck sweatshirts drove him crazy. And since he hadn't totally cooled off yet from the passionate, if imaginary, kiss with Jessica, he was ready to get back outside.

"We need to get going," he said. "It's Jess's first time, so we want good seats."

And so started a debate between Joe and Marie that lasted all the way to the rink as to what constituted good seats. And since Joe was in the shotgun seat next to Rick and Marie was in the backseat with Jessica, it meant the older man spent a lot of time turned in his seat, yelling past Rick's ear.

"You sit close and you can hear everything and practically smell the sweat," Joe said.

"But if you sit near the top, you can see *everything*," Marie argued.

"I'd like to see everything," Jessica said, "but it's hard to resist the smell of sweat."

She said it so sincerely, Rick had to choke back a laugh. He didn't offer an opinion, though. Truth be told, the other guys from the station and their families would have staked out a section already. They'd take the best four seats that were left together.

Getting inside, dropping the bags of toys in the collection box, and making their way to those seats was probably quite the adventure for Jess, though. It didn't seem as if they could walk ten feet before she had to be introduced to somebody else. When they finally found the guys from his station, though, he was pleasantly surprised by how many of their names she remembered.

He knew she'd met some of them a couple of times—at the station when Marie stopped by, and then at the bar—but the first time had been nothing but a barrage of names, and some of them hadn't been at Kincaid's the other night. Remembering names was probably a skill that helped make her good at her job, he thought. It made people feel valued.

Another thing that surprised him was how often he had to stop himself from touching her. He wanted to put his hand on the small of her back to guide her through the crowd. Or lace his fingers through hers when they were talking to people. And maybe if she'd been any other woman, he would have. But whenever the temptation got too strong, he'd remember they were there with Joe and Marie. And they were trying not to do the kissing thing anymore, by mutual agreement.

"Aidan!" he heard her say, and watched her shake the other guy's hand. "It's good to see you again."

Then he watched her greet everybody else, amazingly able to keep them all straight. Aidan was engaged to Lydia, who was Scott's sister. And their dad, Tommy, was in attendance, as well. And Scott and Lydia's sister, Ashley, who was married to Danny Walsh. He wondered if she'd made a spreadsheet or something in advance and studied it.

"I had a great time at your bar the other night," she told Tommy, who grinned at the praise. "And the burger was to die for."

"I'm glad you liked it," the old, retired firefighter said, his chest puffing a little. "Heard you played a little pool with the guys."

Rick hoped that was all he'd heard, but Jess just smiled. "Did you close down to come for the game? It looks like you're all here."

"Nope. Karen's watching the place for us tonight. She's a friend of Rick's."

"We should find some seats," Rick said before that conversation could go any deeper. "Good to see you, Tommy."

They finally found an empty stretch of bleacher long enough for the four of them. Rick had assumed Jessica would sit between her grandparents, but Joe went in first, with Marie on his heels. Jessica sat next to her, leaving Rick at her side on the end. It wasn't a big deal, except for the fact he was going to spend the entire game with his thigh pressed against hers.

"How do you remember everybody's names?" he asked her while they waited for things to get under way.

"It's just a knack I have. I tend to remember details about people pretty easily if I'm trying. When I was growing up, I always wanted to be an event planner. Even now, one of my favorite things to do is plan the annual holiday party we throw for our employees and some of our clients. Doing it at a distance isn't as fun, but I still get to handle the details."

"How come you didn't do that, then, if that's what you wanted to be and you're good at it?"

She laughed. "My father would never have gone

for that. And what's the point of building a successful business if your only child is organizing baby shower party favors or wedding venues?"

"So you have to live his dream because you're an only child?"

She gave him a sharp sideways look and he shut his mouth. Luckily, the announcer chose that moment to turn their attention to the ice, and Jessica not only laughed but clapped her hands for the guy dressed as Santa on skates.

As always, the crowd noise rose to earsplitting decibels during the team introductions. The police department's team skated out first, followed by the fire department. Judging by the explosion of sound when Aidan and Scott were introduced, Lydia and Ashley were sitting not too far behind them and off to the left.

Once the game started, it quieted a little, though. He watched the play, but he was also very aware of Jess's long leg pressed against his. Especially when, about halfway through the game, she tilted the rest of her body toward his to ask a question.

"How come they're not punching each other?"

Rick leaned closer, because there was no way he could have heard her correctly. "Did you ask me why they're not punching each other?"

"Yes, or hitting each other with the sticks or something. Except for sometimes pushing each other into the walls, they're not hitting each other at all."

So he *had* heard her correctly. "I have to say, you

keep this bloodthirsty side of yourself pretty well hidden."

"I've seen highlights during news broadcasts, of course, and when I found out we were coming here, I read up on hockey on the internet. I thought there would be fighting and blood and stuff."

"It's a charity game being played by guys whose calling in life is to help people."

"Yes, I get that. Protect and serve and all that." She waved her hand. "But this is hockey. I had expectations."

He forced himself not to laugh at her, because he didn't want her to feel foolish. But it was hard when that pretty face seemed so genuinely dismayed by the lack of violence. "Sorry to disappoint you, but the game's not over yet. There's still a chance Kincaid could get riled up. He's got a bit of a temper."

"Scott and Aidan are both from your station, so how come you didn't play?" She gave him a slow once-over that would have made his cheeks red if he was the blushing kind. "Not good enough?"

His eyebrow arched and he held her gaze until she proved she *was* the blushing kind. "Oh, I'm good enough, honey. Trust me."

"Don't call me honey."

"Don't question my manhood."

She *really* blushed then. "I didn't question your... manhood. I questioned your ability to play hockey."

"Same thing."

"What an incredibly guy thing to say."

"Thank you."

She turned her attention back to the ice with an exasperated sigh, and he had to stifle a chuckle. When he nudged her knee with his, she crossed her arms and tilted her chin a little, so it was clear she was ignoring him. But a smile played with the corner of her mouth and that was good enough.

He might have been tired earlier in the day but now, as far as he was concerned, this game could go on all night.

JESSICA COULDN'T REMEMBER enjoying an event as much as she enjoyed the hockey game. Of course it didn't hurt that the fire department won and the crowd had managed to set a new record for tickets sold *and* the number of toys collected for charity.

She probably shouldn't have had a steamed hot dog, though. Or the nachos. Or the popcorn or the cotton candy. And she didn't even want to think about how much soda she'd had. But as best she could tell, questionable food choices and sports were a package deal.

When it was time to leave, she stood and put her hands to her back to stretch. She had no idea how Joe and Marie managed to sit on the bleachers for so long, but maybe they were just used to it. And her leg felt cold without the constant hot pressure of Rick's thigh against hers. At first, she'd felt compelled to draw her knee away to give him more space and to save herself from the distraction, but there simply hadn't been enough room.

When the crowd they were being swept along with

finally got through the exit, the cold night air was like a slap in Jessica's face. It hadn't been cold when they left the house and she had a shirt on under the sweatshirt, so she hadn't bothered with a coat.

"I'll go get the car," Rick told Joe and Marie, who were chatting with friends on the sidewalk. "Save you the walk. And it'll take a bit in this traffic, so you'll have time to visit."

"Take Jessica with you," Marie said. "I can tell she's already freezing."

While she wanted to protest and try to at least pretend she could hang with the native New Englanders, the idea of a warm car and a nicely contoured seat was too much temptation to resist. She walked up the street next to Rick, trying to remember how far away the car was parked and hoping they got there before she embarrassed him by freezing to death in the midst of a bunch of people who didn't even look cold.

Then she stepped in a shallow puddle. Or rather, she stepped onto it. Her foot slipped on the ice and she would have landed hard on her ass if not for Rick's quick reflexes. In a flash, his arm was looped under hers and he yanked her upright before she could actually fall. It wasn't comfortable, but it was better than a busted tailbone.

"Thanks. I guess I should add ice being slippery to my journal of things I learned in Boston."

"I can throw you over my shoulder if you want. I've had professional training."

She gave him a look that might have scorched that

fancy fire coat he wore. "Do they give classes on being a caveman at the fire academy?"

"That part just comes naturally to some of us. But they have to teach us how to lift with our legs and not with our backs, I guess."

This was ridiculous. Jessica was freezing, and now Rick had threatened to throw her over his shoulder.

Okay, that wasn't really fair, she forced herself to admit. He'd *offered* to throw her over his shoulder. A small distinction, but one he'd probably consider an important one. "I think I can manage on my feet, thank you."

"Let me know if you change your mind. Practice keeps the skills sharp."

She realized they'd continued on walking, and his arm was still tucked under hers, with his hand curled around her elbow. Whether he was afraid she'd slip on ice or if he just liked it there, she couldn't be sure. But she certainly didn't mind it, so she just kept walking.

"Did you have a good time tonight?"

"I definitely did, though I ate a lot of foods I don't think were meant to go together."

"Any food eaten while watching sports is exempt from any kind of nutritional standards." He smiled at her, his teeth gleaming in the dim light. "Especially if you're actually at the arena or stadium in person. Ask any sports fan."

"I should watch a game on TV. With professional hockey players, I mean."

"Just so you know, there's not always fighting and blood in professional hockey, either."

She rolled her eyes at him. "Not for the fighting. I had a really good time tonight and I think I could become a fan."

"It's too bad you're not staying longer. I could probably get Bruins tickets."

"I'm not sure which team I'm supposed to root for. I think I've heard the news talk about Ducks. Does that sound right?"

His expression made it clear he didn't think much of that. "You've gotta be a Boston Bruins fan. Your family's from here. This is where you were introduced to hockey. And why have a duck when you can have a bear?"

"There probably aren't many Bruins fans in San Diego."

"That just makes you exceptional in a city with very little taste."

She laughed and bumped against him, taking him off guard and knocking him a couple of steps sideways. Since his arm was hooked in hers, she went with him. He nudged her back and she was tempted to rest her head against his arm as they walked. It was nice, just the two of them.

But then she saw the car and it brought reality back. This wasn't a date. It was a family outing planned before she'd even arrived. And they'd agreed they weren't going to kiss anymore, so there would be no kiss good-night.

Once she was in the car and the engine started generating enough heat to spare some for the vents, Jessica sighed and snuggled into the comfort. Considering how many people had told her it wasn't even cold yet and she should experience January and February, she should probably be thankful she was going home soon.

"The Bruins play Monday night," Rick said as he worked the car through the traffic toward where they'd left Joe and Marie. "I'll be watching it if you want to come up and watch it with me."

Okay, that sounded *almost* like a date. "You don't watch the games with Joe?"

He shook his head. "He follows the Bruins box scores and he likes the charity games, like tonight, but he doesn't watch many of the games until postseason. He's more of a baseball guy."

"Okay." She probably should have said no, but that wasn't what came out of her mouth. "I'll bring some junk food."

"Sounds like a plan."

A plan. Not a date. Just a plan, like friends would make. But it was a plan she was already looking forward to.

TEN

On Sunday afternoon, Rick glanced out his window and happened to notice the side door to the garage was open. Since he was too bored to watch television, but not bored enough to reach out to his friends and see if anybody was doing anything interesting, he decided he'd take a walk down and see what Joe was up to.

Rick found him in front of the work bench along the back wall of the garage, rummaging through one of the many chock-full drawers in the various storage towers and toolboxes. "Hey, Joe. Looking for something specific?"

"No, just looking. When did I accumulate all this junk?"

Rick shook his head. "Before I got here, although I've probably helped contribute to the collection since I moved in."

"Why would I ever think I needed to save some of this?" He held up a bolt that had seen better days, judging by the fact the nut screwed onto it looked rusted right to the threads.

"You never know what you might need." Rick was pretty sure it was just a guy thing. He'd never met a garage-owning man yet who didn't have jars and cof-

fee cans full of miscellaneous metal things. "Soak it
in some oil and it'll work just fine."

"Can you imagine how long it would take us to
muck out this house if we sold it?"

"Are you considering selling?" He wasn't sure if
the subject had been temporarily tabled or if he just
wasn't in the loop, but he hadn't heard much about it
since they filled him in after the appointment with
the doctor.

Joe shrugged and opened another drawer. "We're
not *not* considering it."

Rick wondered if Jessica had been talking to them,
or if they were just naturally working themselves toward that direction. "It's a big house. Needs a lot of
upkeep and I know the utility bills and the taxes must
be a bitch."

"I hate surrendering to it. It's like an admission I
might be getting old."

"Hell, half the people you grew up with sold their
houses and bought condos in Florida ten years ago
or more."

Joe snorted. "We went to Florida once. I hated it."

"Well, there are plenty of options around here.
Maybe something away from the city, where it's quiet,
and you and Marie can sit on a doublewide swing and
listen to the birds sing or whatever."

"I like this neighborhood. We know where everything is and we can walk to almost anything we want.
I'm a city boy at heart. But it is a big house, and Marie's not getting any younger."

It struck Rick how Joe wouldn't admit to being

too old to take care of the house, but maybe he'd consider selling it for Marie's sake. "How does she feel about it?"

"Same as I do, mostly. We like it here and don't really want to move. But we also don't want the other to end up in a bind if something happens, you know?"

"You don't have to rush into anything. And the most important thing is that the two of you are on the same page about it and screw what anybody else thinks."

"Yeah. Jessica helped Marie set up an appointment with a real estate agent for Wednesday. She says we can't really think about our options without a solid idea of what we might be able to get for the house."

"She's probably right." She hadn't mentioned the real estate agent to him at all, and it had to have been set up before the hockey game. Even if they'd made the appointment on Friday while he was working, it seemed odd she didn't say anything to him.

"I guess Jessica's flying back to San Diego on Thursday," Joe continued. "Marie's going to be heartbroken, even though she knew it was coming eventually, but I told her we'd finally break down and get her one of those smartphones. Waste of money if you ask me, but they can send text messages to each other and do that video chat thing."

She was leaving Thursday. She hadn't mentioned that to him, either. He knew she'd go soon, since her company was having its Christmas party, but he hadn't known which day. "I don't think you have to worry about Jess not staying in touch. It's meant a lot to her, getting to know you."

"We wish she didn't live so damn far away."

"I know, but I bet she'll fly out a few times a year to visit. If not more."

"I hope so. It's been just Marie and I for so long, so it's nice to have family. Even if Davey had come back, it would've been hard to forgive him for the hell he's put his mother through. But Jessica, she's not like him. And we're both so thankful to have her now, even if we won't get to see her all the time. It's nice knowing we have somebody good out there in the world with our name."

Rick had no doubt the Broussards would be changing their wills any day, if they hadn't already started the process, and he didn't blame them a bit. They were the kind of people who would have left the house and any money they had to their son simply because he was their son. But knowing they'd be gifting their property to Jessica would make them much happier.

"What do you suppose this went to?" Joe asked, holding up an oddly shaped chunk of metal.

Rick took it from him to give it a closer look. "I have no idea."

He and Joe ended up killing almost two hours in the garage, looking through containers and sorting piles of junk. They didn't really accomplish anything, but sometimes that wasn't the point. Especially on a lazy, early winter Sunday. The days of digging out hydrants, snow-related accidents, clearing roofs and extra shifts were right around the corner. Spending a couple of hours with a good friend, sorting bolts and talking about everything and nothing was a good way to relax.

Of course he managed to get dirty enough so when it was time to call it quits, he needed a shower. After stripping down and tossing his dirty clothes in the hamper, Rick turned on the shower and set it to pretty damn hot. The shower was huge, as was the entire master bathroom because Joe and Marie had given him the freedom to remodel however he wanted as long as he paid for it. And being a big guy who'd gone from growing up in a house with a small shower to renting an apartment with an even smaller shower, the bathroom was where he'd spent the most money.

He let the hot water beat against his skin for a couple of minutes before grabbing the shampoo and scrubbing his hair. Even as his muscles relaxed, his mind turned to Jess and the fact she'd be leaving Thursday. In just a few days, she'd be getting on a plane to San Diego and he didn't know when—or really even if—she'd be back.

Last night had almost gotten the better of him. When he'd taken her arm to keep her from falling, he should have let go as soon as she was steady and kept his hands to himself. But they'd just kind of kept talking and kept walking, and he liked the contact. Then she'd gotten flirty, bumping his shoulder because he was being funny, and he'd thought about kissing her.

He thought about kissing her a lot. Her mouth fascinated him, and he could only imagine how it would feel to press his lips against hers. The feel of her hair tangled in his fingers. The softness of her skin.

After rinsing the shampoo out of his hair, Rick grabbed the bar of soap and lathered up. He scrubbed hard at his arms, which he'd managed to get greasy as well as grimy, and then rinsed the soap away. It wasn't so easy to push the image of Jessica away, though, and he found himself wishing she was in the shower with him. It was definitely built for two.

Rick braced one hand against the tile wall and closed the fingers of his other hand around his dick as he imagined the hot water running down her naked body. The steam would make the hair around her face damp and her skin would be tender and flushed. He'd kiss her while pressing her back against the tiles, and he didn't have to imagine that. He knew how her mouth felt and how she tasted. But now, in his mind, he slid his hand between her legs.

Picturing her blue eyes widening, he wondered if she'd be shy and whisper his name. Or maybe she'd be bold and demanding, her head thrown back with abandon.

Stroking himself harder, he imagined the feel of her slick, hot flesh under his palm. The sounds she'd make when he slid his fingers over her clit. Her nipples would be hard in his mouth, and he'd suck each in turn until she squirmed against his hand. He'd whisper in her ear, telling her all the things he was going to do to her, while she came. And then, when the last shudder faded away, he'd turn her around and have her brace her hands against the tile as he slowly eased his cock into her.

With a groan, Rick came, his dick pulsing in his hand as he stroked and the fantasy faded. Then he leaned his forehead against the shower wall and closed his eyes. The relief would be temporary, he knew. He wanted the real Jessica, naked and under him, and jerking off to imaginary her wasn't enough anymore.

AFTER CLIMBING THE two flights of exterior stairs to Rick's small deck, Jessica raised her fist to knock on his glass sliding door, only to realize she didn't have to knock. She could see him, and he was looking straight at her.

He was also almost naked.

Obviously fresh out of the shower, he had a towel wrapped around his waist, but there was plenty of skin for her to look at. And look she did. She wasn't sure if it was his job or the gym or both, but his body was so well toned he could be on a magazine cover. Not so ripped it would be a vanity point, but he was definitely in shape.

And his calves were almost as impressive as his biceps. That was probably from going up and down the huge ladder on his truck and climbing stairs, but she'd never really noticed a man's legs before. She certainly noticed his.

Whose bright idea had it been for them to put an end to any making out when they'd only gotten as far as kissing?

Then she realized he was waving her in and felt stupid. Gawking at the man through his door wasn't one of her finer moments and she hoped he'd let it go without commenting. She opened the door and stepped inside, sliding it closed behind her.

"Sorry," he said. "I wasn't expecting company."

"Marie sent me up to ask you for…a thing."

"A thing?" He grinned. "A specific thing, or can I just grab whatever's at hand and give it to you?"

She sighed and held up her hands in defeat. "Look, you know you're an attractive guy. You know I like kissing you but we're not doing that anymore. You also know you're only wearing a towel and you smell delicious. I don't think you need to mock a woman for forgetting what she came here for."

"I wasn't mocking you. Just clarifying whether or not any old thing would do."

"Who takes showers at this time of day, anyway?"

"People who get dirty digging around in decades' worth of crap in the garage."

She gave a self-deprecating laugh. "Forget it. You can take showers whenever you want. Just bad timing on my part."

"Okay, to get back to the thing at hand, what was Marie doing when she asked you to come up here?"

"She was looking through a plastic box that had a bunch of recipes in… Oh! She said you borrowed her big slow cooker a few weeks ago and she wants to make a roast this week. It won't fit in her everyday one." She held up a hand. "I didn't even know they came in different sizes or that there was such a thing as an everyday slow cooker."

"She bought a small one because she's usually only cooking for the two of them and it's mostly soups and stews. And she makes a mean chili." He frowned in the direction of the kitchen, as if trying to remember where he'd left it. "Let me throw some clothes on and then I'll dig it out for you."

"Okay." She would have been more than happy to watch him rummage around his kitchen in just the towel, but she could imagine he might feel awkward. Especially if the towel slipped and ended up on the floor.

Flushed, Jessica waited until he'd closed his bedroom door and then looked around the apartment. It had been remodeled at some point, far more recently than the downstairs, and she guessed he'd sunk his own money into it. It was as open concept as the old house's structure allowed, with the living room area flowing naturally into the kitchen. He had a table and chairs set up near the slider, and everything was leather or chrome and glass. The kitchen island and countertops were a dark granite, and he had nice stainless steel appliances. There was a half bath off the kitchen, but she only saw one bedroom door. Considering the footprint of the house, it must be one hell of a master suite.

There were two big bookcases in the living room, stuffed full of books, and some family pictures sat in frames on top of them. She guessed one of the photos was of Rick's brother, along with a woman and two young boys taken on a boat. There was a strong resemblance between him, his brother and their dad, and his mom was pretty, too. She was smiling at the camera in one framed picture, with her husband's arm around her and her two sons bookending them. Her pride was evident in her body language and expression, and Jessica sighed.

She'd be lying if she said her mom abandoning her when she was little didn't hurt. Usually it was a dull, barely there ache. But sometimes it was a gaping wound she knew would never heal. Even though she'd learned with age—and through multiple failed marriages on her father's part—to accept that her mother had probably been leaving her father and not just her, she'd always wondered why she hadn't fought for her. Even if she couldn't handle full custody, she could have stuck around for visitations.

As with his own parents, Jessica's mother wasn't a topic her father wanted to discuss. He'd claimed she was unstable and they were better off without her. But he'd said a lot of bad things about her grandparents, too, and now she knew better. Or at the very least, they weren't the same people they'd been while raising their son. So maybe her dad was wrong about her mom, too.

The big difference, as far as Jessica was concerned, was simple. Joe and Marie hadn't fought to see her because they hadn't known she existed. Her mother had known. She'd made a conscious choice to remove herself from Jessica's life, and no amount of therapy or logical pep talks could ever make her understand.

"You okay?"

She jumped at the sound of Rick's voice, since she hadn't heard his bedroom door open. "What?"

"You look lost in space, and that's not a happy expression."

"I was just looking at your family pictures. You all look really happy. Is that your brother's boat?"

"It's my dad's, actually. But my brother uses it more than anybody else, I guess."

"I've been out on a boat a few times. It's nice at first, and it can be relaxing, but then I get bored and want to go for a walk or something. That doesn't work so well."

He chuckled, but his eyes remained serious. "I'm guessing boat envy didn't put that sadness in your eyes."

"I never have sad eyes."

"Yeah, you do. Maybe you just don't know it."

She turned back to the photos so he couldn't see her face anymore. "Sometimes it's hard seeing family pictures with such happy, obviously proud mothers. And then there's the obvious reaction to seeing three generations smiling together. I guess that's what families are supposed to look like."

"Families look a lot of different ways, and there's no right or wrong or supposed to about any of them."

"Mine has always been just me and my father, and most of the time he seems more like my boss or a business partner. Nobody's ever used a photo of us to sell picture frames, that's for sure."

"I can turn them around if you want."

"You can't be serious," she said, turning to face him with an incredulous look. When she saw his face, she realized he definitely wasn't serious and was simply trying to lighten the mood. Maybe he'd guessed she wasn't used to people being able to see her emotions that way, and that was true. Nobody had ever told her she had sad eyes before.

"Are you coming down for dinner tonight?" she asked, wanting to change the subject.

He shook his head, and she felt a pang of disappointment. "I'm going to meet some of the guys tonight. I don't usually eat with Joe and Marie, actually, even though it probably looks that way. I think having you around made all the meals into special occasions, so she kept inviting me."

"And you accepted so you could keep an eye on me." She realized belatedly how that sounded and felt heat in her cheeks. "So you could make sure I'm not fleecing them out of all their money, I mean."

"I don't think that. I mean, I think your job makes you more inclined to make decisions based on financial reasons and not their emotional well-being, but I don't think you'd ever fleece anybody, never mind Joe and Marie."

She tilted her head. "You don't think I can balance fiscal responsibility with their emotional well-being?"

"I think you can, but it's probably not your first instinct." He walked to a cabinet in the kitchen and pulled out a slow cooker, which he set on the island. "Joe told me you set up a meeting with a real estate agent."

"Marie did, actually. And she discussed it with him first."

"But you had a hand in it."

"They're not listing it with her. She's giving them a fair market value appraisal and that's all unless they decide to move forward. How are they supposed to make informed decisions without determining the worth of their most valuable asset?" She walked over to the island. "Unless you're worried about having to find a new place to live."

"I think we already had this conversation. I'm not worried about me. My only concern is Joe and Marie."

"Mine, too." She picked up the slow cooker. "I'll give this to Marie."

"Tell her I said thank you." She nodded and was almost to the door when he spoke again. "Hey. You still going to watch the game with me tomorrow? I'll order pizza."

Maybe if he was questioning her motives because he was a jerk, she'd reconsider. But it was hard to hold his concern for her grandparents against him, especially since she'd know he was still there for them when she left. Just as he'd been there for them before she arrived. "Of course. I'm looking forward to it."

He gave her a look she couldn't quite decipher, but that sent a sizzle through her body. "I am, too."

"Don't look at me like that. We're agreed we're

not moving in the direction that look wants me to go, remember?"

"I remember. And I'm sure if I think long and hard enough, I can remember why we agreed to that."

For once, Jessica was grateful when she stepped outside and the cold air instantly chilled her body. Maybe if she left her window open, she'd actually get some sleep tonight.

RICK WALKED INTO Kincaid's Pub, ready for a beer and a burger and maybe a few games of pool in the back room. Ashley was behind the bar tonight, and that meant Aidan probably wouldn't show up. Lydia worked a lot of nights, so when she took off and he wasn't at the station, he was with her.

"Hey, Rick, where's your girl?" Tommy bellowed from the back corner of the bar, and everybody turned to look at him.

"She's not my girl," he said to the room in general, since most of them were people he knew. "She was at the game with her grandparents. So was I. That was the extent of us being there together."

When he reached the bar, Ashley set a frosted mug on a coaster in front of him. "Yeah, we could see you guys from where we were sitting. And I heard about your pool lesson the other night. She might not be your girl yet, but that's totally happening."

"She's going back to San Diego on Thursday." It wasn't a total denial of any chemistry they may have witnessed at the bar or at the hockey game, but it should put an end to the speculation.

"Oh." She frowned at him, her expression of annoyance so like Scott's, he almost laughed at her. Scott and Lydia had the fiery Kincaid temperament, like their old man. Ashley tended to be levelheaded and calm, though she'd pop off if she was pushed hard enough. "That's what sexting is for."

"Don't you think I'm a little old for sexting?"

"Of course not." She paused, and then smiled. "Although, if you send her a dick pic, you might want to use a filter."

It's a good thing he hadn't taken a drink of his beer yet, or he might have choked on it. "Gee, thanks a lot."

"And a zoom lens."

Rick turned to see Danny stepping up to the bar. He hadn't seen Ashley's husband when he came in, but he should have known he'd be here. "You two are freaking hilarious tonight."

"I'm not sure why you and my wife are talking about your dick, but that makes you fair game for any insult I want to throw your way." He set his empty mug on the bar. "You didn't bring Jessica with you?"

"And that's why we were talking about his dick," Ashley said as she replaced his empty mug with a full one.

"Okay." Danny took a sip of his beer and then turned to face Rick. "Since she's not here with you, are we talking about your literal dick or are you *being* a dick?"

"I'm done with this conversation." Rick picked up his beer and headed for the alcove at the back of the bar where the pool table was.

A game was going on, but there were quite a few guys gathered around to watch. Rick shook hands with Scott and Gavin, plus there were several guys from a nearby station and two police officers he recognized. Of course Danny followed him back, but luckily didn't bring up the conversation they'd been having at the bar.

Once Scott lost and no longer had the run of the table, he grabbed his half-empty beer mug and walked over to sit with Rick at the small round table he'd claimed. "How's it going?"

Rick shrugged. "It's going, I guess."

"You going to play tonight?"

"I don't think so. Not really in the mood. Is Aidan with Lydia tonight?"

"Yeah, since we'd talked about getting together tonight, Danny wanted in. And Ashley said if Danny was going to be here, she may as well work and Lydia could have a night off. It's not like Sundays are hectic." Scott tipped his chair back onto two legs so it balanced against the wall. "How are things going with Jessica and the Broussards?"

Rick had an instant flashback to the moment he'd spotted Jess outside his door, her hand frozen in midair, just shy of knocking. Considering what he'd just been up to in the shower, he wasn't surprised to feel a rush of heat in his cheeks but, luckily, she hadn't been looking at his face.

"Things are good," he said. "But she's leaving Thursday."

Maybe if he said it enough times, he'd be able to

figure out how he felt about it. He should be thankful things would go back to normal around the house. But the idea of not seeing Jessica whenever he popped in downstairs didn't sit well.

"For good?"

Rick shrugged. "I'm sure she'll come back to visit Joe and Marie, so I'll see her around here and there. You seeing anybody new?"

Scott sighed and dropped his chair back onto four legs. "No. I think I'm going to stop trying to see anybody for a while."

"Interesting. And unlike you."

"Yeah. But maybe I spend too much time with women who don't see marriage in our future—or see marriage for the wrong reasons—and it's keeping me from finding the right one."

Rick knew he'd been burned recently by a young woman who'd pressured Scott for a ring, but only because she wanted access to his benefits and was even willing to get pregnant to get him to the altar. She hadn't been, but he was pretty sure that girl was a turning point for Scott.

"I don't think I have a right one," Rick said before taking a long swig of his beer.

"From what I hear, she might be right under your nose. Literally, like she's sleeping one floor below you."

He had to guess Scott had gotten that little tidbit from his sisters, since he'd been on the ice the entire game and hadn't seen them together. And Scott hadn't seen the kiss in the pool room, but Aidan had probably filled him in. "Pretty sure the right woman for me would at least live in the same time zone."

"Good point." Scott sighed and raised his mug. "Here's to being not the marrying kind."

Rick touched his mug to Scott's and then took another drink. "Well. This is kind of depressing."

"Yup." Scott nodded. "Another night alone in our apartments to look forward to. Might as well order some burgers and then stay here until they throw us out."

Rick agreed, but he was thinking about tomorrow night, when he wouldn't be alone in his apartment. And he might feel low at the moment and she might be leaving on Thursday, but Jess, hockey and junk food was a potent combination he'd spend the next twenty-four hours thinking about.

ELEVEN

JESSICA DID A little yoga in her room after wrapping up her work late Monday afternoon. And she even threw in some bonus planking just because she hadn't been back to the gym with Rick but had continued to stuff herself with Marie's cooking.

The fact it was a good excuse to take a shower at that time of day was purely coincidental, she told herself. And since she was taking a shower anyway, she went ahead and shaved her legs while she was in there. A little scented body cream and she was ready to go watch a hockey game.

She felt silly, though, when she had to go down to the kitchen to get the bag of junk food she'd bought at the corner market during her lunch break. Marie was there, preparing dinner for her and Joe, and she breathed in deeply.

"You smell lovely, honey."

"Thanks. I took a shower." That sounded awkward. "I was doing yoga in my room and I'm out of shape so I got sweaty, so I wanted to clean up."

Marie gave her a knowing look. "You don't want to watch hockey if you don't smell pretty."

Jessica laughed and took a seat at the table. "It's

good to take a shower after yoga. It keeps the muscles limber. Honest."

"Mmm-hmm." Marie hit the button to turn the oven off and cracked the door to let the accumulated heat escape. "Are you sure you don't want to eat with us?"

"Rick said he'd order pizza. You're supposed to eat junk food with hockey."

"Pizza's not junk food," Joe said as he walked into the kitchen.

"I should make homemade pizza soon," her grandmother said. "I haven't done that in ages."

Jessica frowned. "Isn't the whole idea of pizza that not only does somebody else make it, but they deliver it to your house?"

"Mine's better."

She didn't doubt that. Marie was an amazing cook and Jessica had never realized how much her own skills were lacking until she came here. She might look like a younger version of her grandmother, but the cooking gene had definitely skipped her. "I'm going to go answer some last-minute emails while you guys eat. Everybody's trying to clear their desks before the holiday party on Saturday kicks off the holiday pseudo-break."

"Pseudo-break?" Joe asked, pulling out his chair. "That doesn't sound like time off, exactly."

"It's the closest we get to time off. We close the office for the week Christmas falls in, but the market doesn't take time off, so we all have to stay on top of things from home. And we have a lot of top clients who expect us to be as dedicated to work as they are."

"All work and no play is no way to live," Joe said sternly.

"Hey, you're talking to a woman who's in Boston about to watch her first Bruins game while her office in San Diego is going nuts. I'm learning." She'd been walking past him, but on impulse, she leaned over and kissed his cheek.

He smiled and grabbed her hand, giving it a little squeeze. Then he let it go without saying anything. By now Jessica knew he wasn't emotionally demonstrative, so the small gesture spoke volumes.

"You going to watch the news with us before you go upstairs?" he asked.

"Of course." She gave them a small wave and then took her phone out to the couch, where she dealt with emails and read articles she'd bookmarked until it was time for the news.

She had trouble focusing on the broadcast because her gaze kept straying to the time displayed on their cable box. The snow in the forecast caught her attention, but it didn't look as if it would amount to very much in New England terms, so she didn't worry about it. If Joe didn't comment on the forecast, she knew there was nothing to worry about.

When it was finally time, she said good-night to her grandparents, since they'd already be in bed by the time the game ended, and grabbed the paper bag of snacks. Then, after taking a deep breath—telling herself a hockey game was no big deal, really—she went up the stairs to Rick's apartment.

As soon as he opened the door, Jessica knew they'd reached a point of no return. They were either going to drop the futile game they'd been playing, dancing around their attraction for each other, or they were going to fully commit to absolutely no more kissing or touching and mean it.

She doubted he'd been doing yoga in his bedroom but Rick had definitely just gotten out of the shower. And he was freshly shaven. That was slightly disappointing since she'd spent a lot of time wondering how that scruffy jaw would feel against her skin.

But both of them taking showers late in the day meant eating pizza in front of the television wasn't the only thing on their minds.

"Black sweater?" He grinned as he stepped back to let her in. "Good choice."

She hooked her thumb under the yellow bra strap and pulled it out far enough so he could catch a glimpse of it. "It was the closest I could come to black and yellow."

His gaze seemed locked on the thin strip of her bra and his jaw tightened. "Black and gold."

She frowned and released the bra strap, which slid back into place. "The colors look like black and yellow."

"I know. But it's gold. Trust me." The grin reappeared. "But that bra definitely qualifies."

"Oh, good. I'd hate to get disqualified from fandom for the wrong color underwear." She handed him the paper bag. "I brought junk food to go with the pizza."

He led the way to the island, where he unloaded the bag. She'd bought chips and dip and a bag of pretzels. Two different kinds of cookies. A variety of artificially flavored cupcakes packaged in pairs. And at the bottom of the bag, a bottle of liquefied cheese in a squeeze bottle.

"You really know how to bring the junk food." He held up the squeezable cheese. "What are you going to do with this?"

"I'm not sure. Maybe dip the pretzels in it?"

"Maybe I should have ordered a small pizza."

She laughed. "We don't have to eat it all. I only brought it because you're supposed to eat junk food with sports, though I would have preferred nachos. And cotton candy. I bet if you bring it to work, it won't go to waste."

"Go to waste? I'll be lucky if it makes it to the kitchen. What do you want to drink with your pizza? Beer, soda or water?"

"I'll take a soda." She wasn't a big beer drinker and the two she'd had at Kincaid's Pub filled her quota for a while.

He went to the fridge and grabbed them each a soda. "The pizza's already on the coffee table and the game's about to start."

Jessica ate a slice of pizza while they went through a big lead-in for the game. The announcers talked about a lot of people she'd never heard of and used terms that meant nothing to her, but she enjoyed watching them skate around on the ice before they got ready to drop the puck, as the guy on TV said.

Then, after all the talking, the referee dropped the puck between two hockey players and they all erupted into action. It was so fast-paced she had a hard time keeping track of the puck and she winced every time somebody got slammed into the glass enclosure, but it was still fun. Every once in a while Rick would yell at the television, making her smile.

Several times, she opened the browser on her phone to search for the definition of a term so she could get a better handle on what was happening. She'd first done it after the tenth or so time she heard *icing*, and she was looking up *penalty kill* when Rick caught her.

"What are you doing? You're not working during a game, are you? That's absolutely not allowed."

She looked up from her phone. "No, I'm not working. I'm looking things up on Google."

"Things?"

"Yes, *things*. I don't know what the announcers are talking about and that makes it hard for me to follow. If I look up some of the terms as they use them, it's easier to understand the game."

"You could always just ask me." He winked. "I know what most of the words mean."

She lowered the phone to her lap and shrugged. "Isn't it annoying if you're trying to watch the game and somebody's asking you really basic questions about it the whole time?"

"Or maybe I look at it like I'm sharing my knowledge of the game so somebody else will learn to love it, too. Sharing the passion, so to speak."

Laughing, she locked her phone screen and tossed it onto the coffee table, trying not to think too much about Rick sharing his passion with her. Hockey. He'd been talking about hockey. "If I was some guy who'd come over to watch the game with you and had to ask what icing means, would you feel the same way?"

"No." He didn't even pretend to think about it. "I'd tell him to shut up and read a book about the game before he came back again."

"So I guess I'm special, then?"

"Absolutely." He gave her a look that seemed to say whether they were talking about hockey or anything else, he did think she was special.

The sizzle of sexual attraction she expected every time she and Rick locked eyes came, but this time it was wrapped in a warm, emotional feeling that scared the crap out of her.

Not at all sure how to respond—either to his words or to her reaction to them— she turned back to the game. As confusing at it was, at least she knew the final objective of the men on the screen. Get the puck in the other team's goal more times than they got it in yours.

But in real life, she wasn't sure what the objective was anymore. Maybe she needed men in suits with microphones to narrate it for her.

SOMETHING HAD SPOOKED HER, Rick thought, and based on the way her expression had changed, he had to guess it was when he said she was special.

What he couldn't figure out was why. She had to know he liked her. It wasn't a coincidence they'd both showered before this game—something he'd noticed as soon as he opened the door. Hell, he couldn't keep himself from kissing her, even when they'd agreed not to, and he wasn't in the habit of kissing women he didn't like.

Maybe she didn't know how to take a compliment like that, which was sad. She was smart and funny and beautiful and caring and the people in her life should have been telling her that all along.

"Do you want another slice of pizza?" he asked, hoping to get her to look at him so he could see her face.

"I don't know. I'd hate to be too full to try that liquid-cheese-in-a-bottle stuff." She turned to look at him and he was relieved to see her humor reached her eyes. Whatever had bothered her seemed to have been fleeting.

"I can't believe you've never had it."

"I can't believe you *have.*"

"We all have things in our past we're not proud of." He paused to watch the Bruins' goalie block a dangerous shot, and then turned back to her. "Right?"

She shrugged. "My closet is skeleton and squeezable cheese free, I think."

"Oh, come on. You must have had a rebellious phase or dated questionable guys or something."

"Not that I recall. I think my father has even approved of all the boyfriends I've had, and I guess that's probably unusual."

It was probably unusual for most women, he thought, but not for her. She didn't seem to like making waves with her father. "I have a feeling I don't fit into your usual taste in men."

"No, not really. I usually date younger guys who wear suits and ties to work. They drive environmentally conscious compact cars or sedans that mimic the look of luxury cars they hope to afford someday."

"Younger guys, huh?" Great. No pressure or anything.

"Not a lot younger, but a few years, usually."

"I guess younger guys probably have a lot of stamina."

"I will neither confirm nor deny," she said in a prim voice before amusement ruined the effect. "I think it's mostly because my friends are a little younger, too, so I meet younger guys. And in my field, a lot of the guys my age are already married. Plus, like you said, there's the stamina thing."

"Funny." He took her hand and ran his thumb across her palm. "I guess there's something to be said for stamina. Although there's probably something to be said for experience, too. You learn things as you go along."

"Really? What kind of things?"

"I guess I could list them for you." He stopped making circles against her palm and linked his fingers with hers. "Or I could show you."

She arched an eyebrow at him. "And miss the rest of the hockey game?"

"There's a game on?"

She laughed and then it faded away to a sigh. "And are we supposed to agree in advance it won't happen again?"

Rick already knew there was a good chance he'd want her again before he'd even caught his breath from the first time. "How about we agree to just enjoy each other's company until you have to get on the plane back to San Diego?"

"That sounds like a plan we can actually stick to," she said, giving him a smile that took his breath away.

He let go of her hand to hit the power button on the television remote before standing up. Then, when she stood, he put one arm around her back and the other behind her knees to sweep her off her feet.

When she squealed and wrapped her arms around his neck, he gave her a quick kiss. "First on that list of things we old guys have figured out? Women like romantic gestures."

JESSICA HAD NEVER been carried before, and certainly never into a man's bedroom. It was thrilling and sweet, and she ran her fingertips over the nape of his neck as he turned sideways to get her legs through the doorway.

There was just enough light from the street shining through the curtain to show her she'd been right about him having one hell of a master suite. The room was big, with a lot of open floor space dominated by a huge bed.

When he set her down on the edge of the mattress, she actually sighed. "Comfy."

"See? Number two is knowing making out on the couch is a lot less comfortable than it looks on TV."

She laughed as he pulled his shirt over his head and tossed it aside. "Is this list written down somewhere?"

"Nope." He stepped between her legs and she ran her hands over his naked stomach and chest. The muscles twitched, and she skimmed her fingernails down his abs just to see them clench.

Rick cupped her face in his hands and bent to kiss her. It was slow, simmering, and she felt her pulse quicken in anticipation. His tongue flicked over her lips and she opened her mouth to him. She felt as though she could kiss him forever and never grow tired of it.

Then his hands left her face, skimming down over her shoulders and arms before his hands cupped her breasts through the soft knit of her sweater. She sucked in a breath when his thumbs brushed over her nipples and she felt his smile against her mouth.

Jessica took matters into her own hands and grabbed the hem of the sweater. She had to break off the kiss to pull it over her head, but she didn't want fabric between her body and Rick's hands anymore.

"God, you're beautiful," he told her, his voice rough. He tucked his hands under her arms and lifted her so she was farther back on the bed before sliding one finger under the strap of her bra. "And I do love this color."

She touched her fingertip to his mouth, intending to trace his lip, but he caught it between his teeth before sucking gently. When he swirled his tongue over the tip, she moaned and pulled her finger free so she could kiss him.

"You do love kissing," he said after a few minutes.

"I've never really thought much about it," she confessed. "I think it's you."

"Good." He nipped at her lip. "I like kissing you."

He kissed her mouth again before moving to her jaw and the hollow at the base of her throat. Then he unhooked the yellow bra and slid it over her arms so he could kiss her breasts. She dug her fingers into his biceps when he closed his mouth over one nipple and then the other, sucking hard enough to make her squirm.

His fingers skimmed over her stomach to the button of her jeans. He popped it with one hand and then worked the zipper down. "I don't want to stop touching you long enough to get these off of you."

"The sooner you get them off, and get yours off, the sooner you can be inside of me."

He groaned against her breast, then ran his tongue over a nipple. "Are you in a hurry?"

"For you to be naked? Absolutely."

He chuckled before pushing up off the bed. It only took him seconds to pull her jeans and socks off, though he did take a moment to appreciate the yellow lace panties before adding them to the pile of clothes on the floor.

Then he stripped out of his jeans and boxer briefs, and Jessica had a moment to fully appreciate his ruggedly built body before he stretched out alongside her. He ran his hand over the flat of her stomach and she laughed.

"You'd think a man as experienced as yourself would know better than to touch a woman's stomach like that. It makes us self-conscious."

"I love every inch of your body." He rolled so he was looking down at her. "Did you just call me old?"

She reached down and ran her fingers up the length of his erection, watching his jaw clench. "Definitely not."

"Jesus, Jess. You can't do that."

She closed her fingers around him. "I want you now."

"I think I'm supposed to be proving a point about experience versus stamina or something and you are not helping."

Still stroking him, but not with too much pressure, she captured his bottom lip between her lips and kissed him again. "Just kissing you feels amazing. I don't want to wait anymore."

He shifted his weight so he could reach his nightstand and open the drawer to pull out a condom. Jessica reluctantly stopped touching him long enough for him to put it on, and then he was kissing her again. Rough and demanding, he kept kissing her while reaching between their bodies to guide his cock into her.

Jessica dug her fingernails into his shoulders as he slowly filled her, each slow stroke deeper than the one before until she'd taken him completely. He pushed her hair away from her face and his gaze locked with hers as he moved his hips.

She said his name and he smiled, a slow grin that made her smile back at him. "That feels so good."

"*You* feel so good." He cupped one of her breasts and lowered his mouth to hers, kissing her just the way she liked as he moved between her thighs.

Jessica wrapped her legs over his, her heels digging into his calves. "Please, Rick."

"Please what?" he said against her mouth.

"Faster."

He obliged and she scraped her fingernails over his back as he thrust into her. Her back arched off the bed as she came, biting down on the side of her hand to keep from screaming his name.

He hooked his hand under her knee and lifted so he could thrust harder and it was only a moment before he found his own release with a guttural moan.

Jessica, still breathless from her own orgasm, ran her hands over his back as he came. Then he buried his face in her neck and pressed small kisses against her skin. Smiling, she stroked his hair as their breathing slowly returned to normal.

Then he tossed the condom in the trash basket under the nightstand and rolled onto his back, pulling her with him. She pressed her body along the length of his, loving the feel of his naked skin.

"I'm so glad we didn't agree not to do this again," she murmured after a few minutes.

He ran his fingers through her hair, making her shiver. "No shit. Although, even if we had, I'd be trying to break it in about fifteen minutes or so."

She kissed his chest. "I should come watch hockey with you more often."

"God, I hope they play Wednesday."

TWELVE

"HEY." *THUMP. THUMP.*

Rick opened his eyes to see Jeff Porter standing over him, kicking the base of the couch. The station was relatively quiet from what he could hear, so resting his eyes hadn't turned into sleeping through alarms. "What?"

"You have company," Jeff said. "Downstairs."

Swinging his feet to the floor, Rick sat up so fast he was surprised he didn't get dizzy. "Jess is here?"

"Jess? You mean your landlords' granddaughter?" Jeff narrowed his eyes. "You sure jumped to that conclusion pretty quickly."

It made sense he'd wake up thinking of Jess, since he'd nodded off thinking about her. "Is it her or not?"

"Sorry, guy, but it's not her."

Rick scrubbed his hands over his face, trying to shake off not only the lingering sleepiness, but the disappointment, as well. It was probably stupid to be sorry she hadn't shown up at the station when he'd spent last night with her. And if she was smart, she'd told Joe and Marie she had a lot of work to do and holed up in her bedroom to catch up on her sleep. They hadn't gotten much last night.

"Who is it?" he asked Jeff after pushing himself to his feet.

"As much as we'd all get a kick out of seeing your face when you're caught off guard, I like you today so I'll give you the heads-up. It's the friendly lady with the nightgown and the false alarms."

"Shit." It had been a couple of weeks since the last time she'd called for help she didn't need, so he'd put her out of his mind.

"She's carrying a plastic container, so there might be food in it for us. Maybe even the freshly-baked-from-scratch kind of food."

"If she has baked goods, I'm surprised she didn't leave them in the oven long enough to set her smoke detectors off."

Jeff laughed, but Rick wasn't amused as he walked down to the ground floor and toward the front of the open bay. Aidan and Scott were making a big deal out of inspecting a length of hose, but Rick suspected it was their way of keeping an eye on the woman while having a good excuse not to make conversation with her. While their house hadn't had any problems, there were cases of people taking their infatuation with firefighters to dangerous levels.

The woman in question was clutching her plastic container and looking at everything she could see from the doorway with wide eyes. She was pretty and she'd seemed nice in the past, but Rick knew he had to shut her down as firmly as possible without upsetting her.

"Hi," he said, stepping up to her. "I heard you're looking for me?"

She smiled, her face flushing as she nodded. "I just wanted to stop by and thank you again for helping me."

"We're just doing our jobs, ma'am." He managed to deliver the corny—but true—line with a straight face.

She giggled. "It's Deena. And I still want to thank you. I baked you some muffins. I wasn't sure what kind you'd like, so there are blueberry and cranberry and chocolate chip."

"We're not really supposed to accept gifts, so—"

"I make good muffins," she interrupted, "but they're not worth more than fifty dollars."

So she knew the rules. Maybe she'd looked them up just to be on the safe side, or maybe she had some experience in showing up with muffins for firefighters. He couldn't be sure, but he knew there was no way out of accepting the token thanks without hurting her feelings, which he'd hate to do. And next she'd introduce the possibility of returning soon for the plastic container while dropping strong hints that she wouldn't mind if he dropped it by her place.

"Okay," he said, accepting the box. "We'll all enjoy these, I'm sure."

"I hope so. Maybe I can stop by in a couple of days or whenever you're here and pick up the container."

"Sure." He looked down at the box in his hands. "They won't last that long, though. I'll probably have to hide a cranberry one in my truck to sneak it home to my girlfriend. She loves them."

"Oh, definitely. Like I said, I'm pretty good at muffins." She gave him a smile. "On second thought, the container's one of those disposable ones, so you can just toss it when they're gone. It's not really worth coming back for."

He thanked her again, hoping the relief at extricating himself didn't show on his face, and she seemed happy enough when she waved goodbye to the guys behind him and walked away. As soon as she turned the corner out of sight, Aidan and Scott appeared next to him.

"Did she say chocolate chip?" Scott asked.

"I'm not sharing."

"You told her we'd all enjoy them," Aidan pointed out.

"You two didn't seem to be in a hurry to help me out. An urgent call I needed to take or something would have been nice."

Aidan shrugged and grabbed the container while Rick was off guard. "You were holding your own. If she hadn't taken the girlfriend hint, we would have stepped in."

"Pretty slick, the way you threw that lie in there," Scott added.

He supposed it had technically been a lie. Though he'd spent the night with Jess and would like to spend a lot more nights with her, she was going back to San Diego on Thursday and he had no idea if or when she'd be back. "If anybody knows that claiming to have a girlfriend is a standard way of getting out of a situation, it would be you, Kincaid."

"I'm reformed." When Rick just stared at him, Scott finally snorted. "Okay, I'm thinking about re-forming."

"I think that translates to him running out of women to date," Aidan added.

Rick listened to the two best friends swap insults for a few seconds, and then pulled out his phone to type a message to Jess. Hey, what's your favorite kind of muffin? Blueberry, cranberry or chocolate chip?

The response came so quickly, he guessed she was probably working with her phone in hand. Blueberry.

"Hold on," he said before the guys could wander off. "Give me one of the blueberry ones."

"I thought you liked cranberry," Aidan said. One of the problems with practically living with a bunch of guys was that they got to know you too well, making it hard to put one over on them. "And you said your imaginary girlfriend likes cranberry, too, so who's it for?"

"Don't worry about it. Maybe I just want something different."

His phone chimed in his hand and he looked down at the screen to see another text from Jess. Why?

Leaving the guys to the muffins, Rick walked around to the far side of Ladder 37 and sat in one of the metal folding chairs that were always kicking around. We got a thank-you batch of muffins and I'm saving you one.

I wouldn't bet money on its chances of making it out of the station.

He laughed, and then immediately stifled it because he didn't want to attract attention. If the guys
figured something had finally happened between him
and his landlords' granddaughter, it would go one of
two ways. They'd think he was just getting lucky with
a pretty woman who was sleeping under the same
roof, and that sounded cheap. He didn't like that. Or
they'd think he was getting into a real relationship
and, since he didn't know how to respond to that, he'd
rather not open the door.

Seniority means nothing if I can't keep one muffin
off-limits.

He imagined her smiling at her phone and wanted
to call her so he could hear the smile in her voice, instead. But he didn't want to talk to her with the guys
around, and he had no idea if she was in her room
alone or downstairs with Joe and Marie nearby.

If you declare two of them off-limits, we can have a
muffin date tomorrow.

"Hey, Hunt! Kincaid!" Rick stood and rushed back
across the bays and caught the two of them halfway
up the stairs. "Give me one of the cranberry ones,
too."

Once he'd secured the second muffin, he cradled
the two of them in one hand while texting with the
other. I've got two, so it's a date.

He'd never had a muffin date with a woman be-

fore, but as the remainder of the tour loomed in front
of him, Rick thought maybe he'd never looked forward to a date more.

JESSICA NOT ONLY set her phone down on the table
when Marie walked into the kitchen, but she put it
facedown, as if she'd been doing something she didn't
want her grandmother to see. It was silly, of course.
She and Rick were adults and they were having a conversation about muffins. There was nothing wrong
with that.

Still, she couldn't help but feel it was best if her
grandparents didn't know she and Rick had taken
their relationship to an intimate level. Joe was still
something of a closed book to her, but she had no
doubt Marie would start making them all one big,
happy family in her mind. And when it didn't turn
out that way, she might feel torn between the two of
them and Jessica didn't want that.

"You're still working?" Marie asked, heading to
the refrigerator. "You've been sitting at that table for
hours."

"We had to hire a new caterer for the holiday party
this year and Alicia had some concerns, so she for-
warded the contract and a few email chains to me.
It looks like they want to charge us top-shelf prices
for the bar, but they're not serving top-shelf liquor."

"You serve alcohol? That's not a problem?"

Though Jessica hadn't said too much about her father's life because she felt caught in a weird conflict
of loyalties, she'd said enough so Marie knew alco-

hol was an issue. "Dad never drinks in the office and especially not at the holiday party. Sometimes he'll have a drink if he's out in a social situation, but he never drinks too much unless he's at home."

"That's good. I hope you get your catering issues sorted out so you can enjoy the party."

"I've got a handle on it, I think. I made a couple of phone calls and then followed them up with an email. I think they got the hint."

"I'm going to miss you when you leave," Marie said, sitting at the table with her. "I've gotten used to you being here."

"I'm going to miss you, too. If not for the party, it would have been nice to stay for Christmas." She picked up the pen next to her laptop and fiddled with it. "Maybe I could come back."

"Oh, honey, you are welcome to come back anytime you want. And I'd love to spend the holidays with you. You know that. But I don't want Davey alone, either. We've obviously had troubles, but I'm still his mother and he's been going through a hard time. It would break my heart to imagine him all alone for Christmas."

"This particular hard time is of his own making," Jessica pointed out.

"That's true, but he's going through a divorce and you coming out here hasn't been easy for him, I'm sure, on either a personal or a professional level. You don't want to throw too much at him at one time. Not that his well-being is your responsibility, but I know you've always worried about him."

Marie's immediate willingness to sacrifice her own happiness for her son's despite the fact he'd abandoned them and broken her heart was something Jessica had a hard time understanding. Her father loved her and he'd done his best raising her, but his needs came first. Maybe it was because his needs were so often wrapped up with the needs of Broussard Financial Services, but Jessica couldn't remember the last time she'd been number one on the family priority list.

"You're right, I guess," she said finally. "Before I leave, though, I'd like to get you a smartphone for Christmas. So we can keep in touch."

Marie laughed. "Even that fancy phone of yours will accept calls from an old landline."

"True. But it would be nice to be able to text sometimes, too. And send each other pictures."

"Joe did say maybe I should get one so we can do that."

"I'd love for it to be my gift to the both of you, even though I know you'll have to twist his arm to get him to do a video chat. It would mean a lot to me to keep in touch."

Her grandmother wrapped her arms around her. "I don't care if we have to send carrier pigeons back and forth across the country. We're not losing touch with you."

Jessica blinked back tears and squeezed Marie. "I totally agree. A smartphone would definitely be faster, though. We can go get one today so I can show you the basics before I leave."

"That does sound like fun. And I want you to be

able to send me pictures of your office and your home. I want to see what your life looks like." She let go of Jessica and wiped at her eyes. "Maybe you could sneak me a picture of Davey. Not the fancy picture on his website, but a candid shot from the party or something like that."

"I can try," Jessica said, hedging. She wouldn't try to sneak a picture of her father to send to his parents because that felt like an invasion of his privacy. But she would try her best to get him to agree to let her send one. It seemed like the least he could do at that point. "And I want you to promise you'll keep me in the loop when it comes to your health and any decisions you make about the house."

"Of course we will. I think Joe and I have a lot of conversations about it in our near future, but it's a hard thing to wrap your mind around."

"You can call me anytime to talk about it. It's a big decision."

"The biggest." Marie was quiet for a few seconds, and then she clapped her hands together. "Okay, we only have today and tomorrow left together, so that's enough with tears. Let's go have some fun."

RICK TRIED TO stifle a yawn, but he was bone-tired and he couldn't stop it, though he did cast an apologetic glance at Jessica. "Sorry. I swear it's not you."

"Usually somebody yawning every five minutes in my company would give me a complex, but you had a busy night according to the morning news. And you didn't get a lot of sleep Monday night."

"I don't regret a single second of Monday night," he said, putting his empty paper plate on the coffee table before sitting up straighter on the couch. "How's your muffin?"

"I feel like I shouldn't be enjoying it so much since it was baked for you by a woman who was so infatuated with you she was using false alarms to get close to you." She sighed deeply. "It's a really good muffin, though."

"Maybe I should have tried the muffin *before* I told her I had a girlfriend."

She gave him a stern look that only lasted a few seconds. "I'd throw this at you for saying that, but then I wouldn't be able to eat the rest of it."

"I'll look away while you lick the crumbs off the plate if you want."

"That's sweet of you to leave me some dignity like that." She chewed and swallowed another bite. "So you told her you have a girlfriend."

"Yeah."

"Is that the standard defense when a woman shows up at the station looking for attention from one of you?"

He shrugged, not really sure how to answer that. "We use it a lot, I guess."

"So it's not really specific to you?"

"Considering you'd spent the night before in my bed, it might have been a little specific, I guess."

When she smiled before popping the last bite of muffin into her mouth, Rick realized he'd managed to say the right thing.

"So if you were introducing me to people now, would you still introduce me as your landlords' granddaughter?"

"No. I mean, it might come up, but I want everybody to know you're with me." He watched her smile and dreaded the upcoming separation even more. "Are we going to do the long-distance thing?"

She sighed. "It's a very long distance. And even though I'm going to be visiting Joe and Marie, it's not like I'll be coming back to Boston multiple weekends per month or anything. Maybe it doesn't need definition. We'll just keep in touch and see how it goes."

"I hope it goes good," he said, and then yawned again. "I'm going to miss you."

"I'll miss you, too."

"What time is your flight tomorrow?"

"It takes off at 5:45."

He winced. "In the morning?"

"Yeah, so I'm leaving here about four. I took the early flight so I can get there and run by my house, but still have time to get into the office. I didn't leave myself a lot of time to oversee the last-minute stuff, plus I'm sure my father will want to have a catch-up meeting."

"I can set my alarm and go with you."

She laced her fingers through his and rested her head against the couch. "You don't have to. I still have the rental, anyway, so it's not like you could drive me."

"I could drive the rental and then take a cab back."

"Rick, they won't let you past security, anyway. There's no sense in you losing sleep and throwing your schedule off to drive me to the airport for no reason."

"I don't think there has to be a reason." The reason was spending every last minute he could with her.

She inhaled deeply and then turned her head to look him in the eye. "It's going to be hard enough leaving Joe and Marie. I don't know if I could stand an airport goodbye with you. I'm not very good at that sort of thing."

"So it's easier if you just get up and get in your car and go?"

"Honestly, yes."

He nodded. "Then that's what you should do. But text me when you land so I know you got to California okay."

"I think if we don't get there okay, you'll hear about it on the news."

"Don't say that." Once she'd put her plate down, he pulled her closer so she was tucked against his side and kissed the top of her head. "Just text me when you get there."

"You want me to sit like this so I can't see you yawn, don't you?"

"I swear it's not personal."

"Why don't you go to bed for a while and then you can come down and have dinner with us."

"Sounds good. Why don't you come to bed with me?"

She laughed, and he felt her head shake even though he'd closed his eyes. "I think it would be hard not to take those yawns personally."

"Just to lay down with me," he muttered. He was

losing the sleep battle and he wanted to go stretch out on his bed. But he didn't want to lose a minute with Jess, even if he was asleep for it. "I'll sleep better."

She got to her feet and grabbed his hands to help him to his feet. "I still have some packing to do and I have to figure out what I'm leaving here, but I'll lay down with you for a little while."

His last thought before he slipped into a heavy sleep with his body curled around Jessica's was how much he didn't want her to go.

THIRTEEN

EVEN THOUGH SHE practically tiptoed through the house, Jessica wasn't surprised when Marie shuffled into the kitchen in her well-worn slippers and bathrobe just before four o'clock the next morning.

"I almost missed you."

Her throat tight, Jessica took her hand off the doorknob and set her carry-on bag on top of the suitcase. "I told you not to bother getting up."

"You're not leaving this house without a hug from your grandmother. But I know you didn't want a big emotional scene so I made sure I only left enough time for a quick goodbye."

They met in the middle of the kitchen, and tears spilled over Jessica's cheeks as her grandmother wrapped her arms around her. "I'm going to come back and visit as soon as I can."

"I can't wait. I love you, honey."

"I love you too…Gram."

"I like the sound of that." After a big sniffle, Marie pulled back and wiped the tears off Jessica's face. "Your grandfather's not good at this sort of thing, so I let him sleep, but he loves you, too."

"Give him a kiss from me when he wakes up."

"I will. Now you go before you miss your plane. We don't want to have to do this again tomorrow."

After another quick hug, Jessica slung her carry-on over her shoulder and grabbed her suitcase. "Bye, Gram."

She managed to get the door closed and walk down the ramp without her eyes welling up again, but she stopped walking when she reached the driveway.

Rick was leaning against the rental, his shoulders hunched against the cold. The frigid air made his eyes sparkle and his cheeks were pink, and he looked utterly delicious for four o'clock in the morning. His smile was full of warmth and understanding as he uncrossed his legs and made his way across the driveway to take her suitcase.

"I take it Marie got up to see you off," he said, swiping at a leftover tear on her jaw with his thumb.

"Neither of you listen worth a damn." She was going for light and funny, but there was too much emotion clogging her throat to pull it off. "You should go back to bed."

"I might, after your plane takes off. I'm going to spend every minute I can with you before you go, so give me your keys."

He started the car before popping the trunk and made her get into the passenger seat to keep warm while he stowed her bags. Then he slid the driver's seat back a few more inches and got in.

"Got everything?"

She nodded because she wasn't sure she'd be able to speak. This was exactly what she'd been hoping to avoid when she told everybody to stay in bed. If she hadn't hugged Marie or felt that kick in her chest when she saw Rick leaning against the car, maybe she would have been able to lie to herself about how much she didn't want to leave.

Once he'd backed the car out onto the street and put it in gear, Rick put his left hand on the steering wheel and reached his free hand across to take hers. After lacing their fingers together, he set their joined hands on the center console and navigated through the still sleepy streets.

Jessica leaned her head against the headrest, trying to blink back tears as his thumb stroked her index finger. How the hell had this happened? She'd come here to fulfill her curiosity about her father's parents and help them plan for their future, and her entire life had changed.

She had grandparents now—*real* grandparents—and she had this guy she'd only known a couple of weeks, but already couldn't imagine not seeing tomorrow. Or the next day. Or any day in the near future.

"Hey." His voice was soft and he didn't say anything else until she turned her head to look at him. "You're going to text me to let me know you landed okay, right?"

"Yeah."

"Good. And I know you like to text because it's fast and easy, but I want to hear your voice sometimes, too."

Some of the tightness in her chest eased. "So you really think we can make a long-distance thing work?"

"Honestly, I don't know." He squeezed her hand. "I hope so. But I do know I'm not ready to just say 'hey, that was fun, thanks' and not talk to you again."

"I'm not, either."

He took his eyes off the road for a second to smile at her. "We'll figure it out as we go along, then."

They talked a little bit, mostly about Marie and Joe, until they reached the airport, where the conversation turned to where the hell they were supposed to be going.

"I thought you'd have this, being from here," she teased.

"I'm not from the airport." He moved over a lane so abruptly she almost squealed. "Trust me. Nobody has any clue where they're going here."

He finally navigated successfully to the rental car building, then waited with her luggage while she turned the car in. During the shuttle ride to the terminal, he was quiet. But he held her hand and she liked that. She'd forgotten how comforting the gesture could be, and she tried to draw strength from it so she wouldn't cry when it was time for him to leave.

After checking her suitcase at the curb, they went inside and she decided they had time to grab a coffee together before she had to get in the security line. Even if it was only a few minutes, she'd take them.

"Did you leave your car at the airport on the other end?" he asked when they'd found a spot to drink their coffees and watch people.

"I wasn't sure how long I'd be, so I took a cab. I'll

just take one to the house and drop off my luggage before I go to the office."

"How do you think your father's going to be?"

She shrugged. "I think he's had time to come to terms with what happened."

"He shouldn't really have to come to terms with you visiting your grandparents, you know."

"I do know that." She shrugged again. "But he didn't want me to know them and I knew that when I got on the plane here. And I stayed when he wanted me to go back. I guess the details aren't important. What matters is that I did something I knew would upset him and complicate his life."

Rick frowned. "You defied him."

"It's not that, exactly. That makes him sound like a tyrant, when in reality, the manipulation is much more subtle. And it's as much my fear of making him unhappy as it is control on his part."

He reached over and squeezed her knee. "That's not really how family's supposed to work, Jess."

"Aren't you the one who told me families look a lot of different ways, and there's no right or wrong or supposed to about any of them?"

He nodded, his mouth curving in a smile. "You got me there."

Usually when she was in an airport, waiting for a flight, time seemed to slow to a crawl, but the minutes flew by and all too soon they had to throw away their empty cups and head toward the security checkpoint.

"Don't forget to text me when you land."

"I won't forget to text you." She'd probably do

nothing but think about him for the entire flight, so it wasn't likely she wouldn't be thinking about him when the plane touched down.

He put his hand on the back of her neck and kissed her gently. She sucked in a breath, trying to shove down the emotion, but tears blurred her vision.

"No tears," he murmured against her lips. Then he pulled back and gave her a crooked grin. "No sad eyes."

"I told you it would be harder for me to leave if you were here."

"Good." His hand fisted in her hair, tilting her head back so she looked into his eyes. "I want it to be hard for you to leave me because it's sure as hell hard to let you go."

"We were supposed to just enjoy each other's company until I got on the plane."

"We did. We enjoyed each other's company a lot, I guess."

She sighed, letting herself imagine for a few crazy seconds what would happen if she just didn't get on the plane. They'd go back to the house and after spending a few minutes with Marie and Joe, they'd go upstairs to Rick's apartment. It was so tempting she almost opened her mouth to tell him she wasn't leaving.

But even if she took her father out of the equation, she had a life in San Diego. And responsibilities. She was supposed to be hosting the company Christmas party in two days for people who'd worked hard for her and her father for years and who'd helped make it possible for her to spend the past two weeks in Boston without any prior notice.

And, whether he should be part of the equation or not, she had to consider her father. He was probably on shaky ground and the holidays were coming. If Marie could worry about him being alone after all he'd put her through, Jessica wasn't going to beat herself up about doing the same.

"You have to go," Rick said quietly, and she realized she'd been staring up at him, saying nothing.

As much as she wanted to share her reluctance with him, it wouldn't change anything and would only make it harder. "I'll text you."

He kissed her one more time and then ran his finger down her cheek. "Bye, Jess."

"Bye," she whispered as he turned and walked away.

She watched him until he disappeared from her sight, knowing by the set of his head and shoulders he wouldn't look back. If he did, he'd probably come back and want to kiss her again and she'd never leave.

Smiling, Jessica moved into the line and waited her turn for the security screeners. Once she was through, she'd buy a muffin and some fruit, and then open her laptop to work until it was time to board. Hopefully between the work waiting for her and the last-minute party details, she could distract herself long enough to get on the plane without any more tears.

Hours later, her mind addled by the time zones and her heart heavy, Jessica unlocked the door to her condo and stepped into what had been her home for several years. With nobody to please but herself, it was decorated in a simple, classic style with warm colors and an eye for comfort over style. An end unit, it had a lot of light, a tandem garage and access to a pool.

It felt empty now, but she knew that feeling would fade. This was her home and when she was in her favorite pajamas, curled up on the couch with a drink and a book, she'd remember everything she loved about this house and her life.

But right now, with the brief text exchanges to let Marie and Rick know she'd landed still fresh in her mind, all she could think about was what she'd left behind in Boston.

RICK MADE IT through most of Friday without taking anybody's heads off their shoulders—although Gavin came close when he balked at doing some housekeeping—but he started getting restless as the sun went down.

He hadn't slept well the night before because he'd been tossing and turning, thinking about Jess. He'd known he would miss her. He hadn't guessed just how much, though.

Rather than stare at the television screen or listen to whatever conversations the other guys were having, he went down one floor to the office space he shared with Danny Walsh and tried to catch up on some paperwork. But his mind kept wandering and finally he just rocked back in his chair and closed his eyes.

Jess hadn't wanted to leave him. He'd seen it in her

eyes and felt it in the way she'd kissed him goodbye.
Maybe she'd been caught up in the moment, though.
Coming to Boston had been quite the emotional trip
for her and maybe their relationship had gotten tangled up in that.

Back in San Diego, surrounded by her everyday
life, maybe she felt differently. The intensity of her
feelings—whatever they might be—would fade and
eventually so would the memories. She'd realize long-
distance relationships seldom worked out. He didn't
like to think that, but this wasn't his first rodeo and
he knew it was a possibility.

Or maybe she was all the way on the other side
of the country thinking about him. Maybe she was
even wondering if he'd started moving on the minute
she got on the plane. After a moment of hesitation,
he pulled out his cell phone.

Hey, you busy?

He waited for the dialogue bubble to pop up, letting him know she was typing a reply, but instead her
name flashed on the caller ID as the phone vibrated
in his hand. "Hello."

"Hi. I figured since you sent a text, you must not
be too busy to talk. You're working, right?"

Just the sound of her voice soothed his ragged
nerves and he smiled for the first time that day. "I'm
in the office pretending to do paperwork."

"I'm in my office, too, but I'm pretending to read
emails."

"What are you really doing?"

He heard her small, breathless laugh. "Honestly? I'm staring out my huge window at San Diego, wishing I was still in Boston."

"I wish you were still in Boston, too," he confessed, feeling the tightness in his chest ease. There was no cooling off in her voice—no sign she was ready to put some distance between them and move on.

"Why did my dad have to choose California? Why not Connecticut? Or New York, if he really wanted a city?"

He chuckled. "I don't know but, even with the gas mileage in that truck of mine, I'd be driving to see you."

There was silence for a few seconds and then she sighed. "That would have been nice. Have you seen Joe and Marie since I left?"

"I saw them yesterday, and I talked to Joe on the phone today. They miss you, of course, but Marie's telling everybody about the fancy phone her granddaughter bought her and showing off the pictures she already has stored on it."

"I sent her a few I had on my phone, just so she'd have them. She wants me to send her a picture of my father, too."

"Will you?"

"I'll ask him. I think he should, really, but I'm leaving it up to him. I can't get in the middle of their relationship and start playing mediator. I have him and I have them. I hope they don't always have to be separate, but I'm not sacrificing one for the other."

"Good for you." He was glad she seemed confident about balancing those relationships. Especially since it was good for her to have Joe and Marie in her life. "How's the party planning going?"

She told him all about it and while normally it wasn't the kind of thing he cared about, he was content to listen to her talk. Because it was something she enjoyed, her voice was animated and he smiled as he listened to her.

Then, because it was just his luck, the alarm sounded. She must have heard it because she paused in midsentence. "You have to go."

"I'm sorry."

"Will you call me tomorrow?"

He was on his feet, but he'd called on his cell phone, so he took it with him. "Isn't your party tomorrow? Call me when it's over."

"It doesn't usually wrap up until eight. By the time I get home it'll be almost midnight for you."

"I'll take a nap. I want to hear about your party."

"Okay, I'll call you. But you can't put on your gear one-handed, so you have to hang up now."

She was right. "I'll talk to you tomorrow."

"Good night, Rick."

After reluctantly shoving the phone in his pocket, he stepped into his boots. Then he pulled up the pants and yanked the suspenders over his shoulders, before grabbing the coat and his helmet.

He crossed paths with Scott on their way to their respective trucks. "Giving the long-distance thing a shot, huh?"

Rick shrugged. "Since she lives in California, it's the only shot I've got."

As he climbed up into the cab of L-37, he was a mess of mixed emotions. On the one hand, she'd asked him to call her tomorrow. There was no out of sight, out of mind thing going on with her.

But on the other, it really sucked that he'd finally met a woman who turned him so inside out she had to be the one, and she was on the other side of the country.

FOURTEEN

As usual, the Broussard Financial Services holiday party went off without a hitch. Jessica sipped the cranberry margarita that would be her one and only drink for the night and watched her coworkers mingle. The clients who'd attended had already made their exits and now that it was just the BFS employees, the atmosphere was very relaxed.

"You did a wonderful job, as usual."

She turned to face her father, who she hadn't heard approaching thanks to the expensive carpet. "Thank you."

"I shouldn't have doubted you'd pull it off, even from Boston."

She was surprised he mentioned Boston. Between her arrival at the office late Thursday afternoon and now, he'd managed to avoid the topic, as if she'd simply been on vacation or out sick. "Like I said before, as long as I have my phone and my laptop, it doesn't matter where I am."

He pulled out his phone and started tapping the screen. "I'm texting you a photo."

"Why? I'm standing right here, so just show it to me."

"You'll see."

When her phone chimed, she pulled up the text to find a picture of her and her father, taken earlier in the night. They'd obviously been having a discussion, but had turned toward whoever took the picture. They were both smiling and Jessica was surprised to find herself a little choked up. They might not be a picture-frame-selling family, but this was probably the first genuine, happy family photo of them.

"Derek took that and when I saw it, I asked him to text it to me. It's a nice picture of us."

"It is." She saved it to her phone's photo album.

"You asked me earlier if you could send a picture to your grandparents—to my mother—and I think she'd like that one."

Jessica nodded, smiling when she imagined Marie's reaction to the image. And it was a moment she really wanted to share with her grandparents, and with Rick. David Broussard might not have been a good son and he certainly had some faults as a parent, but she wanted them to know she and her father did have a good relationship overall. "She'll love it. Thank you."

"Let me know. What she says, I mean."

"I will." She glanced around and saw that they were almost alone, but not quite. But her father seemed vulnerable tonight—maybe even nostalgic—and she had a question she wanted to ask him. "Can we step into your office for a minute?"

"Of course."

His mouth tightened and she knew he was bracing himself for something unpleasant. Maybe he thought she was going to tell him she was leaving the company and heading back to Boston for good.

As he closed the door behind them, she wondered what his response would be. And for a moment, she was actually tempted to say the words. But then her father was staring at her expectantly, and she lost the nerve to turn her life upside down.

"I have a question for you," she began, "and I want you to answer it. And not like you've answered my questions in the past. I don't want you to deflect or try to make me feel bad for asking or anything else."

"I'll try."

She took a deep breath. "How come my mother didn't fight for custody of me? Or at least visitation?"

Even though he had to know something serious was on her mind, her father still looked taken aback by the question. "I'd rather not discuss this, Jessica. I don't like talking about that time in my life."

"Yeah? Well, I didn't like growing up without a mother and I'd really like to know why I did."

He blinked, clearly surprised by her tone, but she didn't apologize for it or try to make excuses. She simply waited him out.

"It was because of me," he said finally. She'd already guessed that much and was going to push him for more, but then he spoke again. "I discovered cocaine in college. It brought your mother and I together and, if I'm being honest, is a big part of the wedge between my parents and I, even though I'm quite sure they never knew about the drugs."

"They don't know about that, no." She wasn't sure about Marie, but Joe would have mentioned it.

"She managed to clean up a little when she got pregnant with you, but not totally. It's a miracle you were born so perfect. But it didn't last and we were destroying ourselves and each other and we were going to destroy you in the process. I lost a great job at a financial firm and it was a wake-up call. I got clean, but she couldn't and eventually she took off. It was hard to stay clean but it was easier without her, so I let her go."

Jessica stared at the liquid in her glass, swirling it a little as tears blurred her eyes. "Why couldn't you just tell me that?"

"What father wants his daughter to know he was a cocaine addict?"

"I would rather have *known* my father did drugs in college than spend my entire life wondering why my mother didn't want me."

He flinched. "I'm sorry, Jessica. I didn't…I don't know what else to say. I've done some thinking lately and I'm a self-centered person, I guess."

She took a sip of her drink to hide the snarky *really?* smile as that thought popped into her head. But then she forced herself to let it go because it wouldn't help. "I guess if you're aware of it now, you can work on it."

"I'm going to try."

There was a knock on the door and Sharon poked her head in. "Everybody's getting ready to leave and they want to say goodbye."

Her father surprised her by giving her a quick hug,

and then they went out to close out the holiday party. She was exhausted, but she smiled and wished everybody a happy holiday as they trickled toward the door. Once they were gone, she could go home. And then she could talk to Rick.

She managed to lock her door and kick her heels off, but she had her phone in her hand when she sank onto her couch. Even her pajamas could wait. She pulled up the photo of her and her father and sent it in a text to Rick.

Can't send this to Marie until tomorrow because it's late, but it was a nice night. Calling now but wanted to send pic.

He answered on the second ring, and she felt the familiar thrill at hearing his voice. "You look happy in that picture. You had a good time?"

"I did. I always enjoy the party, but it was also great that my father said I could send that picture to Marie and Joe. I thought about having it printed and framed for them for Christmas, but she was so hopeful I'd get a picture of him at the party that I can't handle how disappointed she'd be between now and then."

"I wouldn't wait, either. And just having it will be a great Christmas gift for her, even if it's a little early. And, hey, if it's in a frame, it's awkward to carry around the neighborhood, showing all her friends."

Jessica laughed, turning sideways on the couch to put her feet up. "Did you do anything fun today?"

"I slept. Then I shoveled snow. Did some errands. Basically, no. Until now, of course."

"I couldn't wait for everybody to leave so I could get home and send you the picture. And talk to you."

"I love the picture. I won't even crop Davey out of it," he said. She laughed, shaking her head even though he couldn't see her. "Anything else happen?"

"My father and I talked a little bit, but that's not fun stuff. The cranberry margaritas were delicious. I wish I didn't have a one-drink rule at the company parties."

"Jess." The way he said her name cut off her chatter. "You can tell me the not-fun stuff, too. I want to hear about it."

She smiled and pulled the throw blanket off the back of her couch to cuddle with. It wasn't Rick, but at least it would keep her bare legs warm. "I asked him about my mom."

They talked for a while about her mother, and about her father's seemingly sudden bout of self-awareness. Then he caught her up on hockey news. The sport still didn't make a lot of sense to her, but she was learning and she loved hearing him talk about it.

Until she heard him trying to stifle a yawn and realized it was now the middle of the night in Boston. "You should go to bed."

"Yeah. You have plans for tomorrow?"

"Not really. I might hit the fitness center for a while in the morning and then I'll probably hang around here. Go through my mail. Spend some quality time with Netflix."

"I'll call you tomorrow, then. Probably late afternoon your time."

"I'll be here. Good night."

"Sweet dreams, Jess."

They definitely would be. Sweet, agonizingly sexy dreams that would make her wake in the morning feeling unsettled and longing for him. Long-distance relationships were hell on sleep.

ON CHRISTMAS DAY, Rick sat on the battered couch in the basement of his parents' house, once the playroom and then the teen hangout and finally the man cave. But when John's boys came along, it had circled back to playroom again.

He usually worked the holiday, but at the last minute the LT from a nearby station had ended up in a bind. Due to a traveling in-law situation, a very pregnant wife and the potential for more family drama than any one guy should have to handle, his family had to celebrate on the twenty-third. If he couldn't get the day off, he was probably going to have to run away from home. So Rick had worked his tour, spent Christmas Eve with the Broussards and had landed with his family for the big day itself.

Presents had been opened and there was wrapping paper everywhere. And Rick had managed to get himself on the family shit list by gifting his nephews big superhero Lego sets. They'd been opened over their mother's objection and were now strewn from one end of their grandparents' house to the other. Now he, his brother and the kids were banished to the basement to digest dinner while their dad napped in his recliner and the women relaxed before dessert.

"When are you going to settle down, Rick?" John waved a hand at his sons. "It's time for my boys to have some cousins with the same last name as them because they are *seriously* outnumbered by my in-law's kids right now."

He laughed. "I'm not getting married just so there can be even teams in backyard football games."

"Are you at least seeing anybody?" John took a sip of his soda. "I was pretty surprised you and Karen broke up, to be honest."

"We're just good friends. And I've been seeing somebody for a few weeks. Kind of. Right now I'm not seeing much of her in the literal sense." John frowned and made a hand motion for him to continue. "She's Joe and Marie's granddaughter and she came out from San Diego to meet them and help them with some financial stuff."

"Ah. And now she's back in San Diego, so you're seeing her, but not literally. Got it."

Rick pulled out his phone and checked the time. "I'll be seeing her literally in a few minutes. I sent a note with her Christmas present that she couldn't open it until we were in a video chat so I can see it. She should be calling anytime."

"You sent her a Christmas present?"

"I would have sent it home with her, but I'm surprised her suitcase didn't explode at the seams as it was."

"Did she send you a Christmas present?"

"She left one with Joe and Marie and sent me the other." He smiled at the memory of the awkwardly wrapped snow shovel, with the bent handle that was supposedly better for the back.

That had made him laugh, but the book that came in the mail had touched him. His favorite mystery series was in hardcover on the top shelf of his bookcase, except for the first book, which he'd picked up in paperback on a whim at a yard sale his mom had dragged him to. He'd bought the rest in hardcover but never got around to hunting down the hard-to-find first one. Jessica must have noticed, because she'd sent it to him.

"Did you open them already?"

"Yeah. There was no note with mine saying not to."

"You would have anyway. Growing up, you always found your presents and peeked because you couldn't stand waiting."

Rick laughed, and then his phone rang. He saw that it was Jess. He tried to get to the steps so he could go up and find a private spot, but the boys were blocking the way and then he stepped on a Lego. That hurt like a son of a bitch in stocking feet and he wasted a few precious seconds trying not to swear in front of the kids. Rather than risk missing her call, he answered it where he stood.

"Merry Christmas," she said, and he could tell she was on her laptop, sitting at her table.

"Merry Christmas, Jess. I'm trying to find a quiet spot, but my brother and my nephews are in the room at the moment."

"Hi, Jess," John called out, so Rick had to turn his phone so Jess could "meet" him. And then the boys each had to talk to the pretty lady, including telling her every single thing they got for Christmas. He cut them off when they started gearing up to tell her everything they'd eaten, though.

"Okay, it's my turn to talk to her."

"Upstairs," John said. "It must be almost time for you two to top off your sugar highs."

"Sorry about that," he said once he was finally alone in the basement. He sat back on the couch, trying to find a comfortable spot. It was a little awkward holding the phone at the right angle, but he didn't care.

"They're so cute. And very excited about their gifts."

"They can be a handful, but they're not usually this wound up. Christmas does that to them, I guess." He shifted so his knee was helping to support his hand. If he'd been thinking, he would have brought his laptop. "John's after me to have some kids. He says it's so they're not outnumbered by the cousins on my sister-in-law's side, but I think he just wants me to suffer with him."

"Do you want kids?"

He could tell by the way she didn't look directly at the camera that it wasn't just a polite question. "Yeah, I want to be a dad. I've always assumed I would be someday, though I guess I should start watching the clock pretty soon."

She laughed. "You're not *that* old."

"What about you?"

"I'm not that old, either." He arched his eyebrow at her, making her smile. "I think I want kids. For a long time I guess I've been afraid of being a parent because I don't really have stellar role models and I used my career as an excuse, but now I feel like the person I am matters more than the people my parents are."

"I like the person you are."

"Is that why you're tormenting me by not letting me open my Christmas present?"

He laughed. "Yes. I only torment people I like."

"You also cheat and open your gifts before Christmas."

"It was Christmas Eve, and I still love my book." He'd called her once she'd texted her dinner with her father was over and confessed that he'd opened his gift early. "Go ahead and open yours now."

She held up the box, which she must have had set just out of the camera's view and then ripped open the paper. When she'd sliced the tape and lifted the lid of the box, her laughter came through his phone's speakers so clearly, it was almost like being in the room with her.

Almost, but not quite.

"This is perfect." She lifted out the copy of *Hockey For Dummies* he'd bought her, and flipped through the pages before setting it aside. Then she held up the Bruins hockey jersey the book had been resting on.

"If you're going to be a Bruins fan, you should look the part."

"Thank you." She pulled the jersey over the V-neck tank top she was wearing and then blew him a kiss.

"You have no idea how sexy you look right now."

"I'll wear it to watch hockey games," she said. Then her smile turned decidedly naughty. "Maybe it's *all* I'll wear to watch hockey games."

He groaned and dropped his head back against the couch. "You're killing me, Jess."

"Maybe I'll send you a picture of me in my jersey later."

There was no telling where that conversation might have gone—especially considering it was a video chat—if he hadn't heard the thump of his nephews' feet on the stairs. "I'm about to have juvenile company again, but definitely send me that picture."

With privacy and quiet out of the question, they ended the chat with a promise to talk the next day. Ignoring the knowing look his brother shot him as he joined them again, Rick told his nephews he was in the mood to build some Lego sets.

A week later, when he should have been sleeping in preparation for a busy New Year's Day tour, he made sure he was awake at midnight. Usually he and Jessica talked early enough so he didn't stay up late, so he had to set an alarm. He punched in the text message so when the clock ticked over to the New Year, it was ready to send.

Happy New Year, Jess.

A few seconds later, he got a response. Happy New Year to you, too! Shouldn't you be sleeping?

They say what you're doing when the clock strikes midnight is what you'll be doing all year. I was thinking of you.

Long seconds ticked away as he watched the bubble with the dots indicating she was typing a response. I was thinking of you, too. I would have sent you a text letting you know that, but I know you work tomorrow, so I thought you'd be sleeping and I didn't want to wake you.

Are you at home right now? He hated this impersonal way of communicating.

The phone rang in his hand and he answered it. "Hey, you."

"Happy New Year."

Her voice was quiet, but it didn't sound as if he'd awakened her. "Happy New Year. You didn't have to call. I know it's late."

She laughed. "Not here."

"Oh, that's right. Well, at midnight in Boston, I was thinking of you."

"And at midnight in San Diego, I'll be thinking of you, too. But I'm telling you now because you said New Year's Day is always busy and you need to sleep now, so I won't text you."

"I do need to sleep. But I'll text you tomorrow. And maybe call on Sunday."

"Okay. Good night, Rick. And I hope you're right

about doing all year what you were doing at midnight."

"I am. Good night, Jess."

When he hung up, he plugged his phone in and pulled the blanket up over his head. He hoped he was a *little* right about that tradition. He had no doubt he'd spend a good chunk of the New Year thinking about Jess.

He just hoped he wouldn't have to spend the entire year doing it from the opposite coast.

Maybe it would be easier if he just cut her loose and didn't contact her. The text messages and phone calls just made him miss her more and with every conversation he was reminded he couldn't hold her and she was living a life thousands of miles from his. But he couldn't imagine not talking to her at all so, for now, he'd take what he could get.

FIFTEEN

JESSICA WASN'T SURPRISED when Marie's name flashed on the screen of her cell phone. Her grandmother had really taken to her new smartphone and they'd talked—or at least sent texts back and forth—every day over the five weeks since she'd returned to San Diego.

Leaning back in her office chair, Jessica hit the button to answer the video call. She knew Marie got a kick out of seeing her dressed up, with the view of San Diego over her shoulder. "Hi, Gram."

"Hi, honey. Are you busy? I hate to bother you at work."

"It's fine. Honestly. I told you before if I'm too busy to talk, I'll just send you to voice mail and call you back when I get the chance. How's everything going?"

"Good." Jessica tried not to visibly wince as Marie moved on the couch and everything blurred for a few seconds. "But your grandfather and I have been talking and we think we're going to have the real estate agent put the house on the market."

For a few seconds, she didn't respond and she hoped her reaction didn't show on her face. Helping them make the decision to sell their house had been her objective when she went to Boston in the first place, but it had been nothing but a building at the time. Now it was her grandparents' home and she felt an emotional connection to it she never saw coming. "And you both want that?"

"Yes. Since you left, the house has felt more empty and it's helped us see how ridiculous it is for the two of us to rattle around in it alone."

She missed rattling around in it with them. "Do you have something else in mind already?"

"Maybe. Joe was talking to some of his buddies at the market and one of them moved into a new senior facility not too far away. It has elevators and you can get housekeeping services if you want. With Social Security and the money from the house, we should be able to afford it."

"You can't make a decision like that unless you *know* you can afford it," Jessica said, because fiscal responsibility had been ingrained in her practically from birth. Then she smiled. "How about I fly out and take a look at the place with you? We can figure out the cost, including any fees above the standard lease amount they might not tell you about up front, and we'll go over your financials again together."

Marie's face lit up. "That would be wonderful. Even though we know about what we can expect to get for the house, what we do with that money is important and you can help us figure that out. And you did a lot more research into the housing market than we did, so maybe you could be here when the real estate agent comes back, too?"

"I'll need a couple of days to make arrangements," she said. "Today's Friday, so I'll need the Monday to wrap things up, too. I'll fly out Tuesday and we'll go from there."

When they'd ended the call, Jessica sighed and leaned her head back against her chair. In a few days she'd be back in Boston and she couldn't wait to tell Rick she was coming.

Just like with her grandmother, she and Rick had talked every day over the past few weeks. Sometimes it was only quick text messages and sometimes they did video chats, but usually there were long phone calls at the end of the day.

She'd gotten so she could hear in his voice how a shift had gone. She could hear when he was smiling or when he was so tired she knew talking to her was the only reason he wasn't already asleep. The time zones were a challenge, and she'd gotten in the habit of leaving on time every day, willing to bring her work home so she'd be free to talk to Rick before it was too late on his end.

They'd watched a movie together, their phones on speaker next to them, and last week they'd finally caught a Bruins game on television at just the right time. She ached to physically be with him and touch him, but Rick on the phone was better than no Rick at all.

A sound caught her attention and she lifted her head to see her father standing in the doorway. Judging by the look on his face, he'd been there for at least a few minutes. "Hi, Dad."

"That was my mother."

It wasn't a question, but she nodded. "How much did you hear?"

"Enough to know you're going back to Boston. Do you know how long you'll be away this time?"

So he wasn't going to be stubborn about her going. "I don't know. A couple of weeks, maybe. You already know I can make that work."

"Are they still doing okay, though? Why did they suddenly decide to sell?"

"I don't think it's sudden. It's a conversation they've been having since Joe fell and after so many years in one place, it takes a while to work your way around to the change, I guess." She took a deep breath. "You could have said hello, you know. She would have liked to see your face."

He shook his head so quickly that she guessed it was something he'd considered but already dismissed. "I've been an ass for so many years and I don't know how I'd begin to come back from that. How do I do that, Jessica?"

She smiled. "You knock on the door and when they open it, you say *I've been an ass and I'm sorry* and you go forward from there. You could come with me, you know."

The fact he thought about it, and seriously judging by his expression, was heartening. "I'm not ready quite yet. I want to feel stronger in case it doesn't go well. Even when I was a kid, my old man and I butted heads a lot."

"I think you've both mellowed. And maybe you

won't be as close as some fathers and sons, but being able to get together for Thanksgiving or Christmas once in a while would be a great start. If I ever get married, I'm going to want all three of you there. And if I have a family, I want my kids to have all of you in their lives together."

"I hope that day comes. I really do." He gave her a sad smile. "For now, I'll stay out of the way and let you build your relationship with them, and I'll start by not being *too* put out you're leaving the office again."

"I'm taking the office with me," she reminded him, waving her hand at the laptop and phone on her desk.

"At this rate, it would probably be more efficient to open an office in Boston and expand the business," he said before walking away, and she couldn't tell if he was being snide or sincere.

After grabbing a juice from the minifridge in the corner of her office, Jessica pulled up the ongoing text message thread with Rick and started typing. I'm coming back for a visit.

It didn't take him long to respond, so she pictured him at the fire station, either working in the engine bay or hanging out in the living space upstairs. When?

Probably Tuesday night.

Shit. I'm spending the weekend at my brother's to dog sit for them and going straight to the station on Tuesday. I'll trade shifts and pick you up at the airport.

Then you'll have to work an extra shift while I'm there. You know Marie's not going to let me out of her sight for hours, so get your shift in while I'm with my grandparents. Then I'll sneak upstairs when you get home.

Naked?

She laughed, shaking her head at her phone. I won't sneak up there naked in case I get caught, but I won't wear anything with too many buttons.

I can't wait. I've missed you.

I've missed you, too. Just a few more days.

"I SWEAR, ONE of these years I'm going to carry wads of ten-dollar bills around with me and pay the neighborhood teenagers to shovel." Rick stood straight and stretched his back, glaring at the fire hydrant they'd just shoveled clear of snow. "I'm too old for this shit."

"I know you're old," Scott said, "but it's still pretty damn sad that you think a teenager will pick up a snow shovel for ten bucks."

"Speaking of old, I think Eriksson can shovel out the next one and I'll sit my ass up in the truck." Aidan glared at Chris, who gave them a cheerful wave from behind the wheel.

"Let's go." Rick pulled the map and a pen out of his pocket to check off the hydrant and then they started up the sidewalk to the next one, the truck creeping up the street behind them.

They'd all tossed their bunker coats in the cab a long time ago and were working in just light sweatshirts. Rick probably would have pulled that off, too, except for the fact doing sweaty work in a T-shirt in the cold could get a body in trouble.

Every time it snowed, every single hydrant had to be cleared of snow to below the valve for the hose attachment and at least a couple of feet out. It only took a few minutes to do each one, but there were a *lot* of hydrants in their neighborhood. Even if the snow was deep, the guys from Ladder 37 could find most of them just by memory, but Rick still used the map. If he ever missed one and they were delayed knocking down a fire and somebody got hurt or worse because of the time it took them to get water, he'd never forgive himself.

It wasn't bad today. It was their first time out and it was a nice change of pace. The shoveling part sucked, but it wasn't a bad workout and they shot the shit while they worked. Later in the winter, when the snow came more often and it was bitterly cold and they were doing it for the sixth or seventh time, the mood would be a lot more grim.

When they turned one corner, Rick was heartened to see an exposed hydrant. A pack of kids, with the help of a few adults, were going down the street and shoveling them out. The guys made sure to thank them profusely, and Chris gave them a quick salute with the lights and siren before they trudged on to the next block, where the residents weren't quite as civic-minded.

"You heard from Jessica?" Jeff asked, leaning on his shovel while Rick marked off another cleared hydrant.

"About an hour ago," he said. "She texted me to let me know she finally landed. The weather caused some delays, but she's finally on her way to the house."

"Your house."

"Her grandparents' house."

Jeff shrugged. "Same roof. She just back for a visit?"

"I guess Joe and Marie are ready to talk about selling the house. I haven't talked to them since I heard she was coming back because I was down at my brother's, so I don't know the specifics."

"Oh man, that sucks. That was a wicked good setup for you. Great apartment and low rent."

Rick shrugged as they started toward the next hydrant. "I'll miss the shower, but I can find another place. Hopefully the remodel I did on the place will up the value and help pay them back for all they've done for me over the years."

"I think you did as much for them."

Rick sighed. It *had* been a great setup and not just because he had a great apartment for reasonable rent. Joe and Marie had become like family to him and he actually liked taking care of the place for them. The thought of them selling the house felt a lot like he imagined it would feel if his parents decided to sell the house he and his brother had grown up in. But he also believed it was best for Joe and Marie to down-size, and their well-being came first.

"I might buy a place," Rick said, though it hadn't really crossed his mind until just that second. "I can fix it up the way I want and not worry about whether or not I like the new landlords."

Scott, who'd been listening without comment, paused in the act of stabbing the shovel end into a particularly large snowbank, looking for the clank of metal that would pinpoint exactly where the hydrant was. "You know as soon as you get it just the way you want it, you'll start seeing some awesome woman and you'll want to marry her and then she'll tell you she hates your house. Or the schools suck or there's no place to get her nails done."

"Pretty sure we have more nail places than we do bars now," Jeff said.

That sent the two of them off onto a tangent about manicure and tanning places, and that suited Rick just fine. He didn't want to continue a conversation that included trying to imagine some faceless woman in a strange house she didn't like. Since the beginning of December, the only woman he pictured himself being with was Jess.

He wanted this damn shift to be over so he could see her. The text messages and the phone calls had been nice, but they didn't make him feel the way being in the same room as Jess did. He wanted to see her smile and get her naked in his kitchen.

Eriksson yelled at them from the truck, pounding the outside of the door. "Hey, we've gotta go!"

Rick took a second to get his bearings and circled the hydrant on the map so he'd know where they left off, and then he jogged to the truck. Eriksson hit the siren as they climbed in and pulled away from the curb.

"Looks like we have an electric space heater and shitty extension cord situation," he told them as they pulled on their coats in the confines of the cab. "Home owner thinks it's out, but he's worried about the wall."

Hopefully it would be a quick in and out, Rick thought as Eriksson guided the truck through streets that were even more narrow than usual thanks to the snowbanks. He wasn't sorry to have a break from shoveling, but he needed something to do besides hang around the station and watch the clock.

He still had a lot of hours to kill before he saw Jess again.

"Good morning, honey," Marie said when Jessica wandered into the kitchen in search of coffee the next morning. "It's so good to have you back."

"It's good to *be* back." And it was. Joe and Marie had greeted her with warm hugs yesterday, and then they'd taken her to their favorite Italian restaurant because they decided she needed a big meal after the travel headaches she'd dealt with.

"We got some snow during the night." Marie poured her a mug of coffee and set it on the counter so Jess could add milk and sugar. "Not a lot, but enough so it'll have to be cleaned up. I wonder if I should make a big breakfast. Rick just got home and he should go to bed, but if I know him, he'll be out there with a shovel so Joe doesn't try to do it."

"He, uh… I'm going upstairs to have breakfast with him," Jessica said because she didn't see any way around telling her. "He sent me a text a few minutes ago to let me know he's going to take a shower and then start cooking."

"Oh." The corners of Marie's mouth lifted just enough to give away her amusement. "I'm sure you two have some catching up to do since you've been gone for weeks."

"We'll probably talk about the house. He knows a lot about it, of course."

"I'm sure that must be it." And then her grandmother winked at her.

With no idea what to say to that, Jessica took her coffee to the window and looked out at the new snow. It was pretty, she had to admit, but it was definitely nicer from this side of the window. Late January in Boston was very different than December and, even though she'd dressed for the weather, the cold had threatened to steal her breath when she walked out of the terminal.

She'd just finished her coffee when she heard Rick's truck pull into the driveway, so she rinsed the mug and kissed Marie's cheek. "I won't be too long. You're probably right about Rick wanting to get out there and shovel."

Rather than get bundled up to go outside, Jessica used the staircase up to the third floor that was at the end of the hall opposite her bedroom. They rarely used it because the stairs were steep and narrow, but Joe had told her they hadn't locked the door since Rick moved in, and they liked knowing it could be a fire exit for him if necessary.

After a quick knock, she opened the door and stepped into Rick's kitchen. He'd obviously just walked in because he was still pulling off his sweat-shirt. She'd been anxious walking up the stairs, afraid that somehow it wouldn't be the same now that she'd been gone, despite the fact they'd talked every day. But the look in his eyes and the warm smile made something shift inside of her. He'd missed her. She could see it and she could see that he was as happy to see her as she was to see him.

Tossing the sweatshirt aside, he strode across the room to her and hauled her into his arms. He kissed her, his mouth hot and demanding, until she was breathless and her knees were weak.

"Jesus, I've missed you," he said against her mouth.

She backed away enough to peel off her shirt and bra, then slid the yoga pants she'd thrown on to the floor. He was even faster and by the time she was free of her clothes, he was not only naked but had rolled on the condom he must have stuck in his pocket for this moment.

"I swear that felt like the longest shift I've ever worked," he said, pulling her body hard against his.

"That was the longest five weeks of my life." She wrapped her arms around his neck and lifted her mouth to his.

His hands cupped her breasts, thumbs running across her nipples. "This time I'll just tell you up front I'm going to kiss you and touch you every chance I get."

Jessica ran her hands down his back to the curve of his ass. "While naked, as often as possible."

When he slid his hand between her legs, her knees weakened and they went to the floor. His free hand was between her head and the tile as he kissed her. With a moan she opened her legs as he slipped a finger deep inside her.

"I can't wait," she said, sliding her heels up the back of his legs.

"Good, because I can't, either."

She gasped when his cock drove into her, her back arching off the floor. His fingertips bit into her left hip as he moved, and he leaned on his other arm so he could look down at her. His gaze as he watched her was intense until he raised his eyebrow in that way she found so sexy, and she smiled.

"What?" he asked.

"You have the sexiest eyebrows."

He rocked his hips in a lazy rhythm. "I don't think anybody's ever told me that before. As a matter of fact, I'm sure of it."

"They were one of the first things I noticed about you the day I got here. We were still outside on the sidewalk and I was distracted by what great eyebrows you have."

"I noticed everything about you. Especially your eyes." He grinned. "And your ass. And your legs."

Jessica wrapped those legs around his hips and he thrust deep enough so she moaned. When she ran her hands up his back, the muscles were tight under her palms. The tension in her body built and her breath quickened along with his thrusts.

She cried out as she came, finding the release her body had been wanting for weeks, and it wasn't long before Rick's body stiffened and she felt his orgasm pulsing through his body.

When he collapsed on top of her, his breath hot and ragged against her neck, Jessica wrapped her arms and legs around him, holding him close. For the first time in weeks, she was totally content and the warm rush of happiness was almost as potent as the post-orgasm glow.

But once she'd caught her breath, Jessica became aware of how hard the floor was under her body. She moved a little, and saw the wince on Rick's face when he took some of his weight off of her by shifting it to his arm and hip.

"Are we cuddling," she asked, "or just trying not to admit we might be too old to have sex on a tile floor?"

He chuckled, and then groaned as he pushed himself off the floor. "I was hoping you wouldn't notice my reluctance to try to get up."

He helped her up and, after kissing her again, walked to his bedroom. Just as she finished putting her clothes back on, he returned. He'd thrown on a pair of sweatpants, but skipped the shirt. She didn't mind at all.

"I'll pick up my clothes later," he said when she

looked at them scattered on the floor. "Now that my biggest hunger is taken care of for now, it's time for breakfast. I'm starving. You want an omelet?"

"That sounds delicious." So did the idea of watching her shirtless man cooking her breakfast.

"I missed talking to you," he said, taking a carton of eggs out of the fridge. He set them next to a big mixing bowl and cracked the first egg open. "The phone just isn't the same."

"I missed you, too. What can I do to help?"

"You can grab us some coffee and then sit and talk to me," he said. "And then later, I'm going to drag you outside and teach you how to shovel snow."

She laughed and went to his coffeemaker and poured them each a coffee. "Good luck with that. And Marie was right. She said you should go to bed, but you'd probably shovel snow instead. She was going to make you a nice breakfast to keep you going."

"You should have told me that before I started cracking the eggs." He winked at her. "So I guess you told her you were coming up here to have breakfast with me?"

"I didn't really have a choice." She sat on a bar stool and watched him drop a blob of butter into a frying pan. "Is that okay?"

"Of course. I mean, I guess all I can do is hope they're okay with it. Did you not want to tell her?"

Jessica shrugged. "Joe and Marie are a lot of things, but stupid isn't one of them."

"Very true. So how was your father about you coming out here again? Did he give you a hard time?"

"No, he was really good about it, actually, and said he didn't want to get in the way of me building a relationship with Marie and Joe. I think he's starting to regret a lot of the choices he's made in his life."

"As he should," Rick said, pouring the egg mixture into the pan.

Jessica fought back the automatic reflex to defend her father and said nothing instead. She knew nothing Rick had ever heard about David Broussard would inspire him to like her father, so he'd believe it when he saw it, so to speak.

She changed the subject to the weather while he cooked their breakfasts. It surprised her that a guy who spent as much time outside in the cold as he did wouldn't be jealous of her home city's temperate climate. "You wouldn't even need to own a coat."

He laughed. "I don't mind owning a coat. And I need four seasons. Without cold and snow, how do you know when it's time to start singing Christmas carols?"

"Oh, the department stores will let you know."

The omelets were delicious, but she balked when he told her to go downstairs and borrow some good boots, along with a coat and gloves, from her grandmother. "I have boots and a coat."

"Not for shoveling snow, you don't."

"I don't mind watching out the window."

He laughed and nudged her toward the door. "Meet me outside in ten minutes. You'll have fun, I promise."

Shoveling snow didn't sound at all fun to Jessica,

but spending time with him did. And since he was going to be outside in the cold, she did as he suggested and borrowed Marie's coat and boots. Her grandmother also loaned her some brightly patterned wool mittens with a matching hat.

None of which saved her from the first shock of stepping out the door. It felt even colder than yesterday, when she'd arrived in the city, and she wouldn't have thought that was possible.

When Rick stepped out of the garage with two snow shovels, she shook her head. He was wearing a zip-up hoodie—albeit a thick one—and had gloves on, but no big coat or hat. She knew it was just a matter of her being out of her natural climate, but she thought he might be showing off a little, too.

And there was no way she'd let him—or Mother Nature—get the better of her.

SIXTEEN

RICK HAD TO ADMIT, Jess was either a lot tougher or a lot more stubborn than he'd given her credit for. He would have bet money she'd make it about fifteen minutes before she gave him his shovel back and went inside.

But she made it almost an hour, shoveling snow in the name of working out, and then practicing her snowball-making skills. The first few she tossed in his direction disintegrated on impact, but he made the mistake of showing her how to take the loose snow and really pack it down, breathing on it to help make it sticky. She managed to make a few small snowballs that actually stung a little bit.

"You have a good arm," he said. "If this was good snowball snow, you could hurt somebody."

"Isn't all snow good snowball snow? How can there be bad snow for snowballs?"

He laughed and explained the different between the dry and fluffy snowflakes that fell when it was really cold and wouldn't stick together, and the wet, heavy snow that fell in warmer temperatures and could be packed into snowballs that were practically lethal.

"I think my friends would be a little surprised if

they could see me right now." She laughed, a short self-deprecating sound, while brushing snow off the wool mittens.

"You look beautiful. Your cheeks are all flushed and your nose is red. It's cute."

She gave him a look that let him know she thought he was crazy. "Yes, red noses are all the rage right now. So tell me, what do you do after you shovel snow?"

"Usually, unless I have errands to do, I read for a while. After being outside, it's nice to curl up on the couch with a blanket and a book and relax."

"I just happened to borrow a book from Marie's bookshelf last night."

"Grab it and we'll go snuggle on my couch and read for a while."

The smile she gave him seemed to grab hold of something deep inside of him and squeeze. And that scared him. It had sucked when she'd gone back to California the first time and, even though she'd only been back in Boston a day, he already knew it was going to suck even worse when she left again. Though he was pretty sure it was already too late, he should be trying to put more distance between them, not getting closer.

Rolling his eyes at himself, he put the shovels away. He was pretty sure it was too late. He *knew* it was. And even though he knew living on two opposite coasts was going to be a serious problem they'd have to solve in the future, he didn't see himself giving up on this relationship.

A little while later, they couldn't *get* any closer

and he wouldn't have it any other way. Because she'd caught a chill, she'd curled up on his lap and covered them both with the fleece blanket he kept on the back of the couch. When he'd stretched his legs out, she'd stayed put, using him like a heated recliner.

It was awkward, holding his book open with one hand and turning the pages with his thumb, but he managed because it was worth the effort to have Jess stretched out on top of him. Concentrating wasn't easy, either, and every time he started losing himself in the story, she'd sigh or shift slightly and become the center of his awareness again.

Then she snorted. "I think if I was running for my life, hiding from the bad guys in a warehouse, I wouldn't be in the mood to have sex."

"Duly noted."

She laughed. "How's your book?"

"Not as interesting as the sounds you make reading yours."

"I do *not* make sounds."

His arm was wrapped around her waist, and he squeezed as he kissed the side of her neck. "Oh, you definitely do. A couple of chuckles. A few sighs. And a snort which, judging by the timing, was your opinion of being turned on when somebody's trying to kill you."

"It's so dumb. I mean, if you were in a house that was on fire and you just happened to stumble on a room with no smoke in it, would you feel compelled to stop and have sex in it?"

"No." He paused. "A blow job, maybe, but not sex."

She elbowed him hard enough to make him grunt. "You would not."

"Of course not. With the amount of gear we wear, by the time I could get my dick out, the flames would be knocked down and the guys would be in the truck, laying on the horn."

"Funny." Sighing, she closed the book and tossed it onto the coffee table without getting up. "That's not a very good book."

His was, but she was more interesting to him than any work of fiction, so he did the same. "How long are you planning to stay this trip?"

She thought about it for a few seconds, and then he felt her shrug. "I'm not sure. Marie's left two messages for the real estate agent, but they're playing phone tag. And I'm helping her go through the boxes that represent decades of the worst filing system ever. She has receipts for everything, like the heating system and stuff like that, and prospective buyers will want to know the dates. We just have to find the paperwork."

"So probably at least a week, then?"

"At least. Probably more like two. I told my father it might be a couple of weeks."

Two weeks…maybe. And he had a feeling that they'd be spending a lot of time together over the course of the two weeks. When the time was up and she had to go back to her life in California, he was going to have one hell of a hard time letting her go.

"I should probably go downstairs and let you get some rest or something. You said you shoveled out fire hydrants all day yesterday and then you shoveled snow today. You must be exhausted."

"You're right. I should go to bed." He kissed her neck again, and then gave it a gentle bite. "You should go with me. We can pretend bad guys are chasing us."

She laughed and rolled so she was straddling him on the couch. "Let's see if you're hero material, then."

SINCE THEY'D KEPT in touch a little by way of Facebook and they'd reached out to her when they found out she was back in the city, Jessica met Lydia and Ashley at a tiny Chinese restaurant they said was within walking distance of Joe and Marie's since parking was almost impossible in that area in the winter. Unfortunately, their idea of walking distance didn't factor in the weather and by the time she stepped through the front door, she wished she'd at least called a cab.

They were already there and they waved her over when they saw her. Jessica didn't even take off her coat before sitting down. Her gloved hands were freezing and she rubbed them together, hoping she could get a hot cup of coffee here.

"You look like you want to cry," Ashley said, sympathy heavy in her voice. "I should have told you to take a cab, but I haven't really paid attention to the weather forecasts lately. It's winter. Winter sucks."

"I'd cry, but I'm afraid my eyeballs would freeze if they get that wet." Both women laughed, probably not realizing she was serious.

"So Rick must be glad to have you back on this coast," Lydia said once they'd all ordered coffees and

Jessica had requested a few minutes to thaw out before deciding what she wanted to eat.

She pressed her gloved hands to her cheeks, trying to warm them enough to manage normal facial expressions. "I think so. He seems to be."

"Are you happy to be back?"

"That's…not an easy question to answer," she said honestly. "It's kind of a mess."

"That's why you have friends to talk to," Ashley said. "Sometimes things aren't as messy as they seem when you're the one in it."

"I'm glad to be back because I've missed Joe and Marie. And Rick. But being back also makes it harder because it starts to feel like real life and I like it. But my real life is actually in San Diego, so it screws with my head."

Lydia held up her hands. "This might be overly simplistic, but if you prefer this life to your so-called real life, why not make *this* your real life? We have financial advisors in Boston. Good ones, even, or so I'm told."

"But it's not just switching jobs," Ashley said. "She built that business with her father and she's probably meant to take it over."

"Yes," Jessica said. "Besides my house and my friends, there's loyalty not only to my father and everybody who works for us, but to the plan I had, you know? I mean, I guess it was mostly his plan, but I've invested most of my life into it."

"I guess we know how that feels," Lydia said. She gave Jessica a sympathetic look. "My dad just assumed Ashley and I would run the bar and I hated that. I hated the whole firefighter thing, too. I even left Massachusetts to get away from it all, but I came back to help Ashley out while she and Danny went through their rough patch. Then Aidan was all smoking hot and sweet and sexy and…well, here I am. But this time it's my choice and I have no regrets."

"What do you mean you hated the whole firefighter thing?" Jessica asked because if there was something specifically bad about firefighters, it would probably be helpful to know that now.

Lydia shrugged. "It's a close community, and that's obviously a good thing. But they're a brotherhood and sometimes it feels like they come first, before families. And it can also be claustrophobic at times. My first husband was a firefighter, too, and I took a lot of shit when I got fed up and divorced him. Forgiving the community for circling the wagons around him took me a while."

"But Aidan's not like that?"

"He is to a point. Their lives depend on each other so they have each other's backs to a degree not a lot of people can understand. They're truly brothers."

"And sisters," Ashley added.

"And sisters. But I know Aidan doesn't put anybody else before me and that matters."

"Wow." Jessica drank another gulp of coffee and then peeled her gloves off. She'd give the coat a few more minutes. "I had no idea. So far my experience with…being involved with a firefighter is trying to spot him on the news, which is dumb, of course. I don't know enough about the fire stations to even know what locations he'd respond to."

"It probably seems fun at first," Ashley said. "Trying to spot him on the news, I guess. But it's easy to become obsessed with that. With knowing he's okay, I mean. It makes the waiting harder."

"I agree," Lydia said. "Everything's on social media. People are live-tweeting fires on Twitter and there are Facebook statuses and videos on Snapchat and Instagram. They're actually streaming as it's happening, and that means it's almost like being there at the fire with them, but being helpless to do anything but stand there and watch."

"I don't follow any of it," Ashley said. "If something happens, they'll tell me. Otherwise, the only way to get through each shift is to assume everything's going okay and his training and experience is keeping him safe."

"But you both chose firefighters anyway?" It was a lot to think about.

"The heart wants what it wants," Ashley said.

"My heart isn't the only part of my body that decided it wouldn't settle for less than Aidan Hunt," Lydia added, her snarky smile looking so much like her brother's.

Jessica finally took her coat off to hang on the back of her chair, shoving her hat and scarf into one of the sleeves like she'd seen her grandmother do. "Firefighters seem to have good…endurance."

Lydia and Ashley laughed, but their server chose that moment to see if they were ready to order, probably signaled by Jessica removing her coat. After a quick scan of the menu, they ordered a variety of dishes to share.

"So I take it things are going *really* well with Rick, then?" Lydia asked once they were alone again.

"We're….yeah." She smiled. "Things are going well. It's almost like we weren't even apart for weeks."

Ashley smiled. "I'm glad. He's such a good guy."

"So what's holding you back?" Lydia asked Jessica.

"We're kind of thrown together because of my grandparents. Once they're settled, what brings us together? How many times, realistically, can I travel to Boston in a year?"

"Ideally it'll be love that brings you together. But I don't think many relationships could survive that kind of distance. I mean some do, but probably not many. One of you will have to make a hard choice eventually. And eventually might not be that far away."

And it would be her who made the hard choice. Even though she'd lived in San Diego her entire life, she couldn't picture Rick living there. This place— this community—was a part of who he was and that bond was part of what she loved about him.

"Shit."

Lydia and Ashley both looked at her, but it was Lydia who spoke. Jessica had already figured out she was the more vocal of the two sisters. "What?"

"Nothing."

"No, that was a particularly vehement *shit*. And we're bartenders. We're awesome at picking up those kinds of signals and when somebody hisses *shit* in that way, something's usually wrong."

Jessica sighed. "I think I just realized—like really admitted to myself for the first time—that I'm in love with him."

"Honey, if ever there was cause to bust out a four-letter word, it's being in love with a firefighter," Ashley said, and they both raised their coffee mugs in a toast to her.

USUALLY SATURDAY NIGHT wouldn't be a good time to hit Kincaid's Pub looking for company and a game of pool, but the wind chill was pretty fierce and Rick thought it would keep a lot of people from leaving their homes just to get a beer and some wings.

He sent out a group text that yielded the information he was the only single guy at the station who didn't have a date that night. Aidan had said he might stop by, but Rick didn't see him when he walked in. That was fine. The television was offering up sports highlights and they were company enough.

Karen was covering the bar tonight, which didn't surprise him. He already knew Lydia and Ashley had the night off, since they were going out with Jess, so they had to get somebody to fill in. Even though he owned the place, Tommy preferred sitting at the bar with Fitz to actually *working* the bar and preferred not to do any of the actual manual labor unless it was an unavoidable situation.

"Hey, Rick," she said, setting a beer in front of

him, making the lights flash off her engagement ring. "How you been?"

"Not too bad. Looks like a slow night."

"Trust me, that doesn't break my heart." He knew what she meant. This time of year kept first responders and emergency rooms hopping, so tending the bar on a slow night probably felt like a vacation to her. "You all alone tonight?"

"Everybody had plans or didn't feel like going out in the cold, I guess."

"It wouldn't be so bad if the wind would die down."

"Let me ask you something. The day Joe and Marie were in the ER because he fell and you showed me your engagement ring, I said it happened fast. And you said 'when it's right, it's right.' What did you mean by that? I mean, how did you *know* it was right?" When she looked at him as if he just asked her something outrageous, like her bra size, he looked down and traced the condensation on his mug. "Forget I said anything."

"Rick Gullotti, if you just hinted around that you're even *thinking* about settling down, this moment is unforgettable."

"Exaggerate much?"

"No." She tilted her head to give him a considering look. "I guess you asking that question when your landlords' granddaughter just happened to return to Boston is a coincidence?"

"She won't be my landlords' granddaughter very long since they're selling the house."

"Nice deflection, Gullotti. But I'll let it slide. How

do you feel about them selling? You put so much work into your apartment and now you might have to find a new place and start all over."

He shrugged. "It's just an apartment. And nothing says I'll have to start over. Whoever buys it might want to keep me there, although I'm sure they'll raise the rent. Or there's a possibility we can have the property deed changed so I can buy the apartment as a condo, separate from the rest of the house. I think. I haven't really looked into it yet because I thought I'd have a little more time."

And because it wasn't something he'd wanted to deal with. Not only because he hated paperwork, but because he was afraid if he broached the subject to Joe and Marie, they'd realize he really didn't want to move and they might factor that into their own decision. Now that they'd made their decision, it might be time to look into it.

"So how long is Jessica in town for?"

"A couple of weeks, probably." He took a sip of his beer. "How do you know so much about what's going on?"

She smiled. "You think Aidan catching you kissing a woman in the pool room isn't going to get talked about?"

"It's ridiculous. The city's a little big for such a small-town grapevine."

"The important thing here is that she came back. Focus on that."

"She wants to check out the place Joe and Marie are considering moving into. I guess places like that sometimes tack on a shitload of hidden fees you don't find out about until you've already started the process. She wants to make sure they can afford it."

"She could have done that by phone," Karen pointed out.

He wanted to believe seeing him had factored into Jess's decision to fly all the way across the country again to handle business that probably could be handled by phone and online. "She knows it makes her grandparents feel better having her out here."

"It's nice of her to come all the way to Boston to help them with this. It must be a daunting decision for them."

"Yup."

"But she's getting to know them, right? I mean, she'll still come out here even after the business end is settled?"

Rick knew exactly where Karen was heading with that. "Yeah, she will. Though it's hard to say how often."

"You think she'd consider moving out here? With the right incentive, of course." And she tilted her hand again, letting the light refract off her diamond.

"I doubt it. She's pretty thankful to have Joe and Marie in her life, but it doesn't change the fact she's spent her entire life in San Diego. She has a home and friends and not only does she have a job, but it's a family business. That's not easy to walk away from."

"You're a great guy, Rick. You have no idea how much I used to wish we had that something special I was looking for. If you think she's the one, you need to let her know that. How can she make decisions for her future if she thinks what you two have is just casual sex?"

Just the thought of having that conversation made his chest ache. What if she thought it *was* just casual sex? He'd been told so many times that he wasn't the marrying kind and he'd laughed it off. Hell, there was a time in his life when it had been some kind of misguided badge of honor. But he had a gut feeling hearing Jess say those words to him would hurt like hell.

"She knows it's not just casual," he said. Moment of panicked doubt aside, he was certain Jessica knew she was more to him than a casual fling.

"Have you thought about moving to San Diego?" Karen asked.

"Maybe I should have gone to a different bar," he muttered.

"In other words, you have."

"I don't really see myself doing that. I love it here. I can't imagine leaving Ladder 37. My family's nearby. And there's Joe and Marie. Just because they're moving into a smaller place doesn't mean they don't need somebody looking after them a bit."

Karen shook her head, tossing her bar towel over her shoulder. "You sure are full of reasons why a relationship with Jessica won't work."

"It's called being practical."

"Or being scared."

She walked away before he could argue with that, which was probably a good thing because the words to deny it wouldn't come to him.

SEVENTEEN

THE NEXT MONDAY, Rick looked around his apartment and decided it was as good as it would get. He knew the real estate agent was already downstairs with Joe, Marie and Jess. It was only a matter of time before they'd make their way to his place, so he'd given it a quick cleaning and made sure there was no clutter lying around.

The agent would need to take pictures, he supposed. And probably a ton of notes. And he still hadn't decided if he wanted to broach the subject of restructuring the property so he could buy the top floor. The more he thought about it, the less attractive an option it seemed.

Sure, he'd sunk quite a bit into the renovation. He could afford to since the Broussards lowballed his rent. But he wasn't sure he had the heart to live there without them. Another family living under him wouldn't be the same, whether he liked them or not. And he'd renovated this apartment to suit his taste. There was no reason he couldn't do it again.

When the sliding door opened, he looked up from his seat at the island, expecting to see all of them walk through the door. But it was only Jess and she hurried to close the door behind her. They were heading into a deep freeze, weatherwise, and it was already bitterly cold.

"She didn't leave, did she?" That wouldn't make sense, since the property couldn't be listed without mentioning the third-floor apartment.

"I don't think she's ever going to leave, to be honest. Joe and Marie are really taking her request to give them some history of the house seriously. Every room seems to have a dozen stories."

He opened his arms so she could step into his embrace, then wrapped her in a warm hug. She was shivering a little, just from the walk up to his apartment. "Why didn't you use the inside stairs?"

"I had an opportunity to escape and I took it. I was closer to the back door and was afraid I'd get sucked into another description of what kind of wallpaper was in the kitchen forty years before I was born."

He laughed and kissed the top of her head. "Driving you a little crazy?"

"A little? Measurements. Photos. Facts. I thought it would take maybe half an hour, tops."

"Marie doesn't do anything in a half hour. You should know that by now."

"Are you okay with this?" she asked. He wasn't sure what she meant by that, so he frowned. "The real estate agent, I mean."

"Oh. It would be awfully hard for her to list the house with an entire floor of description missing."

"I'm not asking if you know the logical reason for her presence. I want to know if you're okay with it.

I know I focus on this being Joe and Marie's home, but it's your home and it can't be easy."

"The difference is that Joe and Marie own the house and I rent an apartment. It's the chance you take if you don't buy."

She backed away from him so she could see his face. "That can't be how you really feel."

He shrugged and moved around the island to put the roll of paper towels he'd been using back on the counter. "I love this apartment. And I love the house and I love Joe and Marie. But they're moving on and I will, too."

She looked at him for a long moment, and he could tell she wanted to poke at feelings about the house more. But she must have decided against it because she smiled. "It'll be a shame to give up that master bathroom. Especially the shower. It's so big two people could have sex in there."

The thought of Jess naked against all that white tile made him instantly hard as a rock and Rick was glad he was standing on the opposite side of the island. "Yes. Two people *could* have sex in there."

She shivered and rubbed her hands on her arms. "I bet it's warm in there, too. I think I caught a chill coming up here."

"I'd take you in the bedroom and warm you up, but you know the second I get my hands on you, they'll walk through the door."

"I'd rather not take the chance of getting caught naked by my grandparents and a very nosy lady with a camera, thanks." But she gave him a smile that just intensified the ache. "Rain check."

A few minutes later they heard Joe's heavy tread on the deck and Jess went to open the slider for them. Once they were in out of the cold, Joe introduced the real estate agent to Rick.

"We'll be quick," she promised, and he saw Jess—who was standing behind the trio—roll her eyes.

It bothered him more than he thought, watching the woman take pictures of his home so they could sell it to somebody else. He stayed where he was behind the island, only moving when she wanted to take a shot of the kitchen. Not only did he not care to follow them around the apartment, but every time he looked at Jess, he got that mental flash of her naked and slick and soapy in his shower again.

As Joe and Marie took the agent into his bedroom, Jess joined him at the island. "You okay?"

"Sure. Do I not look okay?"

"You're usually a sociable guy, so it's weird you're not talking."

"They're busy and, unless they want to know what kind of marble vanity top that is, there's nothing I can really add."

She looked at him for a long moment, and then blew an exasperated breath at some hair that had drifted toward her face. "Fine. Don't tell me."

"Okay. It's not fun watching people get ready to sell the place I've made a home, even if I think it's the right thing to do. And I also want to fuck you in my shower. So, yeah, there's a lot going on in my head right now."

She tried unsuccessfully to stifle a chuckle, and then she slid her hand into his. He interlocked their fingers and squeezed as she rested her head against his arm. "I know the house thing is hard. It is for all three of you. The shower thing I might be able to help you with at some point, though."

At some point was going to be about forty-five seconds after the door closed behind her grandparents and their real estate lady, but he didn't bother to tell her that. She'd figure it out when he locked the door and got her naked.

From the other room, he overheard the woman asking about the crown molding and groaned. Assuming he—and his throbbing erection—survived that long.

JESSICA STOOD AT the window, watching the real estate agent leave, and she could still hear the engine out on the road when Rick's arms looped around her waist and he kissed the back of her neck. She shivered and leaned back against him.

"I feel dirty," he said. "We should take a shower."

She laughed, but he didn't. "The lady just left, Rick. Joe or Marie might come up to talk about what she said."

"I locked the door. They'll figure it out."

"Or we could wait until a normal time to take a shower. It's barely evening."

"The thought of you in that shower made my dick so hard I'm afraid I'll be permanently damaged," he said, and she giggled. "Why do you think I stayed behind the kitchen island while they roamed around taking pictures?"

"I thought you were staying out of the way."

"I was. I didn't want to alarm anybody." He nipped at her earlobe, and she felt herself caving.

"I do love that shower."

"Let me give you a really good tour." Sliding his hand under her shirt, he ran his fingers up her spine and then tucked them under her bra strap. "Unless you have something you'd rather be doing."

"Something I'd rather do than be naked with you?" She turned in his arms and, after locking her hands behind his neck, hopped up to wrap her legs around his waist.

He caught her, supporting her ass with his hands, and kissed her before carrying her into the bedroom. There was definitely something to be said for having a guy who had to stay in good physical condition for a living, she thought.

Once he'd set her on her feet, he wasted no time stripping down. "You weren't kidding."

He looked down and then laughed. "I never kid about permanent damage to my dick."

"You're not going to turn that shower on cold, are you?"

"How hot do you like it?"

She pulled her shirt off and tossed it aside. "As hot as you can stand it."

He opened the wide glass door and walked into the massive shower. Jessica continued to strip as he turned the water on, so by the time it was running hot enough for him to step under the stream, she was ready to join him.

After pulling the door closed behind her, she grabbed the bar of soap off the shelf and lathered her hands. He started to turn, but she stopped him with a hand to the shoulder.

"You should let me wash your back."

"Okay, but then I'm washing your front."

She laughed and set the bar back on the shelf before touching him. Her fingertips, slick with soap, glided over his shoulders and down his arms. Then she looped her hands around and washed his chest. Her breasts were pressed against his back, almost aching with the need for him to cup them in his hands.

But she wasn't done with him yet. She slid her hands down his stomach, feeling his abs tighten as her touch skimmed lower.

"Jess." He growled her name, but whether it was a plea or a warning, she couldn't tell. And she didn't care.

She closed her hand around his cock, stroking the hard length of it with her slick hand. He dropped his head back as his hips rocked slightly, but after only a few strokes, he grasped her wrist and stilled her hand.

Then he turned and backed her up against the shower wall. The tile was cold and she arched her back, but there was nowhere to go with his body pressed against hers. He pushed her wet hair away from her face and then kissed her hard.

She opened her mouth to him, surrendering completely as his tongue danced over hers. Then he kissed her chin. The hollow at her throat.

The tile was already warming against her skin and she ran her fingers over his hair when his mouth closed over her nipple. He sucked hard, the sensation sizzling through her body.

Steam was filling the enclosure as the hot water beat down on them, rinsing away the soap and leaving their skin flushed. Or maybe it was his mouth on her body. She didn't know and didn't care. All she knew was the feel of his scruffy jaw on her delicate skin and his hand sliding up her thigh.

He stroked the soft flesh between her legs, and she sucked in a breath when he pressed the heel of his hand against her clit. She ground against his hand, so close to an orgasm she could only whimper. Then he slid two fingers into her and his thumb replaced his palm. As his fingers moved, his thumb brushed over her clit and she dug her fingernails into his shoulders as she came.

When the shuddering stopped, Rick reached around her and turned off the shower. "We've done the tile thing once already and you're right. I'm too old for that shit."

She expected him to grab them some towels, but he pushed open the glass door and lifted her into his arms. "Not on the bed! We're so wet even changing the sheets won't help because we'll soak the mattress."

"Yes, ma'am," he said, setting her on her feet. After grabbing a condom from his nightstand, he kissed her.

She heard the crinkle of the condom wrapper and then he was turning her so she faced the bed. When he put his hand on her back, she leaned forward and braced her palms on the edge of the mattress.

He entered her slowly, each stroke just a little deeper than the one before it. Her fingers curled in the bedspread and she tried not to hold her breath as his hands gripped her hips.

When she finally took all of him, he paused, his breathing fast and shallow. He skimmed his fingers over her back, raking the skin lightly with his nails. She shivered and pushed back against him with a moan.

When his hand slid up her neck and his fingers curled in her hair, she gasped and jerked her hips against his. He jerked hard in response, and she cried out. Every thrust was deep, with one hand on her hip and the other buried in her hair.

Then, just when she thought he was going to come, he stilled. After a few seconds, he withdrew and turned her around. "Screw the bed. We'll sleep on the couch if it gets wet. I want to see your face."

He picked her up and set her on the mattress, then settled himself over her. Brushing her hair away from her face, he looked into her eyes and smiled. "I like that. But I like seeing your face."

She felt a hot flush under his scrutiny, but she didn't look away. Instead she cupped his face in her hands and lifted her head to kiss him. She'd never get enough of kissing this man, she thought.

Rick nudged her knees apart and she sighed against

his lips when he filled her again. "I love the feel of you inside me."

He grinned, his eyes crinkling. "I love the feel of me inside you, too."

Taking his time, he moved his hips in a steady rhythm that made her want to beat her fists on his back. But no matter how she raised her hips or dug into the backs of his thighs with her heels, he wouldn't be rushed.

The entire time, he drove her crazy with his mouth, kissing her mouth and her neck. Kissing her breasts and sucking hard on her nipples, almost but not quite to the point of pain. She squirmed and he reached between their bodies to stroke her clit.

The orgasm hit hard and she moaned as the tremors wracked her body. She clutched at his shoulders and he moved his hips faster. With deep, fast strokes, he pounded into her until his hips jerked and he growled her name.

When he rolled onto his back, they both stared at the ceiling, trying to catch their breath. He captured her hand with his and brought it to his mouth to kiss her palm. "Damn, woman."

She wasn't ready to form words, so she made the same sound she made when she bit into a slab of exceptionally good chocolate cake and closed her eyes.

After a few minutes the mattress dipped and she heard him go into the bathroom. She thought about moving, since she was sideways on the bed, naked with wet hair on top of the covers.

It didn't happen, though, and when Rick came

back, he just stretched out beside her again. He stroked her thigh and turned his head to kiss her shoulder.

"Stay with me tonight."

Since she hadn't even been able to muster enough ambition to turn the right way on the bed, it sounded like a great idea. "You have to go to work soon, so you need to sleep."

"I'll sleep." He rolled onto his side and threw his arm over her. "I want you to sleep *with* me. We can have a very early breakfast together before I leave."

It seemed like a big step and that was ridiculous since her own bedroom was just one floor below them. Technically they lived under the same roof. But it was the right step, she thought. It was foolish for her to get up and creep back to her bed when they both wanted her in Rick's. "I should warn you that going to bed with wet hair doesn't bode well for my morning look."

"Honey, there is no look so bad I wouldn't want to see your face in the morning." He nuzzled his face against her neck. "I might laugh, but I won't be scared off."

She giggled and slapped his arm. "Nice. We should at least turn the right way so our heads are on the pillows."

"Mmm." She could hear his breathing getting slower and deeper as he mumbled. "Five more minutes."

Rick had had a feeling when he walked into the station the next morning it was going to be a doozy of a tour. Whenever the meteorologists started trotting out the record cold temperature graphs and talking in excited voices about the possibility of breaking them, his job got harder.

Some freezing rain had made things interesting, and he knew they'd probably spend most of their time responding to motor vehicle accidents. The tire chains were on the trucks in preparation and there were extra blankets in the cabs in case they were needed by any victims caught without coats.

But then somebody had started a fire in an old warehouse being rehabbed into retail space. Now they were in hell, and it was definitely freezing over.

They'd been first on the scene, but E-59 hadn't even finished laying the lines before additional alarms were struck. They had L-37's ladder in position, but with the relentless freezing drizzle falling out of the sky, it was treacherous and Rick couldn't do anything but pray none of them would slip and fall on it.

The only saving grace was the fact it was an empty building. It was massive and it was going to be a long night of battling the elements along with the flames. Hoses froze. Fittings. Footing was treacherous. Their exposed skin was at risk and if fighting a fire was anything, it was wet. Conditions in which water froze on contact with any surface added a hazardous element there was almost no protection against.

But at least there were no people inside, and that was what Rick tried to focus on as his company worked on breaching the roof.

He lost track of how long they worked on knocking down the flames. There were so many companies involved he couldn't keep track of them all, but that wasn't his job, anyway. That was the incident commander's problem.

Word filtered through they'd transported one guy to the hospital for a possible broken clavicle thanks to slipping on the ice. Rick winced when he heard that because that was a shitty bone to break. Then, a while later, he found out three guys were being transported for smoke inhalation after being rescued from a far corner of the building.

Clearly it was going to be one of those days.

Over time, he noticed the news cameras, and the number of cell phones being held up by the onlookers who could get close enough to catch a glimpse of the fire to impress their Facebook friends. And he wondered if Jess had seen any of it.

She'd be worried. Even to him, the scene looked like something out of a horror movie and he'd served through a lot of winters with Boston Fire. He couldn't imagine what it would look like to somebody who didn't have a lot of knowledge of firefighting *or* freezing rain and subzero temperatures.

His foot slipped on an icy beam and he went down hard, landing on his knee. Letting loose every swear word he knew through gritted teeth, he slowly pushed himself back to his feet and tested his weight on the leg. It was going to hurt like a son of a bitch tomorrow, but it would do for tonight.

That was what he got for letting his attention wander to Jess instead of focusing on the job. No matter how worried she might be, her life wasn't in his hands. He owed it to these guys to stay focused.

"You okay?" Chris Eriksson appeared at his side, his eyebrows drawn together in a way that was almost comical thanks to the tiny icicles clinging to them.

"Yeah, I'll live. We're going to pull out and take a break soon. I saw Porter slip a few minutes ago. He didn't go down, but we're all getting tired and somebody's going to get hurt."

"I could use a hot chocolate. I can see the volunteer truck from here and those foam cups are a thing of beauty, man. Every time I look at them, I want to cry."

Rick laughed and called in to command. It was time for some hot chocolate, dammit.

EIGHTEEN

JESSICA HEARD JOE give a long, low whistle and lowered her book to look up at the television screen. Her heart seemed to stop for a few seconds and she audibly sucked in a breath.

A roaring fire filled the screen and, as she watched, the camera angle pulled back and panned the mass of trucks and firefighters surrounding the scene. And while the flames and smoke dominated the background of the shot, ice was everywhere in the foreground.

It glistened on the fire trucks and on the snow. The camera zoomed in on a group of firefighters gathered around an older guy who was obviously in charge, and Jessica actually gasped. Their coats were encased in ice, and icicles hung from the rims of their helmets. One of the men facing the camera had ice in his mustache, and she felt a frisson of fear for a man she didn't even know.

"They shouldn't be out there like that. It's too cold."

"They've got a job to do," Joe said.

"Once the fire is that big, why can't they just let it burn?"

"And let it jump to the next building and keep

spreading until it takes out an entire city block or more? That building's being renovated, but the others have people living in them, and businesses."

Jessica wanted to argue with him, but she knew he was right. It was their job to put out the fire, regardless of the weather. But there were a lot of firefighters in the city doing that job. "Maybe Rick and the others aren't at that fire. There are probably hundreds of fire trucks in Boston, right?"

Joe shook his head. "I know where that building is and if they weren't first on the scene, they were damn close to it."

"They train for this," Marie said in a soft voice. "When it's colder than usual, like tonight, it's a challenge, but they know what they're doing. Especially Rick. He's been doing it a long time."

Jessica remembered what Ashley had told her about not watching the news or the Facebook and Twitter updates, and now she was beginning to understand why. Jessica knew she could drive herself crazy, staring at the screen and hoping for a glimpse of Rick. She was already straining to hear the voices in the background, barely audible above the news correspondent's.

Forcing herself to sit back against the couch cushion, she wondered who they would notify first if something happened to Rick. His parents were the obvious choice, but it wouldn't surprise her at all if Joe and Marie were first on his list of people to call.

Five minutes later, she watched Aidan Hunt accept a cup of coffee from a volunteer. His expression was grim and the camera cut away as he lifted the cup to his mouth. She wanted to yell at the television. If the camera stayed with Aidan, maybe she'd get a glimpse of the others.

Then the station cut back to regular programming, promising to update on the fire as needed, and she wanted to drive to the scene herself just to make sure he was okay. Instead, she set her book on the table and went into the kitchen. Her mouth was dry, so she poured herself a glass of water and tried to think about anything else but what Rick was doing at that moment.

"I don't imagine it's an easy thing, loving a firefighter." Marie had followed her into the kitchen and, when her grandmother put her arm around her shoulders, Jessica leaned into the embrace.

"You're probably right. I don't know how Lydia and Ashley do it."

"They've had a lot of practice, and their dad was a firefighter, too. And their brother, so they've both done their share of waiting for news. But I meant you."

"I can't be in love with Rick." Too late, she realized how weird that sounded. She should have said she wasn't, not that she couldn't be. She knew she was, of course, but she didn't really want Marie to know it.

"Why can't you?"

"We live on opposite ends of the country, for one thing." It was weak, she knew. In the past two months, she'd spent more time in Boston than in San Diego. Not that it was a sustainable, long-term solution, but she'd proven she could work remotely. "I have a career and a condo and that's…it's just where my life is."

"I think it might already be too late to tell yourself you can't fall in love with Rick. Even your grandfather noticed you two have feelings for each other and he's not exactly a romantic soul."

"I don't know what my father would do without me." But she couldn't help wishing she'd called him back to clarify whether he'd been joking about a Boston office or not before she'd left California this time.

"He's a grown man, Jessica. He's leaned on you long enough."

It wasn't that simple, but she knew she wouldn't get anywhere arguing the point with Marie. She was going to change the subject, maybe suggest they have some ice cream, when her phone vibrated in her pocket. She squeezed Marie before stepping out of her embrace to pull the phone out, and then she felt a rush of relief when she saw Rick's name on the screen.

"It's Rick," she told Marie as she opened the text message.

Only have a sec, but if you see the news, I'm ok.

It looks awful. Be careful.

Yeah. Going back in soon but don't worry.

She couldn't help worrying, but she could tell by his short messages that he didn't have time to hold her hand by phone. Be safe. See you soon.

After she'd reluctantly put the phone back in her

pocket, Jessica looked up to see Marie watching her with a soft expression. "I think the fact he reached out to you during a break in a tough night says a lot, don't you?"

Maybe it did, but the thought of going through this on a regular basis was daunting. And so was the thought of abandoning her father and everything in San Diego to move here. She knew he wouldn't leave Boston. His family was there, and Joe and Marie. And there was the extended family made up of his fellow firefighters and *their* families. He had an emotional investment in his home that was stronger than hers to San Diego, with the exception of her father and a few coworkers and friends she was close to.

Picking up her water glass, she tried again to chase away the dryness in her mouth. The thought of such drastic changes to her life scared her, and it seemed ridiculous to consider it based on the fact he'd texted her tonight.

But the knowledge that when most of the men were probably taking advantage of a short break to reach out to their loved ones at home, Rick had reached out to her thrilled Jessica in a way she couldn't deny.

But he'd said he was going back in, so there was more waiting and more worrying for the time being.

THEY WERE PULLING BACK, given permission by the incident commander to take their break so fresh companies could move in, when the floor shifted under their feet. Suddenly they were scrambling and there was shouting and confusion. The smoke was thick, making it hard to see, but he could hear the unmistakable sound of the floor caving behind them.

He saw the reflective strips on Gavin's coat and they were facing the wrong way, and that meant the kid was getting turned around. Putting his hand on Gavin's shoulder, he shoved him in the right direction and yelled at him to keep moving. Gavin wasn't a rookie, but there were times a situation gone to shit outpaced a guy's experience and this was one of them.

When they got outside, Rick swiveled his head. Boudreau. Porter. Eriksson. But it was the E-59 crew that caught his eye. Grant Cutter was on his knees, gasping for air, but Aidan had his arms around Scotty, who was fighting like hell to go back in.

Danny Walsh.

He could hear the commands and updates flying. The other companies would focus their efforts on beating the fire back while locating Walsh and getting him the hell out. But Scott couldn't go back in and Aidan was losing his grip on him.

"Scotty." Rick stepped in front of him, putting his hand on the man's shoulder. "We need to get out of the way."

"He didn't come out, LT."

"I know." Some of the fight went out of Scott and Aidan steered him toward their engine. Rick walked with them, the rest of their crews following.

"You have to let me go back in. He's my brother-in-law. He's family."

"They'll get him out, Scotty, but we have to stay out of the way and let them do it. You know that."

"Ashley's pregnant. Barely two months, so only the family knows." Scotty sagged onto the ice-coated bumper of the truck, his eyes welling up with tears. "I've gotta bring him back to my sister."

Shit. The word echoed around Rick's mind. *Shit shit shit.*

"I can't go home without Danny, Rick. Not after everything they've been through. Not ever."

"That's not going to happen." Fear knotted his stomach. Fear for the guy he'd worked with for years. Fear for Ashley, who'd just gotten her marriage back on track. And fear for all of them. Danny was family to some of them literally, but to all of them figuratively.

His first instinct was to barge into the building and protocols be damned, like Scotty wanted. That was Danny Walsh in there.

But that first instinct was exactly why he took a deep breath and forced himself to clear his mind. If push came to shove, the guys of L-37 and E-59 would do anything to get Danny out, without regard for their own safety or maybe even the safety of others. And that was exactly why they had to stand back and let the other companies work.

None of them stripped out of their ice-stiffened coats, though. They grabbed fresh tanks and double-checked their gear. If they were needed, they'd be ready in seconds.

As they listened to the radio and to the organized chaos around them, the volunteers brought them coffee and hot chocolate from the canteen truck. Rick thanked them and made sure Scott actually drank his, then turned to scan the scene. They were in an area offset from the main action, where the news cameras were aimed. And there were a lot of trucks forming a barrier. He was pretty sure if Ashley or Lydia were watching the news, they wouldn't be able to tell in a sweeping glance that Danny wasn't standing with them. Tommy Kincaid would be listening to that old scanner he kept at the bar, though, and he might know what was going on. Whether he'd tell his daughters or not before the story had an ending, happy or otherwise, Rick couldn't guess.

Somebody shouted and there was a lot of movement at the side of the building. They started moving in that direction, but stopped when the strident beeping warned them an ambulance was trying to back through the crowd.

"Can you see anything?" Scott rocked onto the toes of the heavy boots, trying to see what was going on.

"It has to be Danny."

The EMTs threw open the back doors and hauled out the stretcher, but they were met halfway by three firefighters supporting the weight of a fourth between them. They had him in a hammock carry and even if the lolling of Danny's head didn't give it away, it was obvious to Rick he wasn't conscious.

All they could do was hope he was alive. The EMTs wasted no time getting him on the stretcher and into the back of the ambulance, and the men who'd carried him out gave helpless looks to Scott as it pulled away.

"He was breathing," one of them finally said.

"I should go to Ashley," Scott said quietly, almost as if he were talking to himself. "She needs to get to the hospital."

"Your dad probably already knows, but I'm going to call him and he and Lydia will take care of Ashley. We have a job to finish, repacking this shit, and you're already a man down. We can't go to the hospital until we can get the trucks out and it's going to be a while, so focus on what we're doing. The doctors will take care of Danny and other guys will show up to wait with the family until we can get there. You know that."

When Scott nodded and Rick was sure he had his head on straight enough to stay put, he left him in the care of the others and moved away to call Tommy at the bar. As he suspected, Danny's father-in-law knew what was going on and had been just about to leave to pick up Ashley at her house.

"Do me a favor," Rick said, "and make sure the second you know something, you let Scotty know. He's pretty messed up."

Once he'd gotten that call out of the way, he let his thumb hover over Jess's number. He wanted to hear her voice in the worst way, but then he tucked the phone away. She was a distraction he couldn't dwell on until this hellish night was over.

After knocking the ice off his coat and helmet, Rick grabbed a fresh coffee from a volunteer and went to check in with the incident commander.

JESSICA WOKE TO a weird sound, and it took her a second to realize it was the glass door sliding open. She was in Rick's bed and she sat up when he closed the door behind him. By leaning out over the bed a little, she could see him, and it was probably a testament to his exhaustion that he didn't even jump when he made eye contact with a person he wasn't expecting to be there. Or maybe he was expecting her to be there because where else would she be when he might need her?

"Hey," she said softly as he stepped out of his boots and tossed his coat on a chair before walking toward her.

He pulled the T-shirt over his head and then paused to take off his jeans and socks. He'd obviously taken a shower at some point after the fire. "Hey."

"You're limping."

"I whacked my knee a good one, but it's not a big deal."

When he reached the bed, she moved over and threw back the covers so he could slide in. He wrapped his arms around her and pulled her close. After dragging the covers up to his shoulder, she relaxed into his embrace.

"We almost lost Danny Walsh tonight," he said against her hair. "Or last night, technically. Whenever the hell it was."

"I heard about it on the news and texted Lydia. She said he'll be okay. Right?"

"He's got a pretty bad concussion, smoke inhalation, a broken arm and he busted his leg in two places, but he'll be okay."

"What happened?" She felt his muscles tense slightly. "Actually, never mind what happened. What matters is that he's going to be okay. Is everybody else okay, too?"

"The rest of our guys are okay. Other companies had a few minor injuries, I guess. A guy slipped on the ice and broke his clavicle, and a few were treated for smoke inhalation, but nothing major considering it was fully involved."

"I know you need to sleep now, but I was worried about you and I just wanted to see you for a few minutes when you got home."

"Do you have any plans for this morning? You need to work?"

She could hear the exhaustion in his voice and knew he'd be asleep in a matter of minutes. "There's nothing that can't wait."

He muttered something she couldn't make out and nuzzled his face into her hair. Then, a few seconds later, she felt his muscles go lax as he nodded off. Despite being an early riser, she'd spent a good chunk of the night tossing and turning herself, so she was content to drift in and out of sleep for a while.

It was almost three hours before he stirred a little and rolled onto his back. Jessica waited until he resumed snoring and then slid out of his bed. He'd wanted the comfort of her being there when he first climbed into bed, but she suspected he'd probably sleep better now if she wasn't lying awake next to him. Every time she shifted, he stirred, and she was restless.

Last night had been scary even before the news broke about Danny. And then she'd been afraid for him and for Ashley.

But when she'd seen Rick limping toward her, his face haggard with exhaustion, the fear had settled into the pit of her stomach. He'd been in just as much danger as Danny Walsh had been, and it could just as easily have been him lying in the hospital this morning.

Rather than roam his apartment alone or sit on his couch in silence, she went down the interior stairs and found Marie vacuuming the living room. Her grandmother hit the off switch when she saw her and gestured for her to sit down on the couch with her.

"Good morning, honey. How's Rick?"

"Exhausted. And he hurt his knee somehow. He was limping when he got home."

Marie squeezed her hand. "He's fine, then."

"He was sound asleep when I left him. I think he will be for quite a while actually. I'm not sure what to do now."

"We'll make a casserole for the Walshes," Marie said. "Something that can be put in the freezer and easily heated in the microwave. Ashley doesn't need to be worrying about meals while her husband's in the hospital."

Jessica followed her into the kitchen. "How many casseroles do you think she'll get?"

Her grandmother laughed as she pulled out her recipe box. "At least two dozen. Probably a lot more.

Most of them will get thrown away when they need the freezer space."

"But we're going to make one anyway?"

Marie shrugged, her eyes serious. "Yes. It's simply what we do."

NINETEEN

RICK KILLED THE snowblower's engine and looked around the driveway. They didn't have any fresh snow, but the snowbanks along the edges were slowly creeping into the parking spaces, so he was using the snowblower to cut them back.

"I guess that woman's right about the driveway looking bigger," Joe said from the open garage door.

It had been the real estate agent, after looking at photos she'd taken, who suggested some snow removal—or at least rearranging—would make the driveway look bigger, and that was supposedly a huge selling point.

Rick's knee wasn't too bad and he was happy to have the physical activity to help take his mind off Danny's accident, so he'd volunteered to do it.

"I don't know what the holdup is," Rick said, pushing the snowblower inside. "She gave you a value on the property last month. Why didn't she just use that to list it?"

"I guess she gave us a pretty close ballpark figure, but to actually list it, she needs all kinds of photos and information. How old the roof is. The furnace. Crap like that. She wants to price it just right."

"That makes sense, I guess. Prospective buyers will want to know that."

"Seems like a pain in the ass to me."

"Yup."

"Marie and I were talking last night. Jessica said the place we're looking at is really reasonable and we could actually swing it even without a huge profit on the house."

"That's good. Means you won't have to worry about it in the future if you end up with surplus in the bank."

"It also means we could sell it to you if you were interested in it. You've taken good care of this old beast—and of us—for years and we'd like to give you an opportunity to think about buying it before we go ahead and formally list it on the market."

And then he named a price that Rick almost couldn't believe he'd heard correctly. "That means a lot to me, Joe. You know I love you guys and this house, but you can't do that. If I want to buy it, and honestly I have considered it, I'll pay you what it's worth."

"What's a building worth? It's the people that matter and you're like family to us, so think about it." Joe gave him a grin. "Besides, you can't go spending all your money or you won't be able to afford gas for that truck of yours."

Rick laughed because it was true, if a little exaggerated. His truck was so bad he'd changed the digital display so it showed the outside temperature instead of the average miles per gallon just because it was depressing, but he couldn't hide the dent it put in his wallet. But he wasn't driving around this city in a compact car for any amount of savings at the pump.

"I told Marie I'd talk to you about it," Joe said. "But we haven't said anything to Jessica. No sense in muddying the waters if you're not even interested to begin with, know what I mean?"

Rick nodded, his gut tightening. By muddying the waters, Joe meant displeasing their granddaughter, who probably wouldn't like them making that big of a financial decision on emotion alone. "I'm definitely interested, but I don't think I want to hide something like that from her. Things are complicated, I guess."

"Things always are, son."

It was several hours before Rick got the chance to speak to Jessica alone. Joe and Marie were busy at the kitchen table sorting through boxes of papers, and he went upstairs to find Jess sitting cross-legged on her bed, scowling at her computer.

"Hi," she said when she noticed him in the doorway. "Have you heard anything about Danny today?"

"Yeah. He's going home, actually. Nothing to be done but rest and let the breaks heal. But no lasting damage."

"He'll be out of work for a while, then?"

"Yeah. Guys will rotate through and cover for him to get the extra shifts, but they'll have to find a long-term replacement for him, unfortunately." It was always hard when somebody new joined a company that had been together a long time.

"At least he'll be okay eventually."

"Yup." He shoved his hands into his pockets, feeling awkward with her for the first time in a long time.

"I wanted to talk to you about something. You got a minute?"

"Of course." She closed her laptop and set it aside. "You look so serious."

"I was talking to Joe earlier about the house, and he surprised me by telling me he and Marie want me to have dibs on buying the house," he said. "Not at the full asking price, though."

"Really? What did they offer it to you for?" When he said the number, he wasn't surprised when her eyebrows shot up. "Not at full asking price? Rick, that's not even half of what it's worth."

"Trust me, I know."

She stared at him so long, he had to fight the urge to squirm. He hadn't done anything wrong and he'd honestly thought they'd put the lack of trust when it came to the house behind them a long time ago. But he could practically hear the wheels turning in her head.

"I wish you'd say something," he told her.

"What do you think I'm going to say? Of course I'm going to recommend they retract the offer and list it with the real estate agent. I'm not letting them get screwed out of money just because they like you."

Screwed. The implication he'd deliberately masterminded the offer to screw over Joe and Marie hurt like a kick to the stomach, and the fact she'd think it of him made him angry. "Worried about your inheritance?"

The color drained from her face and she blinked at him for a few seconds. "Excuse me?"

"If they only get half what the house is worth, they might burn through it and not have anything left to leave you."

"I can't believe you'd say that to me." Red splotches shone on her cheeks, and her eyes sparkled with anger. "I couldn't care less about an inheritance, and I thought you knew me better than that."

"And I thought you knew me better than to think I'd take advantage of Joe and Marie."

"Do you understand my job is to protect people's money? Maximizing investments is what I do, so what kind of financial advisor would I be if I stood back and let my own grandparents take a bath on their house?"

"Your grandparents might not have fancy finance degrees, but they're not stupid and neither wants to leave the other unprotected in the future, so I'm sure they've thought this through."

"They're letting emotion cloud their judgment. Feelings have no place in business."

He rolled his eyes. "Did Davey have that cross-stitched on a pillow for you?"

When her mouth tightened and her eyes went flat, he realized he'd gone too far, but there was no taking it back.

"My success in financial planning has nothing to do with my father and everything to do with my education, instincts and experience. Don't sell me short, Rick."

"I think you're selling your grandparents short."

"I'm sure you'd think so, since you're the person who stands to benefit the most if I'm wrong."

Rick blew out a breath and ran a hand over his hair. This had gone sideways on him in a way he couldn't have imagined. "Look, I don't want to fight with you."

"We've obviously arrived at the conflicting interests phase of our relationship. We always knew it would probably happen. I'll sit down with Joe and Marie today and go through all of their options one more time, including a look at their long-term finances if they choose to sell you their home at a fraction of its value."

"You're phrasing it that way to make it sound worse than it is."

"It's an accurate representation of the situation. I'm sure they'll let you know what their decision is within a day or two."

The dismissal was clear in her voice and he knew in her current mood, he'd probably have better luck beating his head against a brick wall than convincing her he hadn't put Joe and Marie up to anything.

With a heavy heart, he turned and walked away.

"THE LAST THING we wanted to do was cause a problem with you and Rick," Marie said, setting a big bowl of baked macaroni and cheese in front of Jessica.

The comfort food was killing her. And possibly her wardrobe. "You didn't cause a problem with us. We simply have different philosophies when it comes to protecting your investments."

"I know you see this old house as an investment,"

Joe said. "That's your job and with the market the way it is, I guess it is pretty valuable. But to your grandmother and I, it's a home. That's what matters to us and it's important to us that somebody loves it as much as we have. Sometimes there *are* emotions in business, no matter what your father and your business professors told you."

"I've broken down the numbers for you," she said. "You can see the impact it has on your financial future."

"Of course it has an impact," Marie said. "But our future financial security doesn't depend on the full amount. Your numbers show that we can live quite nicely with half the amount."

"That's true. It's not what I recommend, but all I can do is suggest. Ultimately, it's your decision to make."

"I just feel so bad that you're going back to California now," Marie said.

"I was always going back to California, since that's where I live. And now that you've made decisions and have the ball rolling, I don't need to be here. I can handle a lot of things via email."

"What about Rick?"

Jessica looked at her grandfather. "What about him?"

"We're not stupid. We've minded our own business, but it's obvious you and Rick have been in a relationship. If we hadn't offered him the house without talking to you first, what were your plans going to be?"

"I don't know," she said honestly. "We hadn't talked about the future."

"But you must have thought about it," Marie said.

"Of course I had. My father made a comment about opening an East Coast office to expand the business, but I wasn't sure at the time if he was being sarcastic or if he meant it. But the more I thought about it, the more I wanted to seriously consider it. I could still be a part of the family business I've helped build, while being here with you guys. And Rick."

"That can still happen."

"I don't think so. It was fun while it lasted. Now it's time for me to go home and get back to work."

Joe wisely changed the subject to something he'd seen on the news recently before Marie could get too emotional, and Jessica listened to them chatter back and forth until she could escape to her room to start packing.

How was it possible she'd accumulated so much stuff during her two stays in Boston? And ninety percent of it was stuff she couldn't wear in California. She'd planned to leave it behind for her next visit, but if Rick was going to buy the house, that wasn't going to work.

With her mouth set in a grim line, she started sorting the few things she'd carry with her from the majority of it, which she'd ship to her address in San Diego. With one checked bag and her carry-on, she could probably bring home the things she'd want right away.

When she dumped her underwear drawer on the

bed, her gaze fell immediately on the yellow bra she'd
worn to watch the hockey game with him. Picking it
out of the pile, she sat on the edge of the bed, pressed
it to her face and sobbed.

RICK WAS CHECKING the air pressure in Ladder 37's
tires when his cell phone chimed. Technically they
had mechanics who took care of all things mainte-
nance related, but he liked to know what was going
on with his own truck. And it never hurt to make sure
they were doing their jobs properly, either. In frigid
temperatures, especially if they had the chains on,
tire pressure mattered.

He pulled out the phone and read the words on
the screen. Jessica just left for the airport. Her plane
takes off in three hours. Just thought you might want
to know. Love, Marie.

For a second, he was amused by her message.
Someday she'd figure out she didn't have to sign texts
like they were letters because the contact information
came through with it.

Then the message itself hit him like a wrecking
ball. In three hours, a plane was going to take Jess
back to California. If they left things as they were, it
would be over. If there was no more communication
between them, by the time she returned to Boston
again they'd be barely more than polite acquaintances
who'd once been lovers.

He sank onto the bumper, feeling sick to his stomach. It didn't seem possible he could spend the rest of

his life without seeing those eyes smile at him again. He would never kiss her again.

She would be gone and, even if they crossed paths again, what they'd had would be nothing but a distant memory.

"You okay?"

He looked up at Gavin. "What?"

"You look like you got really bad news."

There was no sense in trying to hide anything around these guys. "Jess is on her way to the airport to go back to San Diego."

"Oh, that's too bad. I really liked her."

"Me too, kid. More than liked, actually. I love her."

"Did you tell her that?"

"No."

"Not even on Facebook?"

Rick rolled his eyes. "Seriously, are you even old enough to shave?"

"I'm old enough to know you don't let the woman you love get on a plane without running after her. Have you ever even *seen* a movie, dude?" When Rick glared at him, the tips of Gavin's ears turned red. "Uh, Lieutenant Dude."

"I think all those movies were made before they changed the security procedures."

"You're a Boston Fire officer."

"I don't think Homeland Security's going to rewrite their manual for me."

"I just meant you could probably talk somebody into having her paged for you, but misuse of power's another way to go."

"I had no idea you were trying to be a comedian, kid. You might want to keep the day job, and don't spend so much time with Scotty Kincaid. You're starting to sound like him."

Gavin laughed and walked away, but Rick couldn't stop thinking about what he'd said. So they'd fought about how to handle the Broussards' house. People in love fought sometimes and they got through it.

But Jess didn't know he was a person in love. She didn't know he thought they had something worth fighting for because he hadn't told her. Assuming she knew it—could see in the way he looked at her or feel it in his kisses—wasn't enough. He had to say it.

He ran up the stairs and poked his head into Cobb's office. "I have an emergency, Chief. Okay, not a real medical emergency or anything. But I have to do something."

"Boudreau just shared the latest gossip with me. Go. And don't bother coming back today. I'll cover because you're either going to be worthless and mopey or you'll get the girl and forget to come back, anyway. And don't you dare flip that emergency light switch in your truck. No lights for personal shit."

Rick used the remote start on his truck so it was already running and ready to go when he climbed into the driver's seat. After buckling his seat belt, he gunned the engine and drove through the city as fast as traffic allowed, taking a few shortcuts here and there.

Using his phone's hands-free connection to the truck, he called Marie. "I need her flight info, Marie.

Airline. Gate. I could walk around that airport for three days and not find her without a starting place."

She gave him the information and the hitch in her voice told him she was getting emotional. "Good luck, honey."

When he reached the right terminal, he lucked out and saw a police officer he knew from a charity marathon he used to run back when he thought running was fun. With permission to leave his truck at the curb for ten minutes, he went inside and scanned the lines waiting for security screening. She'd been in a cab and hadn't had that much of a head start on him.

She saw him first. When he found her in line, she was looking at him and those pretty eyes hit him hard. They weren't smiling today. He held out his hands, trying to gesture to her to please just give him a minute.

She hesitated so long, he wasn't sure she was going to give him a chance. Then she made her way back the way she'd gone, squeezing her way past the people in line behind her and trying not to hit anybody with the carry-on bag slung over her shoulder.

"Shouldn't you be at work?" she asked when she reached him.

He wanted to touch her face or to stroke her hair. Something. But he had to earn that right back. "I couldn't let you go without talking to you one more time. I want to apologize for losing my temper when we talked about the house. I felt like you were implying I was trying to screw Joe and Marie over and it hurt."

"I didn't think that and I'm sorry the words I used made you feel that way. It wasn't meant to be personal, but you hurt my feelings, too, so it got messy."

"It was mostly me, Jess. It's no excuse, but the house has been a roller coaster and Danny...the nightmares were bad and I didn't sleep well and it made me oversensitive. I understand that you make those kinds of decisions differently. I really do. I was so stupid and I don't want to lose you because of it."

"I don't...I didn't..." She pressed her lips together, her eyes wide and shimmering with tears.

"I love you." He touched her face then because he couldn't stop himself. Cradling her cheek in his hand, he wiped away a tear with his thumb. "That's the important thing. I love you and I want you to stay with me. I want us to figure out our future together and have children and take them to Joe and Marie's new place for Sunday dinners. I want us to be a family, Jess."

"You say *family* like it should mean something to me. My mother took off when I was three and never looked back. I just met my grandparents and I'm thirty-four years old. How the hell would I know anything about family? You see how I messed things up because emotion is hard for me to balance."

"You don't have to balance. You just love. Like you love Joe and Marie. They're your family and you're taking care of them because you love them. And how about your old man? You know how being a financial advisor or whatever you call it isn't *your* dream. You wanted to be an event planner, and you still do, but you do the finance stuff anyway and you kick ass at it because it's *his* dream and you love him? That's family, Jessica."

"I want the family I see in the picture frames at the store," she said, her eyes shimmering with tears.

"Those are models, Jess. God knows that ain't me. I'm real and I have bad days and sometimes I say stupid things, but I love you." He paused, not knowing what to say next and just hoping the right words would come out. "I love you so much you won't need a picture to capture it because I swear to God you will feel it every day of your life."

"I love you, too," she whispered, and Rick's knees almost buckled from the relief. He'd thought— hoped—she did, but he was afraid he'd blown it so badly she'd never say the words. "I don't know when it happened. Weeks ago? But I know standing in that line, waiting to be thousands of miles away from you, was breaking my heart."

"Don't get on the plane today. Come home with me and let me show you just how much I love you. That way, every time you get on that plane, I'll know you're coming back to me as soon as you can."

"Yes, I'll go home with you." She threw her arms around his neck and smiled up at him. "We'll make our own family."

"I can't wait." He kissed her and then raised his eyebrow because it always made her smile. "As a matter of fact, we should go get started on that right away. You don't absolutely need anything in your checked bag, do you? It's probably zipping around a conveyor belt right now."

Jess reached up and ran her fingertip over his eyebrow. "The only thing I absolutely need is you."

* * * * *

If you fell in love with Shannon Stacey's voice in
CONTROLLED BURN
you're going to love THE KOWALSKIS.
See where it all started in
EXCLUSIVELY YOURS *by Shannon Stacey.*
Available Now.

ONE

"You got busy in the backseat of a '78 Ford Granada with Joseph Kowalski—only the most reclusive best-selling author since J. D. Salinger—and you don't think to tell me about it?"

Keri Daniels sucked the last dregs of her too-fruity smoothie through her straw and shrugged at her boss. "Would *you* want anybody to know?"

"That I had sex with Joseph Kowalski?"

"No, that you had sex in the backseat of a '78 Granada." Keri had no idea how Tina Deschanel had gotten the dirt on her high school indiscretions, but she knew she was in trouble.

An exceptionally well-paid reporter for a glossy, weekly entertainment magazine did not withhold carnal knowledge of a celebrity on the editor-in-chief's most wanted list. And having kept that juicy little detail to herself wouldn't get her any closer to parking her butt in an editorial chair.

Tina slipped a photograph from her purse and slid it across the table. Keri didn't look down. She was mentally compiling a short list of the people who knew she'd fogged up the windows of one of the ugliest cars in the history of fossil fuels. Her friends. The cop who'd knocked on the fogged-up window with a flashlight at a really inopportune moment. Her parents, since the cop was in a bad mood that night. The approximately six hundred kids attending her high school that year and anybody *they* told. Maybe short list wasn't the right term.

"It was 1989," Keri pointed out, because her boss clearly expected her to say something. "Not exactly a current event. And you ambushed me with this shopping spree."

Actually, their table in the outdoor café was surrounded by enough bags to stagger a pack mule on steroids, but now Keri knew she'd merely been offered the retail therapy *before* the bad news. It shouldn't have surprised her. Tina Deschanel was a shark, and any friendly gesture should have been seen as a prelude to getting bitten in the ass.

"Ambushed?" Tina repeated, loudly enough to distract a pair of Hollywood starlets engaging in some serious public displays of affection in a blatant attempt to attract the cheap tabloid paparazzi. A rabid horde that might include Keri in the near future if she didn't handle this correctly.

"How do you think I felt?" Tina went on. "I reached out to a woman who mentioned on her blog she'd gone to high school with Joseph Kowalski. Once there was money on the table, I made her cough up some evidence, and she sent me a few photos. She was even kind enough to caption them for me."

Keri recognized a cue when it was shoved down her throat. With one perfectly manicured nail she hooked the 8x10 blowup and pulled it closer.

A girl smiled at her from the photo. She wore a pink, fuzzy sweater, faded second-skin jeans and pink high heels. Raccoon eyeliner made her dark brown eyes darker, frosty pink coated her lips and her hair was as big as Wisconsin.

Keri smiled back at her, remembering those curling iron and aerosol days. If the EPA had shut down their cheerleading squad back then, global warming might have been a total non-issue today.

Then she looked at the boy. He was leaning against the hideous brown car, his arms wrapped around young Keri's waist. Joe's blue eyes were as dark as the school sweatshirt he wore, and his grin managed to be both innocent and naughty at the same time. And those damn dimples—she'd been a sucker for them. His honey-brown hair was hidden by a Red Sox cap, but she didn't need to see it to remember how the strands felt sliding through her fingers.

She never failed to be amazed by how much she still missed him sometimes.

But who had they been smiling at? For the life of her, Keri couldn't remember who was standing behind the camera. She tore her gaze away from the happy couple and read the caption typed across the bottom.

Joe Kowalski and his girlfriend, Keri Daniels, a few hours before a cop busted them making out on a back road and called their parents. Rumor had it when Joe dropped her off, Mr. Daniels chased him all the way home with a golf club.

Keri snorted. "Dad only chased him to the end of

the block. Even a '78 Granada could outrun a middle-aged fat guy with a five iron."

"I fail to see the humor in this."

"You didn't see my old man chasing taillights down the middle of the street in his bathrobe. It wasn't very funny at the time, though."

"Focus, Keri," Tina snapped. "Do you or do you not walk by the bulletin board in the bull pen every day?"

"I do."

"And have you not seen the sheet marked '*Spotlight Magazine*'s Most Wanted' every day?"

"I have."

"And did you happen to notice Joseph Kowalski has been number three for several years?" Keri nodded, and Tina leaned across the table. "*You* are going to get me an exclusive feature interview with the man."

"Or...?"

Tina sat back and folded her arms across her chest. "Don't take it to that point, Keri. Look, the man's eleventh bestseller is going to be *the* summer blockbuster film of the decade. More A-listers lined up to read for that movie than line up on the red carpet for the Oscars. And he's a total mystery man."

"I don't get why you're so dedicated to chasing him down. He's just an author."

"Joseph Kowalski isn't just an author. He played the media like a fiddle and became a celebrity. The splashy NY parties with that gorgeous redhead—Lauren Huckins, that was it—on his arm. Then Lauren slaps him with a multi-million dollar emotional distress suit, he pays her off with a sealed agreement and then he disappears from the map? There's a story there, and I want it. Our readers will eat him up, and *Spotlight* is going to serve him to them because you have access to him nobody else does."

"Had. I *had* access to him." Keri sighed and flipped the photo back across the table even though she would rather have kept it to moon over later. "Eighteen years ago."

"You were his high school sweetheart. Nostalgia, darling! And rumor has it he's still single."

Keri *knew* he was still single because the Danielses and Kowalskis still lived in the same small New Hampshire town, though Mr. and Mrs. Kowalski lived in a much nicer house now. Very *much* nicer, according to Keri's mother.

"You've risen fast in this field," Tina continued, "because you have sharp instincts and a way with people, to say nothing of the fact I trusted you. But this…"

The words trailed away, but Keri heard her boss loud and clear. She was going to get this exclusive or her career with *Spotlight* was over and she could start fresh at the bottom of another magazine's totem pole. And since her career was pretty much the sum total of her life, it wasn't exactly a threat without teeth.

But seeing Joe again? The idea both intrigued her and scared the crap out of her at the same time. "He's not going to open up his insanely private life to the magazine because he and I wore out a set of shocks in high school, Tina. It was fun, but it wasn't *that* good."

Now she was flat-out lying. Joe Kowalski had set the gold standard in Keri's sex life. An ugly car, a Whitesnake tape, cheap wine and Joe still topped her personal "Ten Ways to a Better Orgasm" list.

Tina ran her tongue over her front teeth, and Keri had known her long enough to know her boss was about to deliver the kill shot.

"I've already reassigned your other stories," she said. It was an act of interference entirely inappropriate for Tina to do to someone of Keri's status at the magazine.

"That's unacceptable, Tina. You're overstepping your—"

"I can't overstep boundaries I don't have, Daniels. It's my magazine, and your promotion to editorial depends on your getting an interview with Kowalski, plain and simple." Then she reached into her purse and passed another sheet to her. "Here's your flight information."

THE RECLUSIVE, MEGA-BESTSELLING author in question was trying to decide between regular beef jerky or teriyaki-flavored when he heard Keri Daniels was back in town.

Joe Kowalski nodded at the cashier who'd actually left a customer half-rung up in an attempt to be the first to deliver the news. It wasn't the first time Keri had been back. If she'd gone eighteen years without a visit home to her parents, Janie Daniels would have flown out to LA and dragged her daughter home by an earlobe.

It was, however, the first time Keri had come looking for him that he knew of.

"She's been asking around for your phone number," the cashier added on, watching him like a half-starved piranha. "Of course nobody will give it to her, because we know how you feel about your privacy."

And because nobody had it, but he didn't feel a need to point that out. But he was surprised it had taken Keri as long as this to get around to looking him up, considering just how many years Tina Deschanel had been stalking his agent.

"Maybe she's on the class reunion committee," Joe told the cashier, and her face fell. Committees didn't make for hot gossip.

Members of the media had been hounding his agent for years, but only Tina Deschanel, who took tenacious to a whole new level, was Keri Daniels's boss. Joe had been watching Keri's career from the beginning, waiting for her to sell him out, but she never had. Until now, maybe.

While he wasn't a recluse of Salinger-esque stature, Joe liked his privacy. The New England dislike of outsiders butting into their lives, combined with his own fiscal generosity—in the form of a ballpark, playgrounds, library donations or whatever else they needed—kept the locals from spilling his business. By the time he struck it big, classmates who'd moved away didn't remember enough about him to provide interesting fodder.

Nobody knew the details of the lawsuit settlement except the lawyers, his family and Lauren—who would be financially devastated should she choose to break her silence. And, as unlikely as it seemed, he and Keri had never been linked together in the media reports his publicist monitored. He managed to keep his private life pretty much just that, despite the hype surrounding the movie.

"You're not old enough for a class reunion," Tiffany said, batting her way-too-young eyelashes at him.

A half dozen of each, he decided, tossing bags of beef jerky into his cart. He had a lot more list than cart space left and he kicked himself for not making Terry come along. She could have pushed a second cart *and* run interference on nosy cashiers. She was good in the role, probably from years of experience.

As if on cue, the loudspeaker crackled. "Um... Tiffany, can you come back to register one, please? I have to pick up my kids in ten minutes."

The girl rolled her eyes and started back toward the front of the town's tiny market, but not before calling over her shoulder, "She's staying with her parents, but I guess you already know where they live."

Yeah, he guessed he did, too. The only question was what he was going to do about it. He and his entire family were preparing to leave town for two weeks, and it would be a shame if he missed out on whatever game Keri was playing.

Assuming it was even true. Not that she was in town, but that she wanted to give him a call. In his experience, if there wasn't enough dirt to keep a small town grapevine bearing fruit, people would just add a heaping pile of manufactured fertilizer.

Joe gave a row of pepperoni sticks the thousand-yard stare. If Keri Daniels *was* looking for his phone number, it had to mean somebody had spilled the beans. The rabid pit bull of a woman she worked for had discovered her star reporter had once been the girl of Deschanel's favorite prey's dreams. If that was the case, he and Keri were heading for a reunion and *this* time Keri could do the begging, just like he had before she'd run off to California.

Two hours later, after he'd unloaded his groceries at his own place, he faced his twin sister across the expanse of their mother's kitchen. Teresa Kowalski Porter was *not* a happy woman.

"You are one dumb son of a bitch."

Whereas he liked to play with words— savor them— Terry just spat them out as they popped into her head.

"I thought you were a moron for putting up with her shit then," she said. "But now you're going back for a second helping?"

"I'm ninety-nine percent sure her boss sent her out here in order to use our history to manipulate me into giving the magazine an interview."

"Keri Daniels never needed any help when it came to manipulating people. And I don't even want to think about that other one percent on an empty stomach."

The entire Kowalski family had once held some resentment toward Keri, but Terry's had festered. Not

only because his sister knew how to hold a grudge—
although she certainly did—but because Keri had
hurt her even before she'd gotten around to hurting
Joe.

Terry and Keri had been best friends since kin-
dergarten, despite how corny their names sounded
when said together. The trouble started during their
freshman year when Mr. Daniels got a big promotion.
Between the new style Daddy's money bought and
a developing body that just wouldn't quit, Keri had
soon started circling with a new group of friends. By
the beginning of sophomore year, Keri had left Terry
in her social dust, and she hadn't been forgiven. Joe's
relationship with Keri had been the only thing to ever
come between him and his twin.

And that's why he'd come to Terry first. "Aren't
you even a little curious about how she turned out?"

"No." She pulled a soda from the fridge and popped
the top without offering him one—never a good sign.
"She broke your heart and now, almost twenty years
later, she wants to capitalize on that and sell you out
to further her career. That tells me all I need to know
about how she turned out, thanks."

Joe kicked out a chair and sat at the kitchen table.
"It's just dinner, Terry. Dinner with somebody who
used to mean a lot to both of us."

"Why are you even talking to me about this, Joseph? I could give a shit less about Keri Daniels. If
you want to have dinner with her, then do it. You're
an adult."

"I need you to cover for me with the family."

Terry laughed, then grabbed a list from the fridge to double-check against the army of plastic bins at her feet. "Okay, *almost* an adult."

"You know Mom's going to be all over my ass about being ready to go day after tomorrow even though I'm the first one packed every year. If I fall off her radar for even a few hours, she'll have a fit."

"You really are a dumb-ass. Mom knows she's in town. Tell her you're going to dinner with the bitch who ripped your heart out of your chest and stomped on it. Do you think three jars of peanut butter are enough?"

"We're only going for two weeks. And I don't want the whole damn town to know I'm going to see her."

"Eight adults and five kids…I guess three will be enough."

"Terry." He waited until she looked up from her list. "Seven adults."

"What? Oh. Yeah." She laughed at herself, but the pain was written all over her face. "Who's the dumb-ass now, huh?"

"He is," Joe said, not for the first time. "Did you call that divorce lawyer my agent recommended yet?"

"I'm putting it off until the trip is over." She held up a hand to ward off the argument she knew was coming. "I never thought I'd say this, but I'd rather talk about Keri Daniels."

"Fine. If she agrees to dinner, I'm going to tell everybody I've got a meeting in Boston tomorrow night. Will you back me up?"

"Why didn't you just tell *me* that, too?" she asked, clearly exasperated now.

"I thought about it. But I kept seeing Keri a secret from you once, sis, and it hurt you when you found out. I didn't want to do it again."

She sighed and Joe tasted victory. "Okay, I'll back you up, but I still think you're a moron. How many jars of pickles did we go through last year?"

"YOU WANT ME to do *what*?"

Joe stretched out on the battered leather couch in his office and tried not to laugh at the tone of horrified shock in his agent's voice. "Dinner date. Reporter from *Spotlight Magazine*. You heard right."

"Did that Deschanel bitch kidnap one of the kids? Threaten your mother? I know people, Joe. I can take care of this for you."

"It's Keri. Keri Daniels."

A loaded pause. "That's great. Sure I want to do that for you, Joe, because with a big movie premiere coming up and a deadline approaching, I absolutely want your head fucked up over your high school sweetheart. And exposing yourself professionally to somebody you've exposed yourself to personally? Great idea."

"Dan. Take a breath."

"Oh, I'm taking so many breaths I'm hyperventilating. I need to put a fucking bag over my mouth. Or maybe put a bag over your head because your brains are leaking out."

"I'm pretty sure Tina Deschanel found out Keri and I dated in high school and I doubt Keri wants to do this any more than I do."

"Then don't do it. Please, for the love of my fifteen percent, don't do it."

"I'm just going to have dinner with her and then she can go back to California and tell her boss she tried."

"Then why don't *you* call her?"

Good question. One he didn't particularly care to share the pathetic answer to with Dan.

After all these years, he didn't want to be reunited with Keri by telephone. He wanted to see her face at the same time he heard her voice. Okay, if he was being honest, he wanted to know if he could see the Keri he'd loved in her.

Worst-case scenario, whatever business she felt she had with him could be conducted over the phone and he wouldn't get to see her at all. It was just curiosity— for old times' sake—but he wanted to see her again.

"I'm famous," he said lightly. "I pay people to make my phone calls for me."

"Bullshit. And speaking of paying people, why are you dumping this on me? Jackie's in charge of publicity and press."

"Her head would explode."

The silence on the other end lasted so long Joe thought his agent might have hung up on him. But no such luck. "Joe, we've been together a long time and, speaking as a guy who's had your back for almost a decade and a half, I think this is even a worse idea personally than it is professionally."

"I know, but I'm going to do it anyway."

KERI SWALLOWED ANOTHER mouthful of non-designer water and resisted glancing at her watch again. Maybe she'd been spoiled by a generous expense account, but meeting in a cheap chain restaurant in the city was too high a price to pay for privacy, in her opinion.

And what was with Joe having his agent contact her to set up the dinner? He couldn't pick up the phone and call her himself? Maybe his overinflated ego interfered with telephone use, so he had to use his agent as though she were a total stranger. As if she didn't know he had a birthmark shaped like an amoeba on his right ass cheek.

Unfortunately, her opinions didn't seem to matter. Tina had made it very clear that if Joseph Kowalski held up a hoop, Keri was to jump through it, wearing a pom-pom hat and barking like a dog if that's what it took to make the author happy.

It really burned her ass to be in this predicament, and just thinking about her boss made her temples throb. The temptation to walk out was incredibly strong but, while she knew she could walk into any magazine editor's office and come out with a job, it would set her back years in her quest to climb to the top of the masthead.

It was only an interview, after all.

There hadn't been a new press or book jacket photo of Joe since his sixth book. That picture had pretty much looked like him, albeit without the grin and dimples. It was one of those serious and contemplative author photos and she'd hated it. But by now, especially considering the coin he was pulling down, he was probably a self-indulgent, fat, bald man with a hunched back from too much time over the keyboard.

She, on the other hand, thought she'd aged well. Nothing about her was as firm as it had been in high school, but she was still slim enough to pull off the pricey little black dress she'd chosen for tonight. Her hair, now sleek and smooth to her shoulders, was still naturally blond, though she would admit to some subtle highlighting.

"Hey, babe," a voice above her said, and just like that the sophisticated woman was gone. She was eighteen again, with big dreams, bigger hair, and an itch only Joe Kowalski could scratch.

She could almost taste the Boone's Farm as she turned, braced for an old, fat Joe and finding...just Joe.

He'd aged even better than she had, the bastard. His face had matured and he had a trace of what men were allowed to call character lines, but he still had that slightly naughtier version of the boy-next-door look. Of course, he wasn't *quite* as lean as he used to be, but it probably wasn't noticeable to anybody who hadn't spent a significant amount of senior year running her hands over his naked body.

All in all, he resembled the boy who'd charmed her out of her pants a lot more than he did the stodgy author she'd hoped to charm into an interview.

"Hi, Joe." She'd stored up a mental cache of opening lines ranging from cute to funny to serious, and every single one seemed to have been deleted. "Thank you for coming."

He slid onto the bench seat across the booth from her. "Time's been pretty damn good to you, if you don't mind my saying so."

No, she didn't mind at all. "You, too. Interesting choice of restaurant, by the way. An eccentricity of the rich and reclusive author?"

He flashed those dimples at her and Keri stifled a groan. Why couldn't he have been fat and bald except for unattractive tufts of hair sprouting from his ears?

"I just like the all-you-can-eat salad bar," he said. "So tell me, is Tina hiding under the table? Waiting to pounce on me in the men's room?"

Keri laughed, partly because it was such a relief to have the topic out in the open. "No, she refuses to leave the city. Says her lungs can't process unpolluted air."

His smoky blue eyes were serious even though his dimples were showing. "Terry's been expecting you to sell me out for your own advantage since I first made the *NYT* list."

Hearing his sister's name made her wince, and knowing she still held such a low opinion of Keri just made her sad. During the very rare moments she allowed herself to dwell on regrets, she really only had two. And they were both named Kowalski.

"I'm being professionally blackmailed," she admitted. "If I don't get an exclusive interview for *Spotlight* from you, I'm out of a job."

"I figured as much. Who spilled the beans?"

Keri pulled the 8x10 from her bag and handed it to him. "I don't know. Do you remember who took that?"

"Alex did, remember? The night we…well, the caption's pretty thorough."

She remembered now. Alex had been a friend of Joe's, but they'd all traveled in the same circle. "But Tina said the blogger who claimed to go to school with you was a woman."

"His name's Alexis now. You wouldn't believe how much he paid for his breasts."

Keri laughed, but Joe was still looking at the photo. Judging by the way the corners of his lips twitched into a small smile and how he tilted his head, Keri figured Tina had been right about the nostalgia angle.

The waitress approached their table, order pad in hand.

Joe still hadn't looked up. "Remember the night you started drinking your screwdrivers without the orange juice and did a striptease on Alex's pool table?"

"I bet the jokes about Alex's pool table having a nice rack went on forever," the waitress said, and *then* Joe looked up.

"You bet they did," he said easily, but he was blushing.

"There must be a whole new slew of jokes about Alex's rack now," Keri said, making Joe laugh.

The waitress tapped her pen on the tab. "So do you guys know what you want?"

And then he did it, just as he always had whenever he'd been asked that question—he looked straight at

Keri with blatant hunger in his eyes and said, "Yes, ma'am, I do."

The shiver passed all the way from her perfectly styled hair to her Ferragamo pumps. Then she watched in silent amusement while he ordered for them both— her regular high school favorite of a medium-well bacon cheeseburger with extra pickles, fries and a side of coleslaw. There was no mention of salad, all-you-can-eat or otherwise.

When the waitress left, she gave him a scolding look. "That's more calories than I've consumed in the last two years, Joe."

He waved away her halfhearted objection. "Let's get down to business."

Keri didn't want to. She was too busy enjoying that sizzle of anticipation she'd always felt when Joe looked at her. Apparently those blue eyes hadn't lost their potency over the past two decades.

Joe leaned back against the booth and crossed his arms. It was probably supposed to look intimidating, but all the gesture really did was draw attention to how tan and incredibly well-defined his biceps were against his white T-shirt. Typing definitely wasn't the only workout his arms got.

"Let's see if I can synopsize our situation," he said. "I never give interviews. You want an interview. No, strike that. You *need* an interview, because the rabid jackal you work for has made it clear your job is on the line. Am I close?"

The sizzle receded to a tingle. "You're in the ball-park."

"I'm not just in the ballpark, babe. I'm Josh Beckett on the mound at Fenway. If I don't give you what you need, you're hiding behind palm trees waiting for drunk pop stars to pop out of their Wonderbras."

And that pretty much killed the last of the lingering tingle. "Payback's a bitch and all that, right, Joe?"

The dimples flashed. "Isn't it?"

Keri just shrugged. She wasn't about to start putting deals on the table or making promises. After years of dealing with celebrities, she usually knew how to handle herself. But this was Joe Kowalski. He'd seen her naked and she'd broken his heart. That changed the rules.

"I'm leaving town tomorrow," he said. "I'll be gone two weeks."

The tingle flared up again, but this time it was a lot more panic and a lot less anticipation. "There's always the telephone or fax or email."

"Not where I'm going."

She laughed. "Would that be Antarctica or a grass hut in the Amazon Basin?"

"I'm not even leaving the state."

Joe had sucked at cards in high school—he had no poker face—but she couldn't read him now. The instincts that had skyrocketed her to the top of the *Spotlight* food chain were giving her nothing, except the feeling he was setting her up for something she might want no part of.

The waitress brought their food, buying Keri a few more minutes to think. One thing Joe had never had was a mean streak—if there was no chance in hell of the interview happening, he wouldn't have agreed to meet her for dinner. He'd never had it in him to humiliate somebody for the sake of his own enjoyment.

Granted, the kind of checks he had to be cashing changed a person, but she'd already seen enough of him—and heard enough from her mother—to know Joe was still Joe. Just with more expensive toys.

That didn't mean he wasn't going to have her jumping through hoops, of course. Probably an entire flaming series of them.

She bit into the bacon cheeseburger and the long-forgotten flavor exploded on her tongue. She closed her eyes and moaned, chewing slowly to fully savor the experience.

"How long has it been since you've had one of those?" Joe asked, and she opened her eyes to find him watching her.

Keri swallowed, already anticipating the next bite. "Years. Too many years."

He laughed at her, and they enjoyed some idle chit-chat while they ate. She brought up the movie and he talked about it in a generic sense, but she noted how careful he was not to say anything even remotely interview worthy.

There would be no tricking the man into revealing something that would get Tina off her back.

"You know," she said, still holding half her cheeseburger, "I *really* want to enjoy this meal more, and I can't with this hanging over my head. What's it going to take?"

"I gave it some thought before I came, and I think you should come with me."

"Where?"

"To where I'm going."

Keri set the cheeseburger on the plate. "For two weeks?"

The length of time hardly mattered, since she couldn't return to California without the interview anyway. But she'd like an idea of what she was signing up for.

"Whether you're there for two weeks or not is up to you. For each full day you stick it out with the Kowalskis, you get to ask me one question."

Keri, unlike Joe, did have a poker face and she made sure it was in place while she turned his words over in her head. "When you say the Kowalskis, you mean…"

"The entire family." The dimples were about as pronounced as she'd ever seen them. "Every one of them."

Her first thought was *oh shit*. Her second, to wonder if *People* was hiring.

Joe reached into the back pocket of his jeans and pulled out a folded sheet of spiral notebook paper. "Here's a list of things you'll need. I jotted it down in the parking lot."

Keri unfolded the paper and read the list twice, trying to get a sense of what she was in for.

BRING: Bug spray; jeans; T-shirts; several sweatshirts, at least one with a hood; one flannel shirt (mandatory); pajamas (optional); underwear (also optional); bathing suit (preferably skimpy); more bug spray; sneakers; waterproof boots; good socks; sunscreen; two rolls of quarters.

DO NOT BRING: cell phone; Blackberry; laptop; camera, either still or video; alarm clock; voice recorder; any other kind of electronic anything.

She had no clue what it meant, other than Joe wanting her half-naked and unable to text for help.

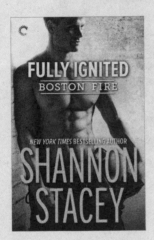
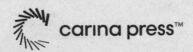

 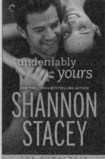 
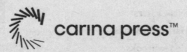

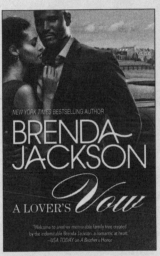

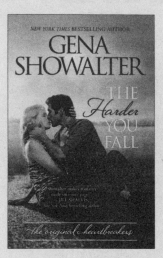